T0042092

NEW YORK REVIEW BOOKS

CLASSICS

THE HAUNTED
LOOKING GLASS

The Haunted Looking Glass is the late Edward Gorey's selection of his favorite tales of ghosts, ghouls, and grisly goings-on. Included are stories by Charles Dickens, Wilkie Collins, M. R. James, W. W. Jacobs, and L. P. Hartley, among other masters of the fine art of making the flesh creep, all accompanied by Gorey's inimitable illustrations.

"[Gorey's] cult of devotees numbers in the millions. . . ."

—*Salon*

"[Gorey's works] tickle the funny bone as they raise hair on the back of the neck."

—*The New York Times*

EDWARD GOREY IN NEW YORK REVIEW BOOKS

Fletcher and Zenobia by Edward Gorey and Victoria Chess
He Was There from the Day We Moved In by Rhoda Levine
Three Ladies Beside the Sea by Rhoda Levine
The Unrest Cure by Saki
Men and Gods by Rex Warner
The War of the Worlds by H. G. Wells

THE HAUNTED LOOKING GLASS

*GHOST STORIES CHOSEN AND
ILLUSTRATED BY EDWARD GOREY*

NEW YORK REVIEW BOOKS

New York

THIS IS A NEW YORK REVIEW BOOK
PUBLISHED BY THE NEW YORK REVIEW OF BOOKS
207 East 32nd Street, New York, NY 10016
www.nyrb.com

Permission to reprint "A Visitor from Down Under" by L. P. Hartley from *The Complete Stories of L. P. Hartley* is granted by The Society of Authors as the literary Representative of the Estate of L. P. Hartley

Library of Congress Cataloging-in-Publication Data
The haunted looking glass : ghost stories / chosen and illustrated by
Edward Gorey.
   p. cm.
 ISBN 0-940322-68-4 (acid-free paper)
 1. Ghost stories, English. I. Gorey, Edward, 1925–
 PR1309.G5 H38 2001
 823'.0873308—dc21

                              00-012341

ISBN 978-0-940322-68-4

Cover illustration by Edward Gorey
Printed in the United States of America on acid-free paper.
20 19 18 17 16 15 14 13 12 11 10

CONTENTS

THE EMPTY HOUSE, Algernon Blackwood   3

AUGUST HEAT, W. F. Harvey   25

THE SIGNALMAN, Charles Dickens   35

A VISITOR FROM DOWN UNDER, L. P. Hartley   53

THE THIRTEENTH TREE, R. H. Malden   75

THE BODY-SNATCHER, Robert Louis Stevenson   93

MAN-SIZE IN MARBLE, E. Nesbit   117

THE JUDGE'S HOUSE, Bram Stoker   135

THE SHADOW OF A SHADE, Tom Hood   159

THE MONKEY'S PAW, W. W. Jacobs   179

THE DREAM WOMAN, Wilkie Collins   195

CASTING THE RUNES, M. R. James   225

About the Authors   253

THE EMPTY HOUSE
by Algernon Blackwood

CERTAIN HOUSES, LIKE certain persons, manage somehow to proclaim at once their character for evil. In the case of the latter, no particular feature need betray them; they may boast an open countenance and an ingenuous smile; and yet a little of their company leaves the unalterable conviction that there is something radically amiss with their being: that they are evil. Willy nilly, they seem to communicate an atmosphere of secret and wicked thoughts which makes those in their immediate neighborhood shrink from them as from a thing diseased.

And, perhaps, with houses the same principle is operative, and it is the aroma of evil deeds committed under a particular roof, long after the actual doers have passed away, that makes the gooseflesh come and the hair rise. Something of the original passion of the evildoer, and of the horror felt by his victim, enters the heart of the innocent watcher, and he becomes suddenly conscious of tingling nerves, creeping skin, and a chilling of the blood. He is terror-stricken without apparent cause.

There was manifestly nothing in the external appearance of this particular house to bear out the tales of the horror that was said to reign within. It was neither lonely nor unkempt. It stood, crowded into a corner of the square, and looked exactly like the houses on either side of it. It had the same number of windows as its neighbors; the same balcony overlooking the gardens; the same white steps leading up to the heavy black front door; and, in the rear, there was the same narrow strip of green, with neat box borders, running up to the wall that divided it from the backs of the adjoining houses. Apparently, too, the number of chimney pots on the roof was the same; the breadth and angle of the eaves; and even the height of the dirty area railings.

And yet this house in the square, that seemed precisely similar to its fifty ugly neighbors, was as a matter of fact entirely different—horribly different.

Wherein lay this marked, invisible difference is impossible to say. It cannot be ascribed wholly to the imagination, because persons who had spent some time in the house, knowing nothing of the facts, had declared positively that certain rooms were so disagreeable they would rather die than enter them again, and that the atmosphere of the whole house produced in them symptoms of a genuine terror; while the series of innocent tenants who had tried to live in it, and been forced to decamp at the shortest possible notice, was indeed little less than a scandal in the town.

When Shorthouse arrived to pay a "weekend" visit to his Aunt Julia in her little house on the sea front at the other end of the town, he found her charged to the brim with mystery and excitement. He had only received her telegram that morning, and he had come anticipating boredom; but the moment he touched her hand and kissed her apple-skin wrinkled cheek, he caught the first wave of her electrical condition. The impression deepened when he learned that there were to be no other visitors, and that he had been telegraphed for with a very special object.

Something was in the wind, and the "something" would doubtless bear fruit; for this elderly spinster aunt, with a mania for psychical research, had brains as well as will power, and by hook or by crook she usually managed to accomplish her ends. The revelation was made soon after tea, when she sidled close up to him, as they paced slowly along the sea front in the dusk.

"I've got the keys," she announced in a delighted, yet half-awesome voice. "Got them till Monday!"

"The keys of the bathing machine, or——?" he asked innocently, looking from the sea to the town. Nothing brought her so quickly to the point as feigning stupidity.

"Neither," she whispered. "I've got the keys of the haunted house in the square—and I'm going there tonight."

Shorthouse was conscious of the slightest possible tremor down his back. He dropped his teasing tone. Something in her voice and manner thrilled him. She was in earnest.

"But you can't go alone——" he began.

"That's why I wired for you," she said with decision.

He turned to look at her. The ugly, lined, enigmatical face was alive with excitement. There was the glow of genuine enthusiasm round it like a halo. The eyes shone. He caught another wave of her excitement, and a second tremor, more marked than the first, accompanied it.

"Thanks, Aunt Julia," he said politely; "thanks awfully."

"I should not dare to go quite alone," she went on, raising her voice; "but with you I should enjoy it immensely. You're afraid of nothing, I know."

"Thanks *so* much," he said again. "Er—is anything likely to happen?"

"A great deal *has* happened," she whispered, "though it's been most cleverly hushed up. Three tenants have come

7

and gone in the last few months, and the house is said to be empty for good now."

In spite of himself Shorthouse became interested. His aunt was so very much in earnest.

"The house is very old indeed," she went on, "and the story—an unpleasant one—dates a long way back. It has to do with a murder committed by a jealous stableman who had some affair with a servant in the house. One night he managed to secrete himself in the cellar, and when everyone was asleep, he crept upstairs to the servants' quarters, chased the girl down to the next landing, and before anyone could come to the rescue threw her bodily over the banisters into the hall below."

"And the stableman——?"

"Was caught, I believe, and hanged for murder; but it all happened a century ago, and I've not been able to get more details of the story."

Shorthouse now felt his interest thoroughly aroused; but, though he was not particularly nervous for himself, he hesitated a little on his aunt's account.

"On one condition," he said at length.

"Nothing will prevent my going," she said firmly; "but I may as well hear your condition."

"That you guarantee your power of self-control if anything really horrible happens. I mean—that you are sure you won't get too frightened."

"Jim," she said scornfully, "I'm not young, I know, nor are my nerves; but *with you* I should be afraid of nothing in the world!"

This, of course, settled it, for Shorthouse had no pretensions to being other than a very ordinary young man, and an appeal to his vanity was irresistible. He agreed to go.

Instinctively, by a sort of subconscious preparation, he kept himself and his forces well in hand the whole evening, compelling an accumulative reserve of control by that nameless inward process of gradually putting all the emotions away and turning the key upon them—a process difficult to describe, but wonderfully effective, as all men who have lived through severe trials of the inner man well understand. Later, it stood him in good stead.

But it was not until half past ten, when they stood in the hall, well in the glare of friendly lamps and still surrounded by comforting human influences, that he had to make the first call upon this store of collected strength. For, once the door was closed, and he saw the deserted silent street stretching away white in the moonlight before them, it came to him clearly that the real test that night would be in dealing with *two fears* instead of one. He would have to carry his aunt's fear as well as his own. And, as he glanced down at her sphinx-like countenance and realized that it might assume no pleasant aspect in a rush of real terror, he felt satisfied with only one thing in the whole adventure—that he had confidence in his own will and power to stand against any shock that might come.

Slowly they walked along the empty streets of the town; a bright autumn moon silvered the roofs, casting deep shadows; there was no breath of wind; and the trees in the formal gardens by the sea front watched them silently as they passed along. To his aunt's occasional remarks Shorthouse made no reply, realizing that she was simply surrounding herself with mental buffers—saying ordinary things to prevent herself thinking of extra-ordinary things. Few windows showed lights, and from scarcely a single chimney came smoke or sparks. Shorthouse had already begun to notice everything, even the smallest details. Presently they stopped at the street corner and looked up at the name on the side of the house full in the moonlight, and with one accord, but without remark, turned into the square and crossed over to the side of it that lay in shadow.

"The number of the house is thirteen," whispered a voice

at his side; and neither of them made the obvious reference, but passed across the broad sheet of moonlight and began to march up the pavement in silence.

It was about halfway up the square that Shorthouse felt an arm slipped quietly but significantly into his own, and knew then that their adventure had begun in earnest, and that his companion was already yielding imperceptibly to the influences against them. She needed support.

A few minutes later they stopped before a tall, narrow house that rose before them into the night, ugly in shape and painted a dingy white. Shutterless windows, without blinds, stared down upon them, shining here and there in the moonlight. There were weather streaks in the wall and cracks in the paint, and the balcony bulged out from the first floor a little unnaturally. But, beyond this generally forlorn appearance of an unoccupied house, there was nothing at first to single out this particular mansion for the evil character it had most certainly acquired.

Taking a look over their shoulders to make sure they had not been followed, they went boldly up the steps and stood against the huge black door that fronted them forbiddingly. But the first wave of nervousness was now upon them, and Shorthouse fumbled a long time with the key before he could fit it into the lock at all. For a moment, if truth were told, they both hoped it would not open, for they were a prey to various unpleasant emotions as they stood there on the threshold of their ghostly adventure. Shorthouse, shuffling with the key and hampered by the steady weight on his arm, certainly felt the solemnity of the moment. It was as if the whole world—for all experience seemed at that instant concentrated in his own consciousness—were listening to the grating noise of that key. A stray puff of wind wandering down the empty street woke a momentary rustling in the trees behind them, but otherwise this rattling of the key was the only sound audible; and at last it turned in the lock and the heavy door swung open and revealed a yawning gulf of darkness beyond.

With a last glance at the moonlit square, they passed quickly in, and the door slammed behind them with a roar that echoed prodigiously through empty halls and passages. But, instantly, with the echoes, another sound made itself heard, and Aunt Julia leaned suddenly so heavily upon him that he had to take a step backwards to save himself from falling.

A man had coughed close beside them—so close that it seemed they must have been actually by his side in the darkness.

With the possibility of practical jokes in his mind, Short-house at once swung his heavy stick in the direction of the sound; but it met nothing more solid than air. He heard his aunt give a little gasp beside him.

"There's someone here," she whispered; "I heard him."

"Be quiet!" he said sternly. "It was nothing but the noise of the front door."

"Oh! Get a light—quick!" she added, as her nephew, fumbling with a box of matches, opened it upside down and let them all fall with a rattle onto the stone floor.

The sound, however, was not repeated; and there was no evidence of retreating footsteps. In another minute they had a candle burning, using an empty end of a cigar case as a holder; and when the first flare had died down he held the impromptu lamp aloft and surveyed the scene. And it was dreary enough in all conscience, for there is nothing more desolate in all the abodes of men than an unfurnished house dimly lit, silent, and forsaken, and yet tenanted by rumor with the memories of evil and violent histories.

They were standing in a wide hallway; on their left was the open door of a spacious dining room, and in front the hall ran, ever narrowing, into a long, dark passage that led apparently to the top of the kitchen stairs. The broad uncarpeted staircase rose in a sweep before them, everywhere draped in shadows, except for a single spot about halfway up where the moonlight came in through the window and fell on a bright patch on the boards. This shaft of light shed a faint radiance above and below it, lending to the objects within its reach a misty outline that was infinitely more suggestive and ghostly than complete darkness. Filtered moonlight always seems to paint faces on the surrounding gloom, and as Shorthouse peered up into the well of darkness and thought of the countless empty rooms and passages in the upper part of the old house, he caught himself longing again for the safety of the moonlit square, or the cozy, bright drawing room they had left an hour before. Then, realizing that these thoughts were dangerous, he thrust them away again and summoned all his energy for concentration on the present.

"Aunt Julia," he said aloud, severely, "we must now go through the house from top to bottom and make a thorough search."

The echoes of his voice died away slowly all over the building, and in the intense silence that followed he turned to look at her. In the candlelight he saw that her face was already ghastly pale; but she dropped his arm for a moment and said in a whisper, stepping close in front of him:

"I agree. We must be sure there's no one hiding. That's the first thing."

She spoke with evident effort, and he looked at her with admiration.

"You feel quite sure of yourself? It's not too late——"

"I think so," she whispered, her eyes shifting nervously towards the shadows behind. "Quite sure, only one thing——"

"What's that?"

"You must never leave me alone for an instant."

"As long as you understand that any sound or appearance must be investigated at once, for to hesitate means to admit fear. That is fatal."

"Agreed," she said, a little shakily, after a moment's hesitation. "I'll try——"

Arm in arm, Shorthouse holding the dripping candle and the stick, while his aunt carried the cloak over her shoulders, figures of utter comedy to all but themselves, they began a systematic search.

Stealthily, walking on tiptoe and shading the candle lest it should betray their presence through the shutterless windows, they went first into the big dining room. There was not a stick of furniture to be seen. Bare walls, ugly mantelpieces, and empty grates stared at them. Everything, they felt, resented their intrusion, watching them, as it were, with veiled eyes; whispers followed them; shadows flitted noiselessly to right and left; something seemed ever at their back, watching, waiting an opportunity to do them injury. There was the inevitable sense that operations which went on when the room was empty had been temporarily suspended till they were well out of the way again. The whole dark interior of the old building seemed to become a malignant Presence that rose up, warning them to desist and mind their own business; every moment the strain on the nerves increased.

Out of the gloomy dining room they passed through large folding doors into a sort of library or smoking room, wrapt equally in silence, darkness, and dust; and from this they regained the hall near the top of the back stairs.

Here a pitch-black tunnel opened before them into the lower regions, and—it must be confessed—they hesitated. But only for a minute. With the worst of the night still to come, it was essential to turn from nothing. Aunt Julia stumbled at the top step of the dark descent, ill lit by the flickering candle, and even Shorthouse felt at least half the decision go out of his legs.

"Come on!" he said peremptorily, and his voice ran on and lost itself in the dark, empty spaces below.

"I'm coming," she faltered, catching his arm with unnecessary violence.

They went a little unsteadily down the stone steps, a cold, damp air meeting them in the face, close and malodorous. The kitchen, into which the stairs led along a narrow passage, was large, with a lofty ceiling. Several doors opened out of it—some into cupboards with empty jars still standing on the shelves, and others into horrible little ghostly back offices, each colder and less inviting than the last. Black beetles scurried over the floor, and once, when they knocked against a deal table standing in a corner, something about the size of a cat jumped down with a rush and fled, scampering across the stone floor into the darkness. Everywhere there was a sense of recent occupation, an impression of sadness and gloom.

Leaving the main kitchen, they next went towards the scullery. The door was standing ajar, and as they pushed it open to its full extent Aunt Julia uttered a piercing scream, which she instantly tried to stifle by placing her hand over her mouth. For a second Shorthouse stood stock-still, catching his breath. He felt as if his spine had suddenly become hollow and someone had filled it with particles of ice.

Facing them, directly in their way between the doorposts, stood the figure of a woman. She had disheveled hair and wildly staring eyes, and her face was terrified and white as death.

She stood there motionless for the space of a single second. Then the candle flickered and she was gone—gone utterly— and the door framed nothing but empty darkness.

"Only the beastly jumping candlelight," he said quickly, in a voice that sounded like someone else's and was only half under control. "Come on, Aunt. There's nothing there."

He dragged her forward. With a clattering of feet and a great appearance of boldness they went on, but over his body the skin moved as if crawling ants covered it, and he knew by the weight on his arm that he was supplying the force of locomotion for two. The scullery was cold, bare, and empty; more like a large prison cell than anything else. They went round it, tried the door into the yard, and the windows, but found them all fastened securely. His aunt moved beside him like a person in a dream. Her eyes were tightly shut, and she seemed merely to follow the pressure of his arm. Her courage filled him with amazement. At the same time he noticed that a certain odd change had come over her face, a change which somehow evaded his power of analysis.

"There's nothing here, Aunty," he repeated aloud quickly. "Let's go upstairs and see the rest of the house. Then we'll choose a room to wait up in."

She followed him obediently, keeping close to his side, and they locked the kitchen door behind them. It was a relief to get up again. In the hall there was more light than before, for the moon had traveled a little further down the stairs. Cautiously they began to go up into the dark vault of the upper house, the boards creaking under their weight.

On the first floor they found the large double drawing rooms, a search of which revealed nothing. Here also was no sign of furniture or recent occupancy; nothing but dust and neglect and shadows. They opened the big folding doors between front and back drawing rooms and then came out again to the landing and went on upstairs.

They had not gone up more than a dozen steps when they both simultaneously stopped to listen, looking into each other's eyes with a new apprehension across the flickering candle flame. From the room they had left hardly ten seconds before came the sound of doors quietly closing. It was beyond all question; they heard the booming noise that accompanies the shutting of heavy doors, followed by the sharp catching of the latch.

"We must go back and see," said Shorthouse briefly, in a low tone, and turned to go downstairs again.

Somehow she managed to drag after him, her feet catching in her dress, her face livid.

When they entered the front drawing room it was plain that the folding doors had been closed—half a minute before.

15

Without hesitation Shorthouse opened them. He almost expected to see someone facing him in the back room; but only darkness and cold air met him. They went through both rooms, finding nothing unusual. They tried in every way to make the doors close of themselves, but there was no wind enough even to set the candle flame flickering. The doors would not move without strong pressure. All was silent as the grave. Undeniably the rooms were utterly empty, and the house utterly still.

"It's beginning," whispered a voice at his elbow, which he hardly recognized as his aunt's.

He nodded acquiescence, taking out his watch to note the time. It was fifteen minutes before midnight; he made the entry of exactly what had occurred in his notebook, setting the candle in its case upon the floor in order to do so. It took a minute or two to balance it safely against the wall.

Aunt Julia always declared that at this moment she was not actually watching him, but had turned her head towards the inner room, where she fancied she heard something moving; but, at any rate, both positively agreed that there came a sound of rushing feet, heavy and very swift—and the next instant the candle was out!

But to Shorthouse himself had come more than this, and he has always thanked his fortunate stars that it came to him alone and not to his aunt too. For, as he rose from the stooping position of balancing the candle, and before it was actually extinguished, a face thrust itself forward so close to his own that he could almost have touched it with his lips. It was a face working with passion; a man's face, dark, with thick features, and angry, savage eyes. It belonged to a common man, and it was evil in its ordinary normal expression, no doubt, but as he saw it, alive with intense, aggressive emotion, it was a malignant and terrible human countenance.

There was no movement of the air; nothing but the sound of rushing feet—stockinged or muffled feet; the apparition of the face; and the almost simultaneous extinguishing of the candle.

In spite of himself, Shorthouse uttered a little cry, nearly losing his balance as his aunt clung to him with her whole weight in one moment of real, uncontrollable terror. She made no sound, but simply seized him bodily. Fortunately, however, she had seen nothing, but had only heard the rushing feet, for her control returned almost at once, and he was able to disentangle himself and strike a match.

The shadows ran away on all sides before the glare, and his aunt stooped down and groped for the cigar case with the precious candle. Then they discovered that the candle had not been *blown* out at all; it had been *crushed* out. The wick was pressed down into the wax, which was flattened as if by some smooth, heavy instrument.

How his companion so quickly overcame her terror, Shorthouse never properly understood; but his admiration for her self-control increased tenfold, and at the same time served to feed his own dying flame—for which he was undeniably grateful. Equally inexplicable to him was the evidence of physical force they had just witnessed. He at once suppressed the memory of stories he had heard of "physical mediums" and their dangerous phenomena; for if these were true, and either his aunt or himself was unwittingly a physical medium, it meant that they were simply aiding to focus the forces of a haunted house already charged to the brim. It was like walking with unprotected lamps among uncovered stores of gunpowder.

So, with as little reflection as possible, he simply relit the candle and went up to the next floor. The arm in his trembled, it is true, and his own tread was often uncertain, but they went on with thoroughness, and after a search revealing nothing they climbed the last flight of stairs to the top floor of all.

Here they found a perfect nest of small servants' rooms,

with broken pieces of furniture, dirty cane-bottomed chairs, chests of drawers, cracked mirrors, and decrepit bedsteads. The rooms had low sloping ceilings already hung here and there with cobwebs, small windows, and badly plastered walls —a depressing and dismal region which they were glad to leave behind.

It was on the stroke of midnight when they entered a small room on the third floor, close to the top of the stairs, and arranged to make themselves comfortable for the remainder of their adventure. It was absolutely bare, and was said to be the room—then used as a clothes closet—into which the infuriated groom had chased his victim and finally caught her. Outside, across the narrow landing, began the stairs leading up to the floor above, and the servants' quarters where they had just searched.

In spite of the chilliness of the night there was something in the air of this room that cried for an open window. But there was more than this. Shorthouse could only describe it by saying that he felt less master of himself here than in any other part of the house. There was something that acted directly on the nerves, tiring the resolution, enfeebling the will. He was conscious of this result before he had been in the room five minutes, and it was in the short time they stayed there that he suffered the wholesale depletion of his vital forces, which was, for himself, the chief horror of the whole experience.

They put the candle on the floor of the cupboard, leaving the door a few inches ajar, so that there was no glare to confuse the eyes, and no shadow to shift about on walls and ceiling. Then they spread the cloak on the floor and sat down to wait, with their backs against the wall.

Shorthouse was within two feet of the door onto the landing; his position commanded a good view of the main staircase leading down into the darkness, and also of the beginning of the servants' stairs going to the floor above; the heavy stick lay beside him within easy reach.

The moon was now high above the house. Through the open window they could see the comforting stars like friendly eyes watching in the sky. One by one the clocks of the town struck midnight, and when the sounds died away the deep silence of a windless night fell again over everything. Only the boom of the sea, far away and lugubrious, filled the air with hollow murmurs.

Inside the house the silence became awful; awful, he thought, because any minute now it might be broken by sounds portending terror. The strain of waiting told more and more severely on the nerves; they talked in whispers when they talked at all, for their voices aloud sounded queer and unnatural. A chilliness, not altogether due to the night air, invaded the room, and made them cold. The influences against them, whatever these might be, were slowly robbing them of self-confidence, and the power of decisive action; their forces were on the wane, and the possibility of real fear took on a new and terrible meaning. He began to tremble for the elderly woman by his side, whose pluck could hardly save her beyond a certain extent.

He heard the blood singing in his veins. It sometimes seemed so loud that he fancied it prevented his hearing properly certain other sounds that were beginning very faintly to make themselves audible in the depths of the house. Every time he fastened his attention on these sounds, they instantly ceased. They certainly came no nearer. Yet he could not rid himself of the idea that movement was going on somewhere in the lower regions of the house. The drawing-room floor, where the doors had been so strangely closed, seemed too near; the sounds were further off than that. He thought of the great kitchen, with the scurrying black beetles, and of the dismal little scullery; but, somehow or other, they did not seem to come from there either. Surely they were not *outside* the house!

Then, suddenly, the truth flashed into his mind, and for

19

the space of a minute he felt as if his blood had stopped flowing and turned to ice.

The sounds were not downstairs at all; they were *upstairs* —upstairs, somewhere among those horrid gloomy little servants' rooms with their bits of broken furniture, low ceilings, and cramped windows—upstairs where the victim had first been disturbed and stalked to her death.

And the moment he discovered where the sounds were, he began to hear them more clearly. It was the sound of feet, moving stealthily along the passage overhead, in and out among the rooms, and past the furniture.

He turned quickly to steal a glance at the motionless figure seated beside him, to note whether she had shared his discovery. The faint candlelight coming through the crack in the cupboard door, threw her strongly marked face into vivid relief against the white of the wall. But it was something else that made him catch his breath and stare again. An extraordinary something had come into her face and seemed to spread over her features like a mask; it smoothed out the deep lines and drew the skin everywhere a little tighter so that the wrinkles disappeared; it brought into the face—with the sole exception of the old eyes—an appearance of youth and almost of childhood.

He stared in speechless amazement—amazement that was dangerously near to horror. It was his aunt's face indeed, but it was her face of forty years ago, the vacant innocent face of a girl. He had heard stories of that strange effect of terror which could wipe a human countenance clean of other emotions, obliterating all previous expressions; but he had never realized that it could be literally true, or could mean anything so simply horrible as what he now saw. For the dreadful signature of overmastering fear was written plainly in that utter vacancy of the girlish face beside him; and when, feeling his intense gaze, she turned to look at him, he instinctively closed his eyes tightly to shut out the sight.

Yet, when he turned a minute later, his feelings well in hand, he saw to his intense relief another expression; his aunt was smiling, and though the face was deathly white, the awful veil had lifted and the normal look was returning.

"Anything wrong?" was all he could think of to say at the moment. And the answer was eloquent, coming from such a woman.

"I feel cold—and a little frightened," she whispered.

He offered to close the window, but she seized hold of him and begged him not to leave her side even for an instant.

"It's upstairs, I know," she whispered, with an odd half laugh; "but I can't possibly go up."

But Shorthouse thought otherwise, knowing that in action lay their best hope of self-control.

He took the brandy flask and poured out a glass of neat spirit, stiff enough to help anybody over anything. She swallowed it with a little shiver. His only idea now was to get out of the house before her collapse became inevitable; but this could not safely be done by turning tail and running from the enemy. Inaction was no longer possible; every minute he was growing less master of himself, and desperate, aggressive measures were imperative without further delay. Moreover, the action must be taken *towards* the enemy, not away from it; the climax, if necessary and unavoidable, would have to be faced boldly. He could do it now; but in ten minutes he might not have the force left to act for himself, much less for both!

Upstairs, the sounds were meanwhile becoming louder and closer, accompanied by occasional creaking of the boards. Someone was moving stealthily about, stumbling now and then awkwardly against the furniture.

Waiting a few minutes to allow the tremendous dose of spirits to produce its effect, and knowing this would last but a short time under the circumstances, Shorthouse then quietly got on his feet, saying in a determined voice:

"Now, Aunt Julia, we'll go upstairs and find out what all this noise is about. You must come too. It's what we agreed."

He picked up his stick and went to the cupboard for the candle. A limp form rose shakily beside him, breathing hard, and he heard a voice say very faintly something about being "ready to come." The woman's courage amazed him; it was so much greater than his own; and, as they advanced, holding aloft the dripping candle, some subtle force exhaled from this trembling, white-faced old woman at his side that was the true source of his inspiration. It held something really great that shamed him and gave him the support without which he would have proved far less equal to the occasion.

They crossed the dark landing, avoiding with their eyes the black space over the banisters. Then they began to mount the narrow staircase to meet the sounds which, minute by minute, grew louder and nearer. About halfway up the stairs Aunt Julia stumbled and Shorthouse turned to catch her by the arm, and just at that moment there came a terrific crash in the servants' corridor overhead. It was instantly followed by a shrill, agonized scream that was a cry of terror and a cry for help melted into one.

Before they could move aside, or go down a single step, someone came rushing along, the passage overhead, blundering horribly, racing madly, at full speed, three steps at a time, down the very staircase where they stood. The steps were light and uncertain; but close behind them sounded the heavier tread of another person, and the staircase seemed to shake.

Shorthouse and his companion just had time to flatten themselves against the wall when the jumble of flying steps was upon them, and two persons, with the slightest possible interval between them, dashed past at full speed. It was a perfect whirlwind of sound breaking in upon the midnight silence of the empty building.

The two runners, pursuer and pursued, had passed clean through them where they stood, and already with a thud the boards below had received first one, then the other. Yet they had seen absolutely nothing—not a hand, or arm, or face, or even a shred of flying clothing.

There came a second's pause. Then the first one, the lighter of the two, obviously the pursued one, ran with uncertain steps into the little room which Shorthouse and his aunt had just left. The heavier one followed. There was a sound of scuffling, gasping, and smothered screaming; and then out on to the landing came the step—of a single person *treading weightily*.

A dead silence followed for the space of half a minute, and then was heard a rushing sound through the air. It was followed by a dull, crashing thud in the depths of the house below—on the stone floor of the hall.

Utter silence reigned after. Nothing moved. The flame of the candle was steady. It had been steady the whole time, and the air had been undisturbed by any movement whatsoever. Palsied with terror, Aunt Julia, without waiting for her companion, began fumbling her way downstairs; she was crying gently to herself, and when Shorthouse put his arm round her and half carried her he felt that she was trembling like a leaf. He went into the little room and picked up the cloak from the floor, and, arm in arm, walking very slowly, without speaking a word or looking once behind them, they marched down the three flights into the hall.

In the hall they saw nothing, but the whole way down the stairs they were conscious that someone followed them; step by step; when they went faster IT was left behind, and when they went more slowly IT caught them up. But never once did they look behind to see; and at each turning of the staircase they lowered their eyes for fear of the following horror they might see upon the stairs above.

With trembling hands Shorthouse opened the front door, and they walked out into the moonlight and drew a deep breath of the cool night air blowing in from the sea.

AUGUST
HEAT
BY
W.F.HARVEY

PENISTONE ROAD, CLAPHAM,

20TH AUGUST, 190—

I have had what I believe to be the most remarkable day in my life, and while the events are still fresh in my mind, I wish to put them down on paper as clearly as possible.

Let me say at the outset that my name is James Clarence Withencroft.

I am forty years old, in perfect health, never having known a day's illness.

By profession I am an artist, not a very successful one, but I earn enough money by my black-and-white work to satisfy my necessary wants.

My only near relative, a sister, died five years ago, so that I am independent.

I breakfasted this morning at nine, and after glancing through the morning paper I lighted my pipe and proceeded to let my mind wander in the hope that I might chance upon some subject for my pencil.

The room, though door and windows were open, was oppressively hot, and I had just made up my mind that the coolest and most comfortable place in the neighborhood would be the deep end of the public swimming bath, when the idea came.

I began to draw. So intent was I on my work that I left my lunch untouched, only stopping work when the clock of St. Jude's struck four.

The final result, for a hurried sketch, was, I felt sure, the best thing I had done.

It showed a criminal in the dock immediately after the judge had pronounced sentence. The man was fat—enormously fat. The flesh hung in rolls about his chin; it creased his huge, stumpy neck. He was clean-shaven (perhaps I should say a few days before, he must have been clean-shaven) and almost bald. He stood in the dock, his short, clumsy fingers clasping the rail, looking straight in front of him. The feeling that his expression conveyed was not so much one of horror as of utter, absolute collapse.

There seemed nothing in the man strong enough to sustain that mountain of flesh.

I rolled up the sketch, and, without quite knowing why, placed it in my pocket. Then with the rare sense of happiness which the knowledge of a good thing well done gives, I left the house.

I believe that I set out with the idea of calling upon Trenton, for I remember walking along Lytton Street and turning to the right along Gilchrist Road at the bottom of the hill where the men were at work on the new tram lines.

From there onwards I have only the vaguest recollection of where I went. The one thing of which I was fully conscious was the awful heat that came up from the dusty asphalt pavement as an almost palpable wave. I longed for the thunder promised by the great banks of copper-colored cloud that hung low over the western sky.

I must have walked five or six miles, when a small boy roused me from my reverie by asking the time.

It was twenty minutes to seven.

When he left me I began to take stock of my bearings. I found myself standing before a gate that led into a yard bordered by a strip of thirsty earth, where there were flowers, purple stock and scarlet geranium. Above the entrance was a board with the inscription:

CHS. ATKINSON   MONUMENTAL MASON
WORKER IN ENGLISH AND ITALIAN MARBLES

From the yard itself came a cheery whistle, the noise of hammer blows, and the cold sound of steel meeting stone.

A sudden impulse made me enter.

A man was sitting with his back towards me, busy at work on a slab of curiously veined marble. He turned round as he heard my steps, and I stopped short.

It was the man I had been drawing, whose portrait lay in my pocket.

He sat there, huge and elephantine, the sweat pouring from his scalp, which he wiped with a red silk handkerchief. But though the face was the same, the expression was absolutely different.

He greeted me smiling, as if we were old friends, and shook my hand.

I apologized for my intrusion.

"Everything is hot and glary outside," I said. "This seems an oasis in the wilderness."

"I don't know about the oasis," he replied, "but it certainly is hot, as hot as hell. Take a seat, sir!"

He pointed to the end of the gravestone on which he was at work, and I sat down.

"That's a beautiful piece of stone you've got hold of," I said.

He shook his head. "In a way it is," he answered; "the surface here is as fine as anything you could wish, but there's a big flaw at the back, though I don't expect you'd ever notice

29

it. I could never make really a good job of a bit of marble like that. It would be all right in a summer like this; it wouldn't mind the blasted heat. But wait till the winter comes. There's nothing quite like frost to find out the weak points in stone."

"Then what's it for?" I asked.

The man burst out laughing.

"You'd hardly believe me if I was to tell you it's for an exhibition, but it's the truth. Artists have exhibitions: so do grocers and butchers; we have them too. All the latest little things in headstones, you know."

He went on to talk of marbles, which sort best withstood wind and rain, and which were easiest to work; then of his garden and a new sort of carnation he had bought. At the end of every other minute he would drop his tools, wipe his shining head, and curse the heat.

I said little, for I felt uneasy. There was something unnatural, uncanny, in meeting this man.

I tried at first to persuade myself that I had seen him before, that his face, unknown to me, had found a place in some out-of-the-way corner of my memory, but I knew that I was practicing little more than a plausible piece of self-deception.

Mr. Atkinson finished his work, spat on the ground, and got up with a sigh of relief.

"There! what do you think of that?" he said, with an air of evident pride.

The inscription which I read for the first time was this:

SACRED TO THE MEMORY
OF
JAMES CLARENCE WITHENCROFT
BORN JAN. 18TH, 1860
HE PASSED AWAY VERY SUDDENLY
ON AUGUST 20TH, 190—
"In the midst of life we are in death"

For some time I sat in silence. Then a cold shudder ran down my spine. I asked him where he had seen the name.

"Oh, I didn't see it anywhere," replied Mr. Atkinson. "I wanted some name, and I put down the first that came into my head. Why do you want to know?"

"It's a strange coincidence, but it happens to be mine."

He gave a long, low whistle.

"And the dates?"

"I can only answer for one of them, and that's correct."

"It's a rum go!" he said.

But he knew less than I did. I told him of my morning's work. I took the sketch from my pocket and showed it to him. As he looked, the expression of his face altered until it became more and more like that of the man I had drawn.

"And it was only the day before yesterday," he said, "that I told Maria there were no such things as ghosts!"

Neither of us had seen a ghost, but I knew what he meant.

"You probably heard my name," I said.

"And you must have seen me somewhere and have forgotten it! Were you at Clacton-on-Sea last July?"

I had never been to Clacton in my life. We were silent for some time. We were both looking at the same thing, the two dates on the gravestone, and one was right.

"Come inside and have some supper," said Mr. Atkinson.

His wife is a cheerful little woman, with the flaky red cheeks of the country-bred. Her husband introduced me as a friend of his who was an artist. The result was unfortunate, for after the sardines and watercress had been removed, she brought out a Doré Bible, and I had to sit and express my admiration for nearly half an hour.

I went outside, and found Atkinson sitting on the gravestone smoking.

We resumed the conversation at the point we had left off.

"You must excuse my asking," I said, "but do you know of anything you've done for which you could be put on trial?"

He shook his head.

"I'm not a bankrupt, the business is prosperous enough. Three years ago I gave turkeys to some of the guardians at Christmas, but that's all I can think of. And they were small ones, too," he added as an afterthought.

He got up, fetched a can from the porch, and began to water the flowers. "Twice a day regular in the hot weather," he said, "and then the heat sometimes gets the better of the delicate ones. And ferns, good Lord! they could never stand it. Where do you live?"

I told him my address. It would take an hour's quick walk to get back home.

"It's like this," he said. "We'll look at the matter straight. If you go back home tonight, you take your chance of accidents. A cart may run over you, and there's always banana skins and orange peel, to say nothing of falling ladders."

He spoke of the improbable with an intense seriousness that would have been laughable six hours before. But I did not laugh.

"The best thing we can do," he continued, "is for you to stay here till twelve o'clock. We'll go upstairs and smoke; it may be cooler inside."

To my surprise I agreed.

We are sitting now in a long, low room beneath the eaves. Atkinson has sent his wife to bed. He himself is busy sharpening some tools at a little oilstone, smoking one of my cigars the while.

The air seems charged with thunder. I am writing this at a shaky table before the open window. The leg is cracked, and Atkinson, who seems a handy man with his tools, is going to mend it as soon as he has finished putting an edge on his chisel.

It is after eleven now. I shall be gone in less than an hour.
But the heat is stifling.

It is enough to send a man mad.

THE SIGNALMAN
by Charles Dickens

"HALLOA! BELOW THERE!"

When he heard a voice thus calling to him, he was standing at the door of his box, with a flag in his hand, furled round its short pole. One would have thought, considering the nature of the ground, that he could not have doubted from what quarter the voice came; but instead of looking up to where I stood on the top of the steep cutting nearly over his head, he turned himself about and looked down the Line. There was something remarkable in his manner of doing so, though I could not have said for my life what. But I know it was remarkable enough to attract my notice, even though his figure was foreshortened and shadowed, down in the deep trench, and mine was high above him, so steeped in the glow of an angry sunset that I had shaded my eyes with my hand before I saw him at all.

"Halloa! Below!"

From looking down the Line, he turned himself about again and, raising his eyes, saw my figure high above him.

"Is there any path by which I can come down and speak to you?"

37

He looked up at me without replying, and I looked down at him without pressing him too soon with a repetition of my idle question. Just then there came a vague vibration in the earth and air, quickly changing into a violent pulsation, and an oncoming rush that caused me to start back, as though it had force to draw me down. When such vapor as rose to my height from this rapid train had passed me, and was skimming away over the landscape, I looked down again, and saw him refurling the flag he had shown while the train went by.

I repeated my inquiry. After a pause, during which he seemed to regard me with fixed attention, he motioned with his rolled-up flag towards a point on my level, some two or three hundred yards distant. I called down to him, "All right!" and made for that point. There, by dint of looking closely about me, I found a rough zigzag descending path notched out, which I followed.

The cutting was extremely deep, and unusually precipitate. It was made through a clammy stone that became oozier and wetter as I went down. For these reasons, I found the way long enough to give me time to recall a singular air of reluctance or compulsion with which he had pointed out the path.

When I came down low enough upon the zigzag descent to see him again, I saw that he was standing between the rails on the way by which the train had lately passed, in an attitude as if he were waiting for me to appear. He had his left hand at his chin, and that left elbow rested on his right hand, crossed over his breast. His attitude was one of such expectation and watchfulness that I stopped a moment, wondering at it.

I resumed my downward way, and stepping out upon the level of the railroad, and drawing nearer to him, saw that he was a dark, sallow man, with a dark beard and rather heavy eyebrows. His post was in as solitary and dismal a place as ever I saw. On either side, a dripping-wet wall of jagged stone, excluding all view but a strip of sky; the perspective one way only a crooked prolongation of this great dungeon; the shorter perspective in the other direction terminating in a gloomy red light, and the gloomier entrance to a black tunnel, in whose massive architecture there was a barbarous, depressing, and forbidding air. So little sunlight ever found its way to this spot that it had an earthy, deadly smell; and so much cold wind rushed through it that it struck chill to me, as if I had left the natural world.

Before he stirred, I was near enough to him to have touched him. Not even then removing his eyes from mine, he stepped back one step, and lifted his hand.

This was a lonesome post to occupy (I said), and it had riveted my attention when I looked down from up yonder. A visitor was a rarity, I should suppose; not an unwelcome rarity, I hoped? In me, he merely saw a man who had been shut up within narrow limits all his life, and who, being at last set free, had a newly awakened interest in these great works. To such purpose I spoke to him; but I am far from sure of the terms I used; for, besides that I am not happy in opening any conversation, there was something in the man that daunted me.

He directed a most curious look towards the red light near the tunnel's mouth, and looked all about it, as if something were missing from it, and then looked at me.

That light was part of his charge? Was it not?

He answered in a low voice—"Don't you know it is?"

The monstrous thought came into my mind, as I perused the fixed eyes and the saturnine face, that this was a spirit, not a man. I have speculated since, whether there may have been infection in his mind.

In my turn I stepped back. But in making the action, I detected in his eyes some latent fear of me. This put the monstrous thought to flight.

"You look at me," I said, forcing a smile, "as if you had a dread of me."

"I was doubtful," he returned, "whether I had seen you before."

"Where?"

He pointed to the red light he had looked at.

"There?" I said.

Intently watchful of me, he replied (but without sound), "Yes."

"My good fellow, what should I do there? However, be that as it may, I never was there, you may swear."

"I think I may," he rejoined. "Yes; I am sure I may."

His manner cleared, like my own. He replied to my remarks with readiness, and in well-chosen words. Had he much to do there? Yes; that was to say, he had enough responsibility to bear; but exactness and watchfulness were what was required of him, and of actual work—manual labor—he had next to none. To change that signal, to trim those lights, and to turn this iron handle now and then, was all he had to do under that head. Regarding those many long and lonely hours of which I seemed to make so much, he could only say that the routine of his life had shaped itself into that form, and he had grown used to it. He had taught himself a language down here—if only to know it by sight, and to have formed his own crude ideas of its pronunciation, could be called learning it. He had also worked at fractions and decimals, and tried a little algebra; but he was, and had been as a boy, a poor hand at figures. Was it necessary for him when on duty always to remain in that channel of damp air, and could he never rise into the sunshine from between those high stone walls? Why, that depended upon time and circumstances. Under some conditions there would be less upon the Line than under others, and the same held good as to certain hours of the day and night. In bright weather, he did choose occasions for getting a little above these lower shadows; but, being at all times liable to be called by his electric bell, and at such times listening for it with re-doubled anxiety, the relief was less than I would suppose.

He took me into his box, where there was a fire, a desk for an official book in which he had to make certain entries, a telegraphic instrument with its dial, face, and needles, and the little bell of which he had spoken. On my trusting that he would excuse the remark that he had been well educated, and (I hoped I might say without offense) perhaps educated above that station, he observed that instances of slight incongruity in such wise would rarely be found wanting among large bodies of men; that he had heard it was so in workhouses, in the police force, even in that last desperate resource, the army; and that he knew it was so, more or less, in any great railway staff. He had been, when young (if I could believe it, sitting in that hut—he scarcely could), a student of natural philosophy, and had attended lectures; but he had run wild, misused his opportunities, gone down, and never risen again. He had no complaint to offer about that. He had made his bed, and he lay upon it. It was far too late to make another.

All that I have here condensed he said in a quiet manner, with his grave dark regards divided between me and the fire. He threw in the word, "Sir," from time to time, and especially when he referred to his youth—as though to request me to understand that he claimed to be nothing but what I found him. He was several times interrupted by the little bell, and had to read off messages, and send replies. Once he had to stand without the door, and display a flag as a train passed, and make some verbal communication to the driver. In the discharge of his duties, I observed him to be remarkably exact and vigilant, breaking off his discourse at a syllable and remaining silent until what he had to do was done.

In a word, I should have set this man down as one of the safest of men to be employed in that capacity, but for the circumstance that while he was speaking to me he twice broke off with a fallen color, turned his face towards the little bell when it did NOT ring, opened the door of the hut (which was kept shut to exclude the unhealthy damp), and looked out towards the red light near the mouth of the tunnel. On both of those occasions, he came back to the fire with the inexplicable air upon him which I had remarked, without being able to define, when we were so far asunder.

Said I, when I rose to leave him, "You almost make me think that I have met with a contented man."

(I am afraid I must acknowledge that I said it to lead him on.)

"I believe I used to be so," he rejoined, in the low voice in which he had first spoken; "but I am troubled, sir, I am troubled."

He would have recalled the words if he could. He had said them, however, and I took them up quickly.

"With what? What is your trouble?"

"It is very difficult to impart, sir. It is very, very difficult to speak of. If ever you make me another visit, I will try to tell you."

"But I expressly intend to make you another visit. Say, when shall it be?"

"I go off early in the morning, and I shall be on again at ten tomorrow night, sir."

"I will come at eleven."

He thanked me, and went out at the door with me. "I'll show my white light, sir," he said, in his peculiar low voice, "till you have found the way up. When you have found it, don't call out! And when you are at the top, don't call out."

His manner seemed to make the place strike colder to me, but I said no more than, "Very well."

"And when you come down tomorrow night, don't call out! Let me ask you a parting question. What made you cry 'Halloa! Below there!' tonight?"

"Heaven knows," said I, "I cried something to that effect——"

"Not to that effect, sir. Those were the very words. I know them well."

"Admit those were the very words. I said them, no doubt, because I saw you below."

"For no other reason?"

"What other reason could I possibly have?"

"You had no feeling that they were conveyed to you in any supernatural way?"

"No."

He wished me good night, and held up his light. I walked by the side of the down Line of rails (with a very disagreeable sensation of a train coming behind me) until I found the path. It was easier to mount than to descend, and I got back to my inn without any adventure.

Punctual to my appointment, I placed my foot on the first notch of the zigzag next night, as the distant clocks were striking eleven. He was waiting for me at the bottom, with his white light on. "I have not called out," I said, when we came close together; "may I speak now?" "By all means, sir." "Good night, then, and here's my hand." "Good night, sir, and here's mine." With that we walked side by side to his box, entered it, closed the door, and sat down by the fire.

"I have made up my mind, sir," he began, bending forward as soon as we were seated, and speaking in a tone but a little above a whisper, "that you shall not have to ask me twice what troubles me. I took you for someone else yesterday evening. That troubles me."

"That mistake?"

"No. That someone else."

"Who is it?"

"I don't know."

"Like me?"

"I don't know. I never saw the face. The left arm is across the face, and the right arm is waved, violently waved. This way."

I followed his action with my eyes, and it was the action of an arm gesticulating, with the utmost passion and vehemence, "For God's sake, clear the way!"

"One moonlight night," said the man, "I was sitting here, when I heard a voice cry, 'Halloa! Below there!' I started up, looked from that door, and saw this Someone else standing by the red light near the tunnel, waving as I just now showed you. The voice seemed hoarse with shouting, and it cried, 'Look out!' Look out!' And then again, 'Halloa! Below there! Look out!' I caught up my lamp, turned it on red, and ran towards the figure, calling, 'What's wrong? What has happened? Where?' It stood just outside the blackness of the tunnel. I advanced so close upon it that I wondered at its keeping the sleeve across its eyes. I ran right up at it, and had my hand stretched out to pull the sleeve away, when it was gone."

"Into the tunnel?" said I.

"No. I ran on into the tunnel, five hundred yards. I stopped, and held my lamp above my head, and saw the figures of the measured distance, and saw the wet stains stealing down the walls and trickling through the arch. I ran out again faster than I had run in (for I had a mortal abhorrence of the place upon me), and I looked all round the red light with my own red light, and I went up the iron ladder to the gallery atop of it, and I came down again, and ran back here. I telegraphed both ways. 'An alarm has been given. Is anything wrong?' The answer came back, both ways, 'All well.' "

Resisting the slow touch of a frozen finger tracing out my spine, I showed him how that this figure must be a deception of his sense of sight; and how figures, originating in disease of the delicate nerves that minister to the functions of the eye, were known to have often troubled patients, some of whom had become conscious of the nature of their affliction, and had even proved it by experiments upon themselves. "As to an imaginary cry," said I, "do but listen for a moment to the wind in this unnatural valley while we speak so low, and to the wild harp it makes of the telegraph wires."

That was all very well, he returned, after we had sat listening for a while, and he ought to know something of the wind and the wires—he who so often passed long winter nights there, alone and watching. But he would beg to remark that he had not finished.

I asked his pardon, and he slowly added these words, touching my arm:

"Within six hours after the appearance, the memorable accident on this Line happened, and within ten hours the dead and wounded were brought along through the tunnel over the spot where the figure had stood."

A disagreeable shudder crept over me, but I did my best against it. It was not to be denied, I rejoined, that this was a remarkable coincidence, calculated deeply to impress his mind. But it was unquestionable that remarkable coincidences did continually occur, and they must be taken into account in dealing with such a subject. Though to be sure I must admit, I added (for I thought I saw that he was going to bring the objection to bear upon me), men of common sense did not allow much for coincidences in making the ordinary calculations of life.

He again begged to remark that he had not finished.

I again begged his pardon for being betrayed into interruptions.

"This," he said, again laying his hand upon my arm, and glancing over his shoulder with hollow eyes, "was just a year ago. Six or seven months passed, and I had recovered from the surprise and shock, when one morning, as the day was breaking, I, standing at the door, looked towards the red light, and saw the specter again." He stopped with a fixed look at me.

"Did it cry out?"

"No. It was silent."

"Did it wave its arm?"

"No. It leaned against the shaft of the light, with both hands before the face. Like this."

Once more I followed his action with my eyes. It was an

action of mourning. I have seen such an attitude on stone figures on tombs.

"Did you go up to it?"

"I came in and sat down, partly to collect my thoughts, partly because it had turned me faint. When I went to the door again, daylight was above me, and the ghost was gone."

"But nothing followed? Nothing came of this?"

He touched me on the arm with his forefinger twice or thrice, giving a ghastly nod each time:

"That very day, as a train came out of the tunnel I noticed, at a carriage window on my side, what looked like a confusion of hands and heads, and something waved. I saw it just in time to signal the driver, Stop! He shut off, and put his brake on, but the train drifted past here a hundred and fifty yards or more. I ran after it, and, as I went along, heard terrible screams and cries. A beautiful young lady had died instantaneously in one of the compartments, and was brought in here, and laid down on the floor between us."

Involuntarily I pushed my chair back, as I looked from the boards at which he pointed to himself.

"True, sir. True. Precisely as it happened, so I tell it you."

I could think of nothing to say, to any purpose, and my mouth was very dry. The wind and the wires took up the story with a long lamenting wail.

He resumed, "Now, sir, mark this, and judge how my mind is troubled. The specter came back a week ago. Ever since, it has been there, now and again, by fits and starts."

"At the light?"

"At the danger light."

"What does it seem to do?"

He repeated, if possible with increased passion and vehemence, that former gesticulation of "For God's sake, clear the way!"

Then he went on. "I have no peace or rest for it. It calls to me, for many minutes together, in an agonized manner,

'Below there! Look out! Look out!' It stands waving to me. It rings my little bell——"

I caught at that. "Did it ring your bell yesterday evening when I was here, and you went to the door?"

"Twice."

"Why, see," said I, "how your imagination misleads you. My eyes were on the bell, and my ears were open to the bell, and if I am a living man, it did NOT ring at those times. No, nor at any other time, except when it was rung in the natural course of physical things by the station communicating with you."

He shook his head. "I have never made a mistake as to that yet, sir. I have never confused the specter's ring with the man's. The ghost's ring is a strange vibration in the bell that it derives from nothing else, and I have not asserted that the bell stirs to the eye. I don't wonder that you failed to hear it. But *I* heard it."

"And did the specter seem to be there when you looked out?"

"It was there."

"Both times?"

He repeated firmly: "Both times."

"Will you come to the door with me, and look for it now?"

He bit his under lip as though he were somewhat unwilling, but arose. I opened the door, and stood on the step, while he stood in the doorway. There was the danger light. There was the dismal mouth of the tunnel. There were the high, wet stone walls of the cutting. There were the stars above them.

"Do you see it?" I asked him, taking particular note of his face. His eyes were prominent and strained, but not very much more so, perhaps, than my own had been when I had directed them earnestly towards the same spot.

"No," he answered. "It is not there."

"Agreed," said I.

We went in again, shut the door, and resumed our seats. I was thinking how best to improve this advantage, if it might be called one, when he took up the conversation in such a matter-of-course way, so assuming that there could be no serious question of fact between us, that I felt myself placed in the weakest of positions.

"By this time you will fully understand, sir," he said, "that what troubles me so dreadfully is the question, 'What does the specter mean?'"

I was not sure, I told him, that I did fully understand.

"What is its warning against?" he said, ruminating, with his eyes on the fire, and only by times turning them on me. "What is the danger? Where is the danger? There is danger overhanging somewhere on the Line. Some dreadful calamity will happen. It is not to be doubted this third time, after what has gone before. But surely this is a cruel haunting of *me*. What can I do?"

He pulled out his handkerchief, and wiped the drops from his heated forehead.

"If I telegraph Danger, on either side of me, or on both, I can give no reason for it," he went on, wiping the palms of his hands. "I should get into trouble and do no good. They would think I was mad. This is the way it would work—Message: 'Danger! Take Care!' Answer: 'What Danger? Where?' Message: 'Don't know. But, for God's sake, take care!' They would displace me. What else could they do?"

His pain of mind was most pitiable to see. It was the mental torture of a conscientious man, oppressed beyond endurance by an unintelligible responsibility involving life.

"When it first stood under the danger light," he went on, putting his dark hair back from his head, and drawing his hands outward across and across his temples in an extremity of feverish distress, "why not tell me where that accident was to happen—if it must happen? Why not tell me how it could be averted—if it could have been averted? When on its second coming it hid its face, why not tell me, instead, 'She is going to die. Let them keep her at home'? If it came, on those two occasions, only to show me that its warnings were true, and so to prepare me for the third, why not warn me plainly now? And I, Lord help me! a mere poor signalman on this solitary station! Why not go to somebody with credit to be believed, and power to act?"

When I saw him in this state, I saw that for the poor man's sake, as well as for the public safety, what I had to do for the time was to compose his mind. Therefore, setting aside all question of reality or unreality between us, I represented to him that whoever thoroughly discharged his duty must do well, and that at least it was his comfort that he understood his duty, though he did not understand these confounding appearances. In this effort I succeeded far better than in the attempt to reason him out of his conviction. He became calm; the occupations incidental to his post as the night advanced began to make larger demands on his attention: and I left him at two in the morning. I had offered to stay through the night, but he would not hear of it.

That I more than once looked back at the red light as I ascended the pathway, that I did not like the red light, and that I should have slept but poorly if my bed had been under it, I see no reason to conceal. Nor did I like the two sequences of the accident and the dead girl. I see no reason to conceal that either.

But what ran most in my thoughts was the consideration how ought I to act, having become the recipient of this disclosure? I had proved the man to be intelligent, vigilant, painstaking, and exact; but how long might he remain so, in his state of mind? Though in a subordinate position, still he held a most important trust, and would I (for instance) like to stake my life on the chance of his continuing to execute it with precision?

Unable to overcome a feeling that there would be something treacherous in my communicating what he had told me to his superiors in the Company, without first being plain with himself and proposing a middle course to him, I ultimately resolved to offer to accompany him (otherwise keeping his secret for the present) to the wisest medical practitioner we could hear of in those parts, and to take his opinion. A change in his time of duty would come round next night, he had apprised me, and he would be off an hour or two after sunrise, and on again soon after sunset. I had appointed to return accordingly.

Next evening was a lovely evening and I walked out early to enjoy it. The sun was not yet quite down when I traversed the field path near the top of the deep cutting. I would extend my walk for an hour, I said to myself, half an hour on and half an hour back, and it would then be time to go to my signalman's box.

Before pursuing my stroll, I stepped to the brink, and mechanically looked down, from the point from which I had first seen him. I cannot describe the thrill that seized upon me, when, close at the mouth of the tunnel, I saw the appearance of a man, with his left sleeve across his eyes, passionately waving his right arm.

The nameless horror that oppressed me passed in a moment, for in a moment I saw that this appearance of a man was a man indeed, and that there was a little group of other men, standing at a short distance, to whom he seemed to be rehearsing the gesture he made. The danger light was not yet lighted. Against its shaft a little low hut, entirely new to me, had been made of some wooden supports and tarpaulin. It looked no bigger than a bed.

With an irresistible sense that something was wrong—with a flashing self-reproachful fear that fatal mischief had come of my leaving the man there, and causing no one to be sent to overlook or correct what he did—I descended the notched path with all the speed I could make.

"What is the matter?" I asked the men.

"Signalman killed this morning, sir."

"Not the man belonging to that box?"

"Yes, sir."

"Not the man I know?"

"You will recognize him, sir, if you knew him," said the man who spoke for the others, solemnly uncovering his own head, and raising an end of the tarpaulin, "for his face is quite composed."

"Oh, how did this happen, how did this happen?" I asked, turning from one to another as the hut closed in again.

"He was cut down by an engine, sir. No man in England knew his work better. But somehow he was not clear of the outer rail. It was just at broad day. He had struck the light, and had the lamp in his hand. As the engine came out of the tunnel, his back was towards her, and she cut him down. That man drove her, and was showing how it happened. Show the gentleman, Tom."

The man, who wore a rough dark dress, stepped back to his former place at the mouth of the tunnel.

"Coming round the curve of the tunnel, sir," he said, "I saw him at the end, like as if I saw him down a perspective glass. There was no time to check speed, and I knew him to be very careful. As he didn't seem to take heed of the whistle, I shut it off when we were running down upon him, and called to him as loud as I could call."

"What did you say?"

"I said, 'Below there! Look out! Look out! For God's sake, clear the way.'"

I started.

"Ah! it was a dreadful time, sir. I never left off calling to him. I put my arm before my eyes not to see, and I waved this arm to the last; but it was no use."

Without prolonging the narrative to dwell on any one of its curious circumstances more than on any other, I may, in closing it, point out the coincidence that the warning of the engine driver included, not only the words which the unfortunate signalman had repeated to me as haunting him, but also the words which I myself—not he—had attached, and that only in my own mind, to the gesticulation he had imitated.

A Visitor from Down Under

L. P. HARTLEY

"And who will you send to fetch him away?"

AFTER A PROMISING start, the March day had ended in a wet evening. It was hard to tell whether rain or fog predominated. The loquacious bus conductor said "A foggy evening" to those who rode inside, and "A wet evening" to such as were obliged to ride outside. But in or on the buses, cheerfulness held the field, for their patrons, inured to discomfort, made light of climatic inclemency. All the same, the weather was worth remarking on: the most scrupulous conversationalist could refer to it without feeling self-convicted of banality. How much more the conductor who, in common with most of his kind, had a considerable conversational gift.

The bus was making its last journey through the heart of London before turning in for the night. Inside, it was only half full. Outside, as the conductor was aware by virtue of his sixth sense, there still remained a passenger too hardy or too lazy to seek shelter. And now, as the bus rattled rapidly down the Strand, the footsteps of this person could be heard shuffling and creaking upon the metal-shod stairs.

"Anyone on top?" asked the conductor, addressing an errant umbrella point and the hem of a macintosh.

"I didn't notice anyone," the man replied.

"It's not that I don't trust you," remarked the conductor pleasantly, giving a hand to his alighting fare, "but I think I'll go up and make sure."

Moments like these, moments of mistrust in the infallibility of his observation, occasionally visited the conductor. They came at the end of a tiring day, and if he could he withstood them. They were signs of weakness, he thought; and to give way to them matter for self-reproach. "Going balmy, that's what you are," he told himself, and he casually took a fare inside to prevent his mind dwelling on the unvisited outside. But his unreasoning disquietude survived this distraction, and murmuring against himself he started to climb the stairs.

To his surprise, almost stupefaction, he found that his misgivings were justified. Breasting the ascent, he saw a passenger sitting on the right-hand front seat; and the passenger, in spite of his hat turned down, his collar turned up, and the creased white muffler that showed between the two, must have heard him coming; for though the man was looking straight ahead, in his outstretched left hand, wedged between the first and second fingers, he held a coin.

"Jolly evening, don't you think?" asked the conductor, who wanted to say something. The passenger made no reply, but the penny, for such it was, slipped the fraction of an inch lower in the groove between the pale freckled fingers.

"I said it was a damn wet night," the conductor persisted irritably, annoyed by the man's reserve.

Still no reply.

"Where you for?" asked the conductor, in a tone suggesting that wherever it was, it must be a discreditable destination.

"Carrick Street."

"Where?" the conductor demanded. He had heard all right,

but a slight peculiarity in the passenger's pronunciation made it appear reasonable to him, and possibly humiliating to the passenger, that he should not have heard.

"Carrick Street."

"Then why don't you say Carrick Street?" the conductor grumbled as he punched the ticket.

There was a moment's pause, then:

"Carrick Street," the passenger repeated.

"Yes, I know, I know, you needn't go on telling me," fumed the conductor, fumbling with the passenger's penny. He couldn't get hold of it from above; it had slipped too far, so he passed his hand underneath the other's and drew the coin from between his fingers.

It was cold, even where it had been held. "Know?" said the stranger suddenly. "What do you know?"

The conductor was trying to draw his fare's attention to the ticket, but could not make him look round.

"I suppose I know you are a clever chap," he remarked. "Look here, now. Where do you want this ticket? In your buttonhole?"

"Put it here," said the passenger.

"Where?" asked the conductor. "You aren't a blooming letter rack."

"Where the penny was," replied the passenger. "Between my fingers."

The conductor felt reluctant, he did not know why, to oblige the passenger in this. The rigidity of the hand disconcerted him: it was stiff, he supposed, or perhaps paralyzed. And since he had been standing on the top his own hands were none too warm. The ticket doubled up and grew limp under his repeated efforts to push it in. He bent lower, for he was a goodhearted fellow, and using both hands, one above and one below, he slid the ticket into its bony slot.

"Right you are, Kaiser Bill."

Perhaps the passenger resented this jocular allusion to his

physical infirmity; perhaps he merely wanted to be quiet. All he said was:

"Don't speak to me again."

"Speak to you!" shouted the conductor, losing all self-control. "Catch me speaking to a stuffed dummy!"

Muttering to himself he withdrew into the bowels of the bus.

At the corner of Carrick Street quite a number of people got on board. All wanted to be first, but pride of place was shared by three women who all tried to enter simultaneously. The conductor's voice made itself audible above the din: "Now then, now then, look where you're shoving! This isn't a bargain sale. Gently, *please*, lady; he's only a pore old man." In a moment or two the confusion abated, and the conductor, his hand on the cord of the bell, bethought himself of the passenger on top whose destination Carrick Street was. He had forgotten to get down. Yielding to his good nature, for the conductor was averse from further conversation with his uncommunicative fare, he mounted the stairs, put his head over the top and shouted, "Carrick Street! Carrick Street!" That was the utmost he could bring himself to do. But his admonition was without effect; his summons remained unanswered; nobody came. "Well, if he wants to stay up there he can," muttered the conductor, still aggrieved. "I won't fetch him down, cripple or no cripple." The bus moved on. He slipped by me, thought the conductor, while all that Cup-tie crowd was getting in.

The same evening, some five hours earlier, a taxi turned into Carrick Street and pulled up at the door of a small hotel. The street was empty. It looked like a cul-de-sac, but in reality it was pierced at the far end by an alley, like a thin sleeve, which wound its way into Soho.

"That the last, sir?" inquired the driver, after several transits between the cab and the hotel.

"How many does that make?"

"Nine packages in all, sir."

"Could you get all your worldly goods into nine packages driver?"

"That I could; into two."

"Well, have a look inside and see if I have left anything."

The cabman felt about among the cushions. "Can't find nothing, sir."

"What do you do with anything you find?" asked the stranger.

"Take it to New Scotland Yard, sir," the driver promptly replied.

"Scotland Yard?" said the stranger. "Strike a match will you, and let me have a look."

But he, too, found nothing and, reassured, followed his luggage into the hotel.

A chorus of welcome and congratulation greeted him. The manager, the manager's wife, the ministers without portfolio of whom all hotels are full, the porters, the lift man, all clustered around him.

"Well, Mr. Rumbold, after all these years! We thought you'd forgotten us! And wasn't it odd, the very night your telegram came from Australia we'd been talking about you! And my husband said, 'Don't you worry about Mr. Rumbold. He'll fall on his feet all right. Some fine day he'll walk in here a rich man.' Not that you weren't always well off, but my husband meant a millionaire."

"He was quite right," said Mr. Rumbold slowly, savoring his words. "I am."

"There, what did I tell you?" the manager exclaimed, as though one recital of his prophecy was not enough. "But I wonder you're not too grand to come to Rossall's Hotel."

"I've nowhere else to go," said the millionaire shortly. "And if I had, I wouldn't. This place is like home to me."

His eyes softened as they scanned the familiar surroundings.

They were light gray eyes, very pale, and seeming paler from their setting in his tanned face. His cheeks were slightly sunken and very deeply lined; his blunt-ended nose was straight. He had a thin, straggling mustache, straw-colored, which made his age difficult to guess. Perhaps he was nearly fifty, so wasted was the skin on his neck, but his movements, unexpectedly agile and decided, were those of a younger man.

"I won't go up to my room now," he said, in response to the manageress's question. "Ask Clutsam—he's still with you?—good—to unpack my things. He'll find all I want for the night in the green suitcase. I'll take my dispatch box with me. And tell them to bring me a sherry and bitters in the lounge."

As the crow flies it was not far to the lounge. But by the way of the tortuous, ill-lit passages, doubling on themselves, yawning with dark entries, plunging into kitchen stairs—the catacombs so dear to *habitués* of Rossall's Hotel—it was a considerable distance. Anyone posted in the shadow of these alcoves, or arriving at the head of the basement staircase, could not have failed to notice the air of utter content which marked Mr. Rumbold's leisurely progress: the droop of his shoulders, acquiescing in weariness; the hands turned inwards and swaying slightly, but quite forgotten by their owner; the chin, always prominent, now pushed forward so far that it looked relaxed and helpless, not at all defiant. The unseen witness would have envied Mr. Rumbold, perhaps even grudged him his holiday air, his untroubled acceptance of the present and the future.

A waiter whose face he did not remember brought him the *apéritif*, which he drank slowly, his feet propped unconventionally upon a ledge of the chimneypiece; a pardonable relaxation, for the room was empty. Judge therefore of his surprise when, out of a fire-engendered drowsiness, he heard a voice which seemed to come from the wall above his head. A cultivated voice, perhaps too cultivated, slightly husky, yet careful and precise in its enunciation. Even while his eyes searched the room to make sure that no one had come in, he could not help hearing everything the voice said. It seemed to be talking to him, and yet the rather oracular utterance implied a less restricted audience. It was the utterance of a man who was aware that, though it was a duty for him to speak, for Mr. Rumbold to listen would be both a pleasure and a profit.

"... A Children's Party," the voice announced in an even, neutral tone, nicely balanced between approval and distaste, between enthusiasm and boredom; "six little girls and six little" (a faint life in the voice, expressive of tolerant surprise) "boys. The Broadcasting Company has invited them to tea, and they are anxious that you should share some of their fun." (At the last word the voice became completely colorless.) "I must tell you that they have had tea, and enjoyed it, didn't you, children?" (A cry of "Yes," muffled and timid, greeted this leading question.) "We should have liked you to hear our table-talk, but there wasn't much of it, we were so busy eating." For a moment the voice identified itself with the children. "But we can tell you what we ate. Now, Percy, tell us what you had."

A piping little voice recited a long list of comestibles; like the children in the treacle well, thought Rumbold, Percy must have been, or soon would be very ill. A few others volunteered the items of their repast. "So you see," said the voice, "we have not done so badly. And now we are going to have crackers, and afterwards" (the voice hesitated and seemed to dissociate itself from the words) "Children's Games." There was an impressive pause, broken by the muttered exhortation of a little girl. "Don't cry, Philip, it won't hurt you." Fugitive sparks and snaps of sound followed; more like a fire being mended, thought Rumbold, than crackers. A murmur of voices pierced the fusillade. "What have you got, Alec, what have you *got*?" "I've got a cannon." "Give it to me." "No." "Well, lend it to me." "What do you want it for?" "I want to shoot Jimmy."

Mr. Rumbold started. Something had disturbed him. Was it imagination, or did he hear, above the confused medley of sound, a tiny click? The voice was speaking again. "And now we're going to begin the Games." As though to make amends for past lukewarmness a faint flush of anticipation gave color to the decorous voice. "We will commence with that old favorite, Ring-a-Ring of Roses."

The children were clearly shy, and left each other to do the singing. Their courage lasted for a time or two and then gave out. But fortified by the speaker's baritone, powerful though subdued, they took heart, and soon were singing without assistance or direction. Their light wavering voices had a charming effect. Tears stood in Mr. Rumbold's eyes. "Oranges and Lemons" came next. A more difficult game, it yielded several unrehearsed effects before it finally got under way. One could almost see the children being marshaled into their places, as though for a figure in the Lancers. Some of them no doubt had wanted to play another game; children are contrary; and the dramatic side of "Oranges and Lemons," though it appeals to many, always affrights a few. The disinclination of these last would account for the pauses and hesitations which irritated Mr. Rumbold, who, as a child, had always had a strong fancy for this particular game. When, to the tramping and stamping of many small feet, the droning chant began, he leaned back and closed his eyes in ecstasy. He listened intently for the final accelerando which leads up to the catastrophe. Still the prologue maundered on, as though the children were anxious to extend the period of security, the joyous carefree promenade which the great Bell of Bow, by his inconsiderate profession of ignorance, was so rudely to curtail. The Bells of Old Bailey pressed their usurer's question; the Bells of Shoreditch answered with becoming flippancy; the Bells of Stepney posed their ironical query, when suddenly, before the great Bell of Bow had time to get his word in, Mr. Rumbold's feelings underwent a strange revolution. Why couldn't the game continue, all sweetness and sunshine? Why drag in the fatal issue? Let payment be deferred; let the bells go on chiming and never strike the hour. But heedless of Mr. Rumbold's squeamishness, the game went its way.

After the eating comes the reckoning.

> Here is a candle to light you to bed,
> And here comes a chopper to chop off your head!
> Chop—chop—chop.

A child screamed, and there was silence.

Mr. Rumbold felt quite upset, and great was his relief when, after a few more halfhearted rounds of "Oranges and Lemons," the voice announced, "Here We Come Gathering Nuts and May." At least there was nothing sinister in that. Delicious sylvan scene, comprising in one splendid botanical inexactitude all the charms of winter, spring, and autumn. What superiority to circumstances was implied in the conjunction of nuts and May! What defiance of cause and effect! What a testimony to coincidence! For cause and effect is against us, as witness the fate of Old Bailey's debtor; but coincidence is always on our side, always teaching us how to eat our cake and have it! The long arm of coincidence! Mr. Rumbold would have liked to clasp it by the hand.

Meanwhile his own hand conducted the music of the revels and his foot kept time. Their pulses quickened by enjoyment, the children put more heart into their singing; the game went with a swing; the ardor and rhythm of it invaded the little room where Mr. Rumbold sat. Like heavy fumes the waves of sound poured in, so penetrating, they ravished the sense; so sweet, they intoxicated it; so light, they fanned it into a flame. Mr. Rumbold was transported. His hearing, sharpened by the subjugation and quiescence of his other faculties, began to take in new sounds; the names, for instance, of the players who were "wanted" to make up each side, and of the champions who were to pull them over. For the listeners-in, the issues of the struggles remained in doubt. Did Nancy Price succeed in detaching Percy Kingham from his allegiance? Probably. Did Alec Wharton prevail against Maisie Drew? It was certainly an easy win for someone: the contest lasted only a second, and a ripple of laughter greeted it. Did Violet Kingham make good against Horace Gold? This was a dire encounter, punctuated by deep irregular panting. Mr. Rumbold could see, in his mind's eye, the two champions straining backwards and forwards across the white, motionless handkerchief, their faces red and puckered with exertion. Violet or Horace, one of them had to go: Violet might be bigger than Horace, but then Horace was a boy: they were evenly matched: they had their pride to maintain. The moment when the will was broken and the body went limp in surrender would be like a moment of dissolution. Yes, even this game had its stark, uncomfortable side. Violet or Horace, one of them was smarting now: crying perhaps under the humiliation of being fetched away.

The game began afresh. This time there was an eager ring in the children's voices: two tried antagonists were going to meet: it would be a battle of giants. The chant throbbed into a war cry.

> Who will you have for your Nuts and May,
> Nuts and May, Nuts and May;
> Who will you have for your Nuts and May
> On a cold and frosty morning?

They would have Victor Rumbold for Nuts and May, Victor Rumbold, Victor Rumbold: and from the vindictiveness in their voices they might have meant to have had his blood, too.

> And who will you send to fetch him away,
> Fetch him away, fetch him away;

> *Who will you send to fetch him away*
> *On a cold and frosty morning?*

Like a clarion call, a shout of defiance, came the reply:

> *We'll send Jimmy Hagberd to fetch him away,*
> *Fetch him away, fetch him away;*
> *We'll send Jimmy Hagberd to fetch him away*
> *On a wet and foggy evening.*

This variation, it might be supposed, was intended to promote the contest from the realms of pretense into the world of reality. But Mr. Rumbold probably did not hear that his abduction had been antedated. He had turned quite green, and his head was lolling against the back of the chair.

"Any wine, sir?"

"Yes, Clutsam, a bottle of champagne."

"Very good, sir."

Mr. Rumbold drained the first glass at one go.

"Anyone coming into dinner besides me, Clutsam?" he presently inquired. "Not now, sir, it's nine o'clock," replied the waiter, his voice edged with reproach.

"Sorry, Clutsam, I didn't feel up to the mark before dinner, so I went and lay down."

The waiter was mollified.

"Thought you weren't looking quite yourself, sir. No bad news, I hope."

"No, nothing. Just a bit tired after the journey."

"And how did you leave Australia, sir?" inquired the waiter, to accommodate Mr. Rumbold, who seemed anxious to talk.

"In better weather than you have here," Mr. Rumbold replied, finishing his second glass, and measuring with his eye the depleted contents of the bottle.

The rain kept up a steady patter on the glass roof of the coffee room.

"Still, a good climate isn't everything. It isn't like home, for instance," the waiter remarked.

"No, indeed."

"There's many parts of the world as would be glad of a good day's rain," affirmed the waiter.

"There certainly are," said Mr. Rumbold, who found the conversation sedative.

"Did you do much fishing when you were abroad, sir?" the waiter pursued.

"A little."

"Well, you want rain for that," declared the waiter, as one who scores a point. "The fishing isn't preserved in Australia, like what it is here?"

"No."

"Then there ain't no poaching," concluded the waiter philosophically. "It's every man for himself."

"Yes, that's the rule in Australia."

"Not much of a rule, is it?" the waiter took him up. "Not much like law, I mean."

"It depends what you mean by law."

"Oh, Mr. Rumbold, sir, you know very well what I mean. I mean the police. Now if you was to have done a man in out in Australia—murdered him, I mean—they'd hang you for it if they caught you, wouldn't they?"

Mr. Rumbold teased the champagne with the butt end of his fork and drank again.

"Probably they would, unless there was special circumstances."

"In which case you might get off?"

"I might."

"That's what I mean by law," pronounced the waiter. "You know what the law is: you go against it, and you're punished. Of course I don't mean you, sir; I only say 'you' as—as an illustration to make my meaning clear."

"Quite, quite."

"Whereas if there was only what you call a rule," the waiter pursued, deftly removing the remains of Mr. Rumbold's chicken, "it might fall to the lot of any man to round you up. Might be anybody; might be me."

"Why should you or they," asked Mr. Rumbold, "want to round me up? I haven't done you any harm, or them."

"Oh, but we should have to, sir."

"Why?"

"We couldn't rest in our beds, sir, knowing you was at large. You might do it again. Somebody'd have to see to it."

"But supposing there was nobody?"

"Sir?"

"Supposing the murdered man hadn't any relatives or friends: supposing he just disappeared, and no one ever knew that he was dead?"

"Well, sir," said the waiter, winking portentously, "in that case he'd have to get on your track himself. He wouldn't rest in his grave, sir, no, not he, and knowing what he did."

"Clutsam," said Mr. Rumbold suddenly, "bring me another bottle of wine, and don't trouble to ice it."

The waiter took the bottle from the table and held it up to the light.

"Yes, it's dead, sir."

"Dead?"

"Yes, sir; finished; empty; dead."

"You're right," Mr. Rumbold agreed. "It's quite dead."

It was nearly eleven o'clock. Mr. Rumbold again had the lounge to himself. Clutsam would be bringing his coffee presently. Too bad of Fate to have him haunted by these casual reminders; too bad, his first day at home. "Too bad, too bad," he muttered, while the fire warmed the soles of his slippers. But it was excellent champagne; he would take no harm from it: the brandy Clutsam was bringing him would do the rest. Clutsam was a good sort, nice old-fashioned servant . . . nice old-fashioned house. . . . Warmed by the wine, his thoughts began to pass out of his control.

"Your coffee, sir," said a voice at his elbow.

"Thank you, Clutsam, I'm very much obliged to you," said Mr. Rumbold, with the exaggerated civility of slight intoxication. "You're an excellent fellow. I wish there were more like you."

"I hope so, too, I'm sure," said Clutsam, trying in his muddleheaded way to deal with both observations at once.

"Don't seem many people about," Mr. Rumbold remarked. "Hotel pretty full?"

"Oh, yes, sir, all the suites are let, and the other rooms, too. We're turning people away every day. Why, only tonight a gentleman rang up. Said he would come round late, on the off chance. But, bless me, he'll find the birds have flown."

"Birds?" echoed Mr. Rumbold.

"I mean there ain't any more rooms, not for love nor money."

"Well, I'm sorry for him," said Mr. Rumbold, with ponderous sincerity. "I'm sorry for any man, friend or foe, who has to go tramping about London on a night like this. If I had an extra bed in my room, I'd put it at his disposal."

"You have, sir," the waiter said.

"Why, of course I have. How stupid. Well, well. I'm sorry for the poor chap. I'm sorry for all homeless ones, Clutsam, wandering on the face of the earth."

"Amen to that," said the waiter devoutly.

"And doctors and such, pulled out of their beds at midnight. It's a hard life. Ever thought about a doctor's life, Clutsam?"

"Can't say I have, sir."

"Well, well, but it's hard; you can take that from me."

"What time shall I call you in the morning, sir?" the waiter asked, seeing no reason why the conversation should ever stop.

"You needn't call me, Clutsam," replied Mr. Rumbold, in a sing-song voice, and rushing the words together as though he were excusing the waiter from addressing him by the waiter's own name. "I'll get up when I'm ready. And that may be pretty late, pretty late." He smacked his lips over the words.

"Nothing like a good lie, eh, Clutsam?"

"That's right, sir, you have your sleep out," the waiter encouraged him. "You won't be disturbed."

"Good-night, Clutsam. You're an excellent fellow, and I don't care who hears me say so."

"Good-night, sir."

Mr. Rumbold returned to his chair. It lapped him round, it ministered to his comfort: he felt at one with it. At one with the fire, the clock, the tables, all the furniture. Their usefulness, their goodness, went out to meet his usefulness, his goodness, met, and were friends. Who could bind their sweet influences or restrain them in the exercise of their kind offices? No one: certainly not a shadow from the past. The room was perfectly quiet. Street sounds reached it only as a low continuous hum, infinitely reassuring. Mr. Rumbold fell asleep.

He dreamed that he was a boy again, living in his old home in the country. He was possessed, in the dream, by a master passion; he must collect firewood whenever and wherever he saw it. He found himself one autumn afternoon in the woodhouse; that was how the dream began. The door was partly open, admitting a little light, but he could not recall how he got in. The floor of the shed was littered with bits of bark and thin twigs; but, with the exception of the chopping block which he knew could not be used, there was nowhere a log of sufficient size to make a fire. Though he did not like being in the woodhouse alone he stayed long enough to make a thorough search. But he could find nothing. The compulsion he knew so well descended on him, and he left the woodhouse and went into the garden. His steps took him to the foot of a high tree, standing by itself in a tangle of long grass at some distance from the house. The tree had been lopped; for half its height it had no branches, only leafy tufts, sticking out at irregular intervals. He knew what he would see when he looked up into the dark foliage. And there, sure enough, it was: a long dead bough, bare in patches where the bark had peeled off, and crooked in the middle like an elbow.

He began to climb the tree. The ascent proved easier than he expected, his body seemed no weight at all. But he was visited by a terrible oppression, which increased as he mounted. The bough did not want him; it was projecting its hostility down the trunk of the tree. And every second brought him nearer to an object which he had always dreaded; a growth, people called it. It stuck out from the trunk of the tree, a huge circular swelling thickly matted with twigs. Victor would have rather died than hit his head against it.

By the time he reached the bough twilight had deepened into night. He knew what he had to do: sit astride the bough, since there was none nearby from which he could reach it, and press with his hands until it broke. Using his legs to get what purchase he could, he set his back against the tree, and pushed with all his might downwards. To do this he was obliged to look beneath him, and he saw, far below him on the ground, a white sheet spread out as though to catch him; and he knew at once that it was a shroud.

Frantically he pulled and pushed at the stiff, brittle bough; a lust to break it took hold of him; leaning forward, his whole length he seized the bough at the elbow joint and strained it way from him. As it cracked he toppled over and the shroud came rushing upwards. . . .

Mr. Rumbold waked in a cold sweat to find himself clutching the curved arm of the chair on which the waiter had set his brandy. The glass had fallen over and the spirit lay in a little pool on the leather seat. "I can't let it go like that," he thought. "I must get some more." A man he did not know answered the bell. "Waiter," he said, "bring me a brandy and soda in my room in a quarter of an hour's time. Rumbold, the name is." He followed the waiter out of the room. The passage was completely dark except for a small blue gas jet, beneath which was huddled a cluster of candlesticks. The hotel, he remembered, maintained an old-time habit of deference towards darkness. As he held the wick to the gas jet, he heard himself mutter "Here is a candle to light you to bed." But he recollected the ominous conclusion of the distich, and fuddled as he was he left it unspoken.

Shortly after Mr. Rumbold's retirement the door bell of the hotel rang. Three sharp peals, and no pause between them. "Someone in a hurry to get in," the night porter grumbled to Clutsam, who was on duty till midnight. "Expect he's forgotten his key." He made no haste to answer the summons; it would do the forgetful fellow good to wait: teach him a lesson. So dilatory was he that by the time he reached the hall door the bell was tinkling again. Irritated by such importunity, he deliberately went back to set straight a pile of newspapers before letting this impatient devil in. To mark his indifference he even kept behind the door while he opened it; so that his first sight of the visitor only took in his back, but this limited inspection sufficed to show that the man was a stranger and not a guest at the hotel.

In the long black cape which fell almost sheer one side, and on the other stuck out as though he had a basket under his arm, he looked like a crow with a broken wing. A bald-headed crow, thought the porter, for there's a patch of bare skin between that white linen thing and his hat.

"Good evening, sir," he said. "What can I do for you?"

The stranger made no answer, but glided to a side table and began turning over some letters with his right hand.

"Are you expecting a message?" asked the porter.

"No," the stranger replied. "I want a room for the night."

"Was you the gentleman who telephoned for a room this evening?"

"Yes."

"In that case, I was to tell you we're afraid you can't have one; the hotel's booked right up."

"Are you quite sure?" asked the stranger. "Think again."

"Them's my orders, sir. It don't do me no good to think."

At this moment the porter had a curious sensation as though some important part of him, his life maybe, had gone adrift inside him and was spinning round and round. The sensation ceased when he began to speak.

"I'll call the waiter, sir," he said.

But before he called the waiter appeared, intent on an errand of his own.

"I say, Bill," he began, "what's the number of Mr. Rumbold's room? He wants a drink taken up, and I forgot to ask him."

"It's thirty-three," said the porter unsteadily. "The double room."

"Why, Bill, what's up?" the waiter exclaimed. "You look as if you'd seen a ghost."

Both men stared round the hall, and then back at each other. The room was empty.

"God!" said the porter. "I must have had the horrors. But he was here a moment ago. Look at this."

On the stone flags lay an icicle, and inch or two long, around which a little pool was fast collecting.

"Why, Bill," cried the waiter, "how did that get here? It's not freezing."

"*He* must have brought it," the porter said.

They looked at each other in consternation, which changed into terror as the sound of a bell made itself heard, coming from the depths of the hotel.

"Clutsam's there," whispered the porter. "He'll have to answer it, whoever it is."

Clutsam had taken off his tie, and was getting ready for bed. What on earth could anyone want in the lounge at this hour? He pulled on his coat and went upstairs.

Standing by the fire he saw the same figure whose appearance and disappearance had so disturbed the porter.

"Yes, sir?" he said.

"I want you to go to Mr. Rumbold," said the stranger, "and ask him if he is prepared to put the other bed in his room at the disposal of a friend."

In a few moments Clutsam returned.

"Mr. Rumbold's compliments, sir, and he wants to know who it is."

The stranger went to the table in the center of the room. An Australian newspaper was lying there which Clutsam had not noticed before. The aspirant to Mr. Rumbold's hospitality turned over the pages. Then with his finger, which appeared even to Clutsam standing by the door unusually pointed, he cut out a rectangular slip, about the size of a visiting card, and, moving away, motioned the waiter to take it.

By the light of the gas jet in the passage Clutsam read the excerpt. It seemed to be a kind of obituary notice; but of what possible interest could it be to Mr. Rumbold to know that the body of Mr. James Hagberd had been discovered in circumstances which suggested that he had met his death by violence?

After a longer interval Clustam returned, looking puzzled and a little frightened.

"Mr. Rumbold's compliments, sir, but he knows no one of that name."

"Then take this message to Mr. Rumbold," said the stranger. "Say, 'Would he rather that I went up to him, or that he came down to me?' "

For the third time Clutsam went to do the stranger's bidding. He did not, however, upon his return open the door of the smoking room, but shouted through it.

"Mr. Rumbold wishes you to Hell, sir, where you belong, and says, 'Come up if you dare!' "

Then he bolted.

A minute later, from his retreat in an underground coal cellar, he heard a shot fired. Some old instinct, danger-loving or danger-disregarding, stirred in him, and he ran up the stairs quicker than he had ever run up them in his life. In the passage he stumbled over Mr. Rumbold's boots. The bedroom door was ajar. Putting his head down he rushed in. The brightly lit room was empty. But almost all the movables in it were overturned and the bed was in a frightful mess. The pillow with its fivefold perforation was the first object on which Clutsam noticed bloodstains. Thenceforward he seemed to see them everywhere. But what sickened him and kept him so long from going down to rouse the others was the sight of an icicle on the window sill, a thin claw of ice curved like a Chinaman's nail, with a bit of flesh sticking to it.

That was the last he saw of Mr. Rumbold. But a policeman patrolling Carrick Street noticed a man in a long black cape, who seemed, by the position of his arm, to be carrying something heavy. He called out to the man, and ran after him; but though he did not seem to be moving very fast, the policeman could not overtake him.

The Thirteenth Tree

R. H. MALDEN

IF, AS I incline to think, architecture in general and domestic architecture in particular is the best expression of the characteristics of the period to which it belongs, there would be a good deal to be said in favor of having been born soon after the year 1570.

Late Tudor or early Jacobean houses always seem to me to exhibit the qualities which I admire most. They are dignified and beautiful without conscious effort. Both inside and out I find them extraordinarily satisfying. "This," I say to myself, "is what a country house ought to be." They look as if they had grown from the soil as naturally as the trees in their parks. They are as they are because the men who planned them were solid, dignified, and sure of themselves.

Castles speak of violence and cruelty, until they have become an anachronism. Then they are sights to be seen rather than houses to live in. Early Tudor houses have something upstart about them; as, it may be suspected, had their owners. The Palladian palaces of the eighteenth century are not free from ostentation. They were meant to display the wealth and taste of their owners, most of whom had probably made the Grand Tour. Despite their dignity and internal comfort I can never feel that they belong to the English countryside. But the type of house which was built about twenty years on either side of the year 1600 always seem to me to escape all these defects. One of them was the scene of the story which I am now going to tell.

It is situated in one of the western counties. That is as much as I shall say about its geographical position, as I do not want to bring the Society for Spectral Investigations, or any similar body, about my ears or those of the neighborhood.

I had known the owner when we were boys. Our paths in life had diverged and for thirty years or more we never met. We came across each other accidentally in London, and both welcomed the opportunity of resuming an old friendship. When he asked me to visit him I was very glad to accept his invitation. Accordingly, a few weeks later, on a fine day early in October, I caught a train at Paddington for my journey westwards.

I had made acquaintance with the first twenty miles of the Great Western in the year 1890, and for some time after that they had been very familiar to me. But I had not traveled by that route for a good many years and was horrified to see how the Great Wen (as Cobbett rudely called London) had spread over what I remembered as a pleasant countryside. One of the few things which did not seem to have altered since I had passed that way last was a building of really exceptional ugliness (a hotel, I believe) close to the station at Slough. For, I think, the first time in my life the sight of it gave me real pleasure.

I had to change three times in the course of my journey and it was nearly five o'clock when I got out at the country station where my host met me. The light was failing when we arrived at the house and I could only see that it was large, and that it promised to be very beautiful.

I was introduced to my hostess and her two daughters, and after tea in the hall in front of a superb log fire in a large open fireplace my host took me to the smoking room.

"I had no idea you were such a territorial magnate," I said to him when we had settled down.

"I never expected to be," he said. "My father was a parson in the north, and I became a solicitor in York—as you know. We lived just outside York for the first fifteen years after I was married. I knew of this place, but never saw it until I succeeded a distant cousin (whom I never saw either) nearly seven years ago. He was unmarried and a queer-tempered old chap by all accounts. Perhaps the fact that he had never seen me influenced his choice of an heir. The place isn't entailed and there were several distant relations beside me. It's a curious thing, but this property has never passed in the direct male line since Sir Robert Newton, whose portrait you'll see in the dining room, bought it and built the house, about the year 1602 I believe. He was Chief Justice of the Queen's Bench. His son was drowned in a pool in the garden. It does not exist now. It was filled in immediately afterwards. No one could ever understand how the boy got into it, or why, having got in, he couldn't get out, as it was quite shallow, I believe, and he was more than a child. There was a daughter who married and brought her family here after her parents' death. But her son was killed at Naseby, leaving several daughters. And so it has gone on. Either there has been no son or he hasn't lived to inherit. My immediate predecessor succeeded a childless uncle, and as we have only two daughters we keep up the tradition. I'm really almost glad I never had a son, as I am sure my wife would be nervous about bringing him here. Indeed, I don't mind admitting that I think I should be. Of course the village people say there's a curse on the place, but they don't know why. I can't think that my respected ancestor—he is my ancestor, if by no means in the direct line—was likely to have done anything to provoke one."

Certainly when I looked at the portrait an hour or two later I could detect nothing evil in it. It suggested that Sir Robert had been a shrewd and kindly person, who would probably be as lenient on the Bench as the law allowed him to be. No doubt he had passed many sentences in his time which we should think harsh or even savage. But that would not have been the view of his contemporaries.

After dinner we sat in the library. It was a large room completely lined with well-filled bookcases whose contents looked as if they would repay examination. There is no saying what may not have wandered into such a place; just as any oyster may contain a pearl of price. I asked whether there was a catalog.

"Not a very good one," was the answer. "In fact I'm not sure that I shan't spend a good part of this winter trying to improve it. You'd like to have a look round it tomorrow, I expect. A good many of the books belonged to Sir Robert. By the way, we've put you in what is said to have been his bedroom. It isn't often used, but we've just had to take up the floors in some of the rooms nearer ours; dry rot, pretty bad too. But I think you'll be quite comfortable there. No; there's no story about it that I ever heard. We don't run to a ghost of any kind."

We went upstairs soon afterwards, and while I was undressing I meditated upon the queer fatality which seemed to have pursued the family for three hundred years. Was it more than a series of odd and unfortunate coincidences? Are there, or have there been, people who had some malign power which they could direct against their enemies? If it were so, how was this power operative after their lifetime? Did it exhaust itself after a period of time or not?

I had finished undressing before I had arrived at a satisfactory answer to any of these conundrums. When I was ready for bed I went to the window, opened it, and drew back the curtains as was my custom. It was a clear night with a good deal of moon. My room was on the first floor at the back of the house, overlooking a part of the garden which I had not seen before. Immediately below me lay a graveled terrace, bounded on the far side by a stone balustrade. On the other side of this, at a lower level and reached by a flight of steps, lay a small formal garden. In the middle was a circular stone basin, where I hoped there might be a fountain. Round the edge stood a number of dark clipped trees—yews or cypresses, I could not tell which. There were twelve of these: one at each corner and two in between. On the far side was a low stone wall separating the garden from the park beyond. Very white it looked in the moonlight; almost as if it were newly built. About the middle there was a dark patch; ivy or creeper I supposed. It made a clump on the coping and then spread sideways, in a way which almost suggested the head and arms of a person in the act of climbing the wall. I thought it rather ugly and decided that if I were the owner I would have it removed. Then I went to bed.

For some reason sleep did not come as quickly as usual and I was visited with the pictures—half dreams and half waking—which belong to the border line of consciousness. Mine made two scenes. In the first I found myself seated in a large old-fashioned traveling coach. Beside me was a figure very much wrapped up. He turned towards me once as if about to speak, and I recognized the original of the portrait in the dining room. Presently we were brought to a standstill by a great concourse of people who seemed to be streaming away from some spectacle. I put my head out of the window to see what it was, but drew it in again quickly. A few yards in front of us was a gallows and there were four bodies dangling from the crossbeam. As I sat down, feeling as if I should be sick, a head was poked in at the window on the other side. It belonged to a young man. The face seemed unnaturally pale. There was something else unusual about it, but I could not take in what it was. The young man said something in a low tone to my companion. I could not catch the words, but they seemed to disconcert him very much. Next moment the face had vanished and we had begun to move again. I woke to find myself murmuring, *"An eye for an eye and a tooth for a tooth."*

The second scene was a churchyard by night. A funeral was taking place. I could see the bearers and the men with the torches and the priest. But there appeared to be no mourners, unless I were one. As the coffin was lowered into the grave some bird of the night gave a long and dolorous screech very close overhead. At this I woke. I think there must have been a hunting owl or a nightjar outside my window. As I did not wish for any repetition of such scenes I got a book and read until I could feel confident that I should sleep soundly.

When I went to my window next morning I received a surprise. There, as was to be expected, was the garden on which I had looked the night before. But there were no trees and no pool, and I could see no growth upon the wall at the bottom. Yet I *knew* that I had seen those things, and that I had not been dreaming at the time. I decided to say nothing about them. When we went out after breakfast, however, I did ask my host whether he knew where the pool in which Sir Robert's son had been drowned had been. But he did not. I noticed that the wall between the garden and the park did not look as new as I had thought it the night before. It seemed to be the same age as the rest of the house, as was to be expected. That might, however, be due to the difference between daylight and moonlight. The day was fine and as the neighborhood was new to me, most of the hours of daylight were passed out-of-doors. After tea, when we were sitting in the library, I asked my host whether he knew why or by whom the curse had been laid upon Sir Robert's descendants.

"Well," said he, "there is a bit of a story about it. But all I know is very incomplete and doesn't explain much. It seems that in the old judge's time there was a woman in the village who was reputed to be a witch. Nothing very out of the way about that. In fact you wouldn't have to look very far to find witches (or reputed ones) in these west-country villages to-day. Her name was Miriam Urch (Urch is quite a common name in these parts) and they say she was at the bottom of it. But I don't know why she should have had a down on the Newtons, and as nothing was ever proved against her she was given Christian burial in the churchyard when her time came. You can see what is said to be her grave close to the north door. I expect it is. Village tradition is generally pretty accurate in such points. They aren't quite sure whether she is always in it though, even now. I believe the rector has had something to say to old Job Dixon the sexton about its untidiness more than once. But *he* says it isn't his fault. There are no other graves anywhere near it, and I don't think there will be as long as there is a scrap of room anywhere else."

No more was said on the topic that evening and the hours after dinner passed pleasantly with a game of bridge with my host and his two daughters. We were all agreed that games are games, and though due respect must be paid to the rules which govern them, they ought not to be transformed into hard and dismal forms of work.

It was near midnight before I found myself in my room, and when I was ready for bed I admit that I hesitated for a moment before drawing back my curtains. Finally curiosity prevailed. If there were anything to be seen I might as well see it. It seemed unlikely that any harm could come to me or to the family through me.

I looked out. The moon shone brilliantly, and there, beyond any possibility of mistake, were the pool and the twelve trees. But were there only twelve? My first impression was that there were more. That was absurd. I counted them again just to make sure, and, as I had thought, there was one at each corner with two in between. But as soon as I looked at them altogether I got the impression that there were more.

But I could not have said where the additional one (I felt sure it was only one) was, nor even whether it was always in the same place. And I noticed that the ivy or whatever it had been on the wall at the bottom, was gone. It might have been cleared away during the day, but I had an uncomfortable feeling that someone or something had come over and was dodging about behind the trees. If so, with what intent?

I began to feel an overpowering desire to go and investigate. Yet I could hardly do that. The door leading to the terrace was doubtless locked and bolted, and I should be sure to disturb someone in getting it open. What could I say if I did? That I thought it a fine night for a stroll and that I always found pajamas the most comfortable wear for a nocturnal ramble? For I felt quite certain—I don't know why—that the trees and pool would be invisible to anyone except myself. All the same, the desire to investigate more closely grew stronger and stronger. I have never seen or experienced hypnotism, but began to feel as I imagine a hypnotic subject does. It seemed as if I was being dragged out by some force which was overpowering my own will, and that if I could not get the door open I should have to jump from my first-floor window. This would never do. As an antidote I began to recite the first thing which came into my head. It happened to be the *Battle of Lake Regillus* from Macaulay's *Lays of Ancient Rome* and not for the first time I blessed the wisdom of my mother who had made us learn quantities of poetry by heart as soon as we could read. This particular poem had been my first major achievement in this line. It had always remained particularly distinct in my memory because the recitation of it had won two new half-crowns from a godfather[1] and thereby had enabled me to understand (for the first and last time in my life) what is meant by "the possession of wealth beyond the dreams of avarice."

---

1. He subsequently became Chief Justice of Trinidad, and was long remembered for his patience with garrulous witnesses, and the fervid eloquence of colored advocates.

I am not quite sure whether I declaimed it aloud or not. But I know that I had only got to the end of the first stanza

But the proud Ides when the squadron rides
Shall be Rome's whitest day

when the spell, which I was quite sure had been malevolent, broke and I was completely my own master again. I felt as one does when a motorcar or bicycle has skidded and disaster in a ditch has been escaped by inches. I stopped at the window because I felt sure that something was going to happen. I did not have to wait long. A figure appeared on the terrace; where it had come from I did not see. When it emerged from the shadow of the house I saw that it was that of a young man; not much more than a boy. He seemed to be dressed as a young gentleman of quality would have been about the year 1600 or a little later. For some reason this did not surprise me. I wondered whether I was spying upon a lovers' meeting. The moonlight was all that could be desired, if the air were a little chilly. But there was no second figure to be seen. He went down the stone steps leading from the terrace to the garden below and advanced to the edge of the pool. He stood there for a minute or two looking down into the water. Perhaps he was admiring the reflection of the moon. Then a very horrid thing happened. A vague black shape darted from behind one of the trees and flung itself upon him. It lay on top of him and had obviously forced him into the pool face downwards with intent to drown him. I tried to shout—though what good that would have done I don't know. But no sound would come. I thought of going to the rescue, but found myself unable to move. Of course that would have been equally futile could I have got there. The next minute a heavy bank of cloud which had been creeping up from the southwest drove across the moon and I could see no more. There was no sound to be heard. How long

85

I remained looking out of the window into blackness and silence, I cannot say. Presently I found that I could move again, so crept into bed. There was nothing more which I could have done. I think I slept more than might have been expected.

Next morning when we went into the library after breakfast, I decided that I must make an effort and tell my host what I had seen. It did need an effort, for I felt very unwilling to speak about it. I don't know why. I don't think I was afraid of being laughed at and if I were told that I had been dreaming I could only reply that I *knew* that I had been awake. Somehow that made me the more reluctant. However, I took the plunge.

He listened to my story very attentively, and obviously took it seriously. When I had finished he said, "I think we know now how poor young Newton came by his end. But who do you suppose it was that fell upon him? Mrs. Urch? If so, why?"

Neither of us said anything more for a little while. I could see that, like Odysseus on more than one occasion, he was this way and that dividing his swift mind. Then he said, "Yes. I think there's sufficient reason. Wait a bit."

We were sitting beside the fireplace as the morning was chilly. He went to the other end of the room, climbed to the top of a short stepladder, and took a smallish tin box from the end of a shelf. I saw that it was tied up with string or tape and that there was a seal over the knot. There was a label attached on which was written, in what looked like an early eighteenth-century hand, "Sir Robert Newton. Secreta. Not to be opened without sufficient reason."

"Well?" I said.

"Well," he replied. "Don't you think there is now?"

Of course I agreed and the string was cut.

The most important part of the contents was a notebook. The handwriting was Elizabethan, and brief inspection satisfied us that the book had belonged to the judge. It was not exactly a diary. By no means were all the entries dated and there did not seem to have been any attempt to produce a complete record of the period covered, which amounted to several years. There were a number of rather cryptic notes, apparently relating to cases which he had tried. Whether these were meant to direct his summing up or were merely private memoranda was not easy to decide. Neither of us was an expert palaeographer, and to decipher them all would obviously take some time. So we put the book aside for the moment.

There were several letters from Lady Newton from which it was to be inferred that she had gone down to the west to supervise the completion and furnishing of the new house while her husband was detained by work in London. These told a not unfamiliar tale of dilatory workmen, of things ordered from a distance which were not delivered on the day appointed and so forth. She also feared that when all done the original estimate would be very much exceeded. (It would have been very interesting had she mentioned the sums, but unfortunately she did not.) These belonged to the years 1599–1600. As one of them referred to the good effect produced by "your visit" it would appear that the judge had made an excursion to the scene of action to see whether he could expedite matters and alleviate some of his wife's troubles.

Underneath there was a largish sheet of paper which had been folded more than once. This proved to be a plan of the house and gardens—obviously by a professional hand. You will not be surprised to hear that in the middle of the small garden below the terrace was a circle of considerable size, which obviously indicated a pool. At a distance of some yards were twelve dots at regular intervals forming a square to show where it was intended to place statues or plant trees or something of the sort. The plan itself did not state what form of ornament the architect had in mind. But I was in a position to say trees, not statues.

There was only one more paper. This was merely a list of

about a hundred names, presumably those of the inhabitants of the village, who were all the judge's tenants. This was dated May 7, 1603, which my host thought must have been very soon after Sir Robert had come to reside permanently in his new home. It suggested that he had begun to devote himself seriously to the duties of a country gentleman. The name of Miriam Urch appeared among them. It was marked with an asterisk but there was no note relating to her to be found. She must have lived alone, as the names were obviously arranged according to their households and there were no other Urches in the village. Beyond establishing the trustworthiness of tradition—up to a point—this did not get us much further. Still, it was something to know that, witch or not, she really had existed. And there did seem to have been some special point of contact, however small, between her and the judge.

At this moment lunch was announced, so our investigation was suspended.

When we felt disposed to resume our researches, I suggested that it might be worthwhile to ask the rector for permission to examine the Register of Burials at the church; supposing it to be in existence. So much was destroyed wantonly during the Commonwealth period that it is not uncommon to find no records prior to 1662. Here, however, we were in luck. The registers were complete from 1558 onwards. May 7, 1603 was our *terminus a quo* and we found the entry of the burial of Miriam Urch on November 4 in that year. She had died on October 31. There was an asterisk in the margin and at the foot of the page (we thought in another hand but could not be sure):

Under Ye Yew tree by Ye north doore.

This was the only note appended to any entry in the volume. It might be presumed that her estate was not sufficient to provide a headstone for the grave and that no one else was prepared to bear the expense. Also that somebody, whether at the time or afterwards, was anxious that the site should not be forgotten.

We turned on. The entries were few as the population of the village was small. We found the burial of Philip Newton, aged 19 years, on November 7, 1604. He had died three days before.

"H'm," I said, "coincidences do happen. But this seems a little too close not to have been arranged. We know, more or less, how it was done. But I wonder why. There must be a story of some kind behind it."

Our only remaining source of information was the judge's notebook, so we returned to that. The next day was so wet that there was nothing to distract us and as we became familiar with his hand we found that we could read most of it without much difficulty. The impression which we had formed on our first cursory inspection was confirmed. There were a number of disconnected memoranda, relating to a variety of matters. Some were dated, but not all. They seemed to cover the last ten or twelve years of his term upon the Bench. Some were concerned with cases which he had heard; others with purely domestic matters. Some were too short to be fully intelligible. It looked as if it had been Sir Robert's practice to put down from time to time whatever happened to be passing through his mind (not necessarily every day) without attempting to keep a systematic diary. One of the longest entries was a very noble prayer (apparently his own composition) that he might be enabled to do justice "in the fear of God and with no fear of man." Shortly after this there was another prayer for forgiveness of any failure. It was clear that he had been a conscientious judge and had set himself a high standard. Interesting as much of this was, it was not relevant to our immediate purpose. We had got to almost the last page before we came upon anything which threw any light on the subject of our investigation.

The last case which he heard before his retirement, or at any rate the last of which there was any record, was of four men for highway robbery committed on Hounslow Heath. Their names were given: Roger Hewitson, William Parrett, Edward Backhouse, and George Urch. The first three were bracketed together with the words *Taken red-handed* written against them. But for some reason the case against George Urch seems to have been less clear. His name was followed by a few jottings:

Taken next day. No good alibi. Identified on oath.

Then followed two or three lines which were quite illegible. Below them the words *Condemned with the others*.

The only other entries were purely personal. After this trial, but at what interval it was impossible to say, both his health and his spirits seemed to have been affected. Twice he recorded *Kept my chamber all day*. Once he had sent for the apothecary (to whom he had paid two shillings and six-pence). Another entry showed that he had paid a visit to the rector of S. Margaret's, Westminster. This ended with the word *Comforted*. From which it would appear that whatever his trouble was it was not entirely physical. At this time his wife and family must have been elsewhere, as he spoke of arranging for his man (whose name was Edward Hilyar) "to lie in the little chamber next to mine"—and more than once "had E.H. to sit with me in the parlor."

It is a reasonable guess that George Urch the highway-man was the son of Miriam Urch and that it was within her knowledge that Sir Robert had sent him to his death. Whether justly or not would not perhaps have concerned her very closely. But the judge's own jottings suggested that there might have been a miscarriage of justice; involuntary on his part. She seems to have had her revenge; if, in the strict sense of the word, she did not live to see it.

We returned to the churchyard. What tradition called her grave could be identified without difficulty as there were no others near it. But there was no vestige of any yew tree. There was, however, a shallow depression, roughly circular and of considerable extent close to it. We had recourse to the rector again, not without apologies. He was able to tell us that he believed that there had been a tree there and that there were one or two old people living in the place who might remember something about it. He promised to ascertain what he could and added that, while he did not wish to appear discourteous, he thought he would be more likely to be successful if he pursued his investigations alone.

He had some information for us next day. There had been a yew tree there, which had been blown down in a terrible storm not long after Victoria became queen. "It were more than two 'underd year old, but it were a good riddance." (No explanation of this was forthcoming.) "Wold rector had roots grubbed and tooken away and burned. When the men got under there was a gurt twod settin', and he spit at they so dellish (query devilishly) that they were frit and run for rector. When they come back he were gone. Never zaw he no more. Rector came back wi' 'em and some things were found; bits o' bone and such-like. Rector he wrapped up they and took they away to burn."

This from a very ancient man whose father had been employed on the work. He had heard his father and mother talking about it once after they thought he was asleep. There had been more said. But that was all he could remember.

(I conjectured that the storm was that of January 6–7, 1839, which seems to have been little less violent than its better-known forerunner of November 1703. It came from the northwest. *Inter alia* it did considerable damage to Bishop Longley's new palace at Ripon.)

The churchwardens' accounts were available and showed considerable expenditure on repairs to the church and work (nature not specified) in the churchyard in the February and March of that year.

"Well," I said, "that's about as much as we are ever likely to know. I doubt whether Mrs. Urch can do any more mischief, if she likes to give a repetition of her original performance now and again. I expect the tree, which would have been quite a small one in her time, was necessary somehow. There seem to be unaccountable but very rigid rules governing these things. Perhaps we shall understand them better someday."

"You may be right," said Phillipson. (I don't think I have mentioned his name before.) "Now I come to think of it, there hasn't been a direct male heir at any time since 1839 for her to try her hand on. All the same I wonder——"

I was not much surprised to hear a few months later that Mr. Phillipson thought the house far too expensive and that he was conveying it to the National Trust and going to live elsewhere.

I believe that it is uninhabited now, so that if Mrs. Urch ever returns to it, no one will be any the wiser or the worse.

I have also heard that the trustees would like to restore the sunken garden according to the plan found amongst Sir Robert's papers. But Mr. Phillipson is opposed to this, and while they think him rather unreasonable they feel bound to respect his wishes.

The Body-Snatcher

ROBERT LOUIS STEVENSON

EVERY NIGHT IN the year, four of us sat in the small parlor of the George at Debenham—the undertaker, and the landlord, and Fettes, and myself. Sometimes there would be more; but blow high, blow low, come rain or snow or frost, we four would be each planted in his own particular arm-chair. Fettes was an old drunken Scotchman, a man of education obviously, and a man of some property, since he lived in idleness. He had come to Debenham years ago, while still young, and by a mere continuance of living had grown to be an adopted townsman. His blue camlet cloak was a local antiquity, like the church spire. His place in the parlor at the George, his absence from church, his old, crapulous, disreputable vices, were all things of course in Debenham. He had some vague Radical opinions and some fleeting infidelities, which he would now and again set forth and emphasize with tottering slaps upon the table. He drank rum—five glasses regularly every evening; and for the greater portion of his nightly visit to the George sat, with his glass in his right hand, in a state of melancholy alcoholic saturation. We called him the Doctor, for he was supposed to have some special knowledge of medicine, and had been known, upon a pinch, to set a fracture or reduce a dislocation; but beyond these slight particulars, we had no knowledge of his character and antecedents.

One dark winter night—it had struck nine sometime before the landlord joined us—there was a sick man in the George, a great neighboring proprietor suddenly struck down with apoplexy on his way to Parliament; and the great man's still greater London doctor had been telegraphed to his bedside. It was the first time that such a thing had happened in Debenham, for the railway was but newly open, and we were all proportionately moved by the occurrence.

"He's come," said the landlord, after he had filled and lighted his pipe.

"He?" said I. "Who?—not the doctor?"

"Himself," replied out host.

"What is his name?"

"Dr. Macfarlane," said the landlord.

Fettes was far through his third tumbler, stupidly fuddled, now nodding over, now staring mazily around him; but at the last word he seemed to awaken, and repeated the name "Macfarlane" twice, quietly enough the first time, but with sudden emotion at the second.

"Yes," said the landlord, "that's his name, Doctor Wolfe Macfarlane."

Fettes became instantly sober; his eyes awoke, his voice became clear, loud, and steady, his language forcible and earnest. We were all startled by the transformation, as if a man had risen from the dead.

"I beg your pardon," he said, "I am afraid I have not been paying much attention to your talk. Who is this Wolfe Macfarlane?" And then, when he had heard the landlord out, "It cannot be, it cannot be," he added; "and yet I would like well to see him face to face."

"Do you know him, Doctor?" asked the undertaker, with a gasp.

"God forbid!" was the reply. "And yet the name is a strange one; it were too much to fancy two. Tell me, landlord, is he old?"

"Well," said the host, "he's not a young man, to be sure, and his hair is white; but he looks younger than you."

"He is older, though; years older. But," with a slap upon the table, "it's the rum you see in my face—rum and sin. This man, perhaps, may have an easy conscience and a good digestion. Conscience! Hear me speak. You would think I was some good, old, decent Christian, would you not? But no, not I; I never canted. Voltaire might have canted if he'd stood in my shoes; but the brains"—with a rattling fillip on his bald head—"the brains were clear and active, and I saw and made no deductions."

"If you know this doctor," I ventured to remark, after a somewhat awful pause, "I should gather that you do not share the landlord's good opinion."

Fettes paid no regard to me.

"Yes," he said, with sudden decision, "I must see him face to face."

There was another pause, and then a door was closed rather sharply on the first floor, and a step was heard upon the stair.

"That's the doctor," cried the landlord. "Look sharp and you can catch him."

It was but two steps from the small parlor to the door of the old George Inn; the wide oak staircase landed almost in the street; there was room for a Turkey rug and nothing more between the threshold and the last round of the descent; but this little space was every evening brilliantly lit up, not only by the light upon the stair and the great signal lamp below the sign, but by the warm radiance of the barroom window. The George thus brightly advertised itself to passers-by in the cold street. Fettes walked steadily to the spot, and we, who were hanging behind, beheld the two men meet, as one of them had phrased it, face to face. Dr. Macfarlane was alert and vigorous. His white hair set off his pale and placid, although energetic, countenance. He was richly dressed in the finest of broadcloth and the whitest of linen, with a great gold watch chain, and studs and spectacles of the same precious material. He wore a broad-folded tie, white and speckled with lilac, and he carried on his arm a comfortable driving coat of fur. There was no doubt but he became his years, breathing, as he did, of wealth and consideration; and it was a surprising contrast to see our parlor sot—bald, dirty, pimpled, and robed in his old camlet cloak—confront him at the bottom of the stairs.

"Macfarlane!" he said somewhat loudly, more like a herald than a friend.

The great doctor pulled up short on the fourth step, as though the familiarity of the address surprised and somewhat shocked his dignity.

"Toddy Macfarlane!" repeated Fettes.

The London man almost staggered. He stared for the swiftest of seconds at the man before him, glanced behind him with a sort of scare, and then in a startled whisper, "Fettes!" he said, "you!"

"Ay," said the other, "me! Did you think I was dead too? We are not so easy shut of our acquaintance."

"Hush, hush!" exclaimed the doctor. "Hush, hush! This meeting is so unexpected—I can see you are unmanned. I hardly knew you, I confess, at first; but I am overjoyed—overjoyed to have this opportunity. For the present it must be how-d'ye-do and good-bye, in one, for my fly is waiting, and I must not fail the train; but you shall—let me see—yes—you shall give me your address, and you can count on early news of me. We must do something for you, Fettes. I fear you are out at elbows; but we must see to that for auld lang syne, as once we sang at suppers."

"Money!" cried Fettes; "money from you! The money that I had from you is lying where I cast it in the rain."

Dr. Macfarlane had talked himself into some measure of superiority and confidence, but the uncommon energy of this refusal cast him back into his first confusion.

A horrible, ugly look came and went across his almost venerable countenance. "My dear fellow," he said, "be it as you please; my last thought is to offend you. I would intrude on none. I will leave you my address, however——"

"I do not wish it—I do not wish to know the roof that shelters you," interrupted the other. "I heard your name; I feared it might be you; I wished to know if, after all, there were a God; I know now that there is none. Begone!"

He still stood in the middle of the rug, between the stair and doorway; and the great London physician, in order to escape, would be forced to step to one side. It was plain that he hesitated before the thought of this humiliation. White as he was, there was a dangerous glitter in his spectacles; but while he still paused uncertain, he became aware that the driver of his fly was peering in from the street at this unusual scene and caught a glimpse at the same time of our little body from the parlor, huddled by the corner of the bar. The presence of so many witnesses decided him at once to flee. He crouched together, brushing on the wainscot, and made a dart like a serpent, striking for the door. But his tribulation was not yet entirely at an end, for even as he was passing, Fettes clutched him by the arm and these words came in a whisper, and yet painfully distinct, "Have you seen it again?"

The great rich London doctor cried out aloud with a sharp, throttling cry; he dashed his questioner across the open space, and, with his hands over his head, fled out of the door like a detected thief. Before it had occurred to one of us to make a movement the fly was already rattling toward the station. The scene was over like a dream, but the dream had left proofs and traces of its passage. Next day the servant found the fine gold spectacles broken on the threshold, and that very night we were all standing breathless by the barroom window, and Fettes at our side, sober, pale, and resolute in look.

"God protect us, Mr. Fettes!" said the landlord, coming first into possession of his customary senses. "What in the universe is all this? These are strange things you have been saying."

Fettes turned toward us; he looked us each in succession in the face. "See if you can hold your tongues," said he. "That man Macfarlane is not safe to cross; those that have done so already have repented it too late."

And then, without so much as finishing his third glass, far less waiting for the other two, he bade us good-bye and went forth, under the lamp of the hotel, into the black night.

We three turned to our places in the parlor, with the big red fire and four clear candles; and as we recapitulated what had passed, the first chill of our surprise soon changed into a glow of curiosity. We sat late; it was the latest session I have known in the old George. Each man, before we parted, had his theory that he was bound to prove; and none of us had any nearer business in this world than to track out the past of our condemned companion, and surprise the secret that he shared with the great London doctor. It is no great boast, but I believe I was a better hand at worming out a story than either of my fellows at the George; and perhaps there is now no other man alive who could narrate to you the following foul and unnatural events.

In his young days Fettes studied medicine in the schools of Edinburgh. He had talent of a kind, the talent that picks up swiftly what it hears and readily retails it for its own. He worked little at home; but he was civil, attentive, and intelligent in the presence of his masters. They soon picked him out as a lad who listened closely and remembered well; nay, strange as it seemed to me when I first heard it, he was in those days well favored, and pleased by his exterior. There was, at that period, a certain extramural teacher of anatomy, whom I shall here designate by the letter K. His name was subsequently too well known. The man who bore it skulked through the streets of Edinburgh in disguise, while the mob that applauded at the execution of Burke called loudly for the blood of his employer. But Mr. K—— was then at the top of his vogue; he enjoyed a popularity due partly to his own talent and address, partly to the incapacity of his rival, the university professor. The students, at least, swore by his name, and Fettes believed himself, and was believed by others, to have laid the foundations of success when he had acquired the favor of this meteorically famous man. Mr. K—— was a *bon vivant* as well as an accomplished teacher; he liked a sly illusion no less than a careful preparation. In both capacities Fettes enjoyed and deserved his notice, and by the second year of his attendance he held the half-regular position of second demonstrator or sub-assistant in his class.

In this capacity, the charge of the theater and lecture room devolved in particular upon his shoulders. He had to answer for the cleanliness of the premises and the conduct of the other students, and it was a part of his duty to supply, receive, and divide the various subjects. It was with a view to this last—at that time very delicate—affair that he was lodged by Mr. K—— in the same wynd, and at last in the same building, with the dissecting rooms. Here, after a night of turbulent pleasures, his hand still tottering, his sight still misty and confused, he would be called out of bed in the black hours before the winter dawn by the unclean and desperate interlopers who supplied the table. He would open the door to these men, since infamous throughout the land. He would help them with their tragic burden, pay them their sordid price, and remain alone, when they were gone, with the unfriendly relics of humanity. From such a scene he would return to snatch another hour or two of slumber, to repair the abuses of the night, and refresh himself for the labors of the day.

Few lads could have been more insensible to the impressions of a life thus passed among the ensigns of mortality. His mind was closed against all general considerations. He was incapable of interest in the fate and fortunes of another, the slave of his own desires and low ambitions. Cold, light, and selfish in the last resort, he had that modicum of prudence, miscalled morality, which keeps a man from inconvenient drunkenness or punishable theft. He coveted, besides, a measure of consideration from his masters and his fellow pupils, and he had no desire to fail conspicuously in the external parts of life. Thus he made it his pleasure to gain some distinction in his studies, and day after day rendered unimpeachable eye service to his employer, Mr. K——. For his day of work he indemnified himself by nights of roaring, blackguardly enjoyment; and when that balance had been struck, the organ that he called his conscience declared itself content.

The supply of subjects was a continual trouble to him as well as to his master. In that large and busy class, the raw material of the anatomists kept perpetually running out; and the business thus rendered necessary was not only unpleasant in itself, but threatened dangerous consequences to all who were concerned. It was the policy of Mr. K—— to ask no questions in his dealings with the trade. "They bring the body, and we pay the price," he used to say, dwelling on the alliteration—"*Quid pro quo.*" And, again, and somewhat profanely, "Ask no questions," he would tell his assistants, "for conscience sake." There was no understanding that the subjects were provided by the crime of murder. Had that idea been broached to him in words, he would have recoiled in horror; but the lightness of his speech upon so grave a matter was, in itself, an offense against good manners, and a temptation to the men with whom he dealt. Fettes, for instance, had often remarked to himself upon the singular freshness of the bodies. He had been struck again and again by the hangdog, abominable looks of the ruffians who came to him before the dawn; and putting things together clearly in his private thoughts, he perhaps attributed a meaning too immoral and too categorical to the unguarded counsels of his master. He understood his duty, in short, to have three branches: to take what was brought, to pay the price, and to avert the eye from any evidence of crime.

One November morning this policy of silence was put sharply to the test. He had been awake all night with a racking toothache—pacing his room like a caged beast or throwing himself in fury on his bed—and had fallen at last into that profound, uneasy slumber that so often follows on a night of pain, when he was awakened by the third or fourth angry repetition of the concerted signal. There was a thin, bright moonshine; it was bitter cold, windy, and frosty; the town had not yet awakened, but an indefinable stir already preluded the noise and business of the day. The ghouls had come later than usual, and they seemed more than usually eager to be gone. Fettes, sick with sleep, lighted them upstairs. He heard their grumbling Irish voices through a dream; and as they stripped the sack from their sad merchandise he leaned dozing, with his shoulder propped against the wall; he had to shake himself to find the men their money. As he did so his eyes lighted on the dead face. He started; he took two steps nearer, with the candle raised.

"God Almighty!" he cried. "That is Jane Galbraith!"

The men answered nothing, but they shuffled nearer the door.

"I know her, I tell you," he continued. "She was alive and hearty yesterday. It's impossible she can be dead; it's impossible you should have got this body fairly."

"Sure, sir, you're mistaken entirely," said one of the men.

But the other looked Fettes darkly in the eyes, and demanded the money on the spot.

It was impossible to misconceive the threat or to exaggerate the danger. The lad's heart failed him. He stammered some excuses, counted out the sum, and saw his hateful visitors depart. No sooner were they gone than he hastened to confirm his doubts. By a dozen unquestionable marks he identified the girl he had jested with the day before. He saw, with horror, marks upon her body that might well betoken violence. A panic seized him, and he took refuge in his room. There he reflected at length over the discovery that he had made; considered soberly the bearing of Mr. K——'s instructions and the danger to himself of interference in so serious a business, and at last, in sore perplexity, determined to wait for the advice of his immediate superior, the class assistant.

This was a young doctor, Wolfe Macfarlane, a high favorite among all the reckless students, clever, dissipated, and unscrupulous to the last degree. He had traveled and studied abroad. His manners were agreeable and a little forward. He was an authority on the stage, skillful on the ice or the links with skate or golf club; he dressed with nice audacity, and, to put the finishing touch upon his glory, he kept a gig and a strong trotting horse. With Fettes he was on terms of intimacy; indeed, their relative positions called for some community of life; and when subjects were scarce the pair would drive far into the country in Macfarlane's gig, visit and desecrate some lonely graveyard, and return before dawn with their booty to the door of the dissecting room.

On that particular morning Macfarlane arrived somewhat earlier than his wont. Fettes heard him, and met him on the stairs, told him his story, and showed him the cause of his alarm. Macfarlane examined the marks on her body.

"Yes," he said with a nod, "it looks fishy."

"Well, what should I do?" asked Fettes.

"Do?" repeated the other. "Do you want to do anything? Least said soonest mended, I should say."

"Someone else might recognize her," objected Fettes. "She was as well known as the Castle Rock."

"We'll hope not," said Macfarlane, "and if anybody does—

well, you didn't, don't you see, and there's an end. The fact is, this has been going on too long. Stir up the mud, and you'll get K—— into the most unholy trouble; you'll be in a shocking box yourself. So will I, if you come to that. I should like to know how any one of us would look, or what the devil we should have to say for ourselves, in any Christian witness box. For me, you know there's one thing certain—that, practically speaking, all our subjects have been murdered."

"Macfarlane!" cried Fettes.

"Come now!" sneered the other. "As if you hadn't suspected it yourself!"

"Suspecting is one thing——"

"And proof another. Yes, I know; and I'm as sorry as you are this should have come here," tapping the body with his cane. "The next best thing for me is not to recognize it; and," he added coolly, "I don't. You may, if you please. I don't dictate, but I think a man of the world would do as I do; and I may add, I fancy that is what K—— would look for at our hands. The question is, Why did he choose us two for his assistants? And I answer, because he didn't want old wives."

This was the tone of all others to affect the mind of a lad like Fettes. He agreed to imitate Macfarlane. The body of the unfortunate girl was duly dissected, and no one remarked or appeared to recognize her.

One afternoon, when his day's work was over, Fettes dropped into a popular tavern and found Macfarlane sitting with a stranger. This was a small man, very pale and dark, with coal-black eyes. The cut of his features gave a promise of intellect and refinement which was but feebly realized in his manners, for he proved, upon a nearer acquaintance, coarse, vulgar, and stupid. He exercised, however, a very remarkable control over Macfarlane; issued orders like the Great Bashaw; became inflamed at the least discussion or delay, and commented rudely on the servility with which he was obeyed. This most offensive person took a fancy to Fettes on the spot, plied him with drinks, and honored him with unusual confidences on his past career. If a tenth part of what he confessed were true, he was a very loathsome rogue; and the lad's vanity was tickled by the attention of so experienced a man.

"I'm a pretty bad fellow myself," the stranger remarked, "but Macfarlane is the boy—Toddy Macfarlane I call him. Toddy, order your friend another glass." Or it might be, "Toddy, you jump up and shut the door." "Toddy hates me," he said again. "Oh, yes, Toddy, you do!"

"Don't you call me that confounded name," growled Macfarlane.

"Hear him! Did you ever see the lads play knife? He would like to do that all over my body," remarked the stranger.

"We medicals have a better way than that," said Fettes. "When we dislike a dead friend of ours, we dissect him."

Macfarlane looked up sharply, as though this jest were scarcely to his mind.

The afternoon passed. Gray, for that was the stranger's name, invited Fettes to join them at dinner, ordered a feast so sumptuous that the tavern was thrown in commotion, and when all was done commanded Macfarlane to settle the bill. It was late before they separated; the man Gray was incapably drunk. Macfarlane, sobered by his fury, chewed the cud of the money he had been forced to squander and the slights he had been obliged to swallow. Fettes, with various liquors singing in his head, returned home with devious footsteps and a mind entirely in abeyance. Next day Macfarlane was absent from the class, and Fettes smiled to himself as he imagined him still squiring the intolerable Gray from tavern to tavern. As soon as the hour of liberty had struck he posted from place to place in quest of his last night's companions. He could find them, however, nowhere; so returned early to his rooms, went early to bed, and slept the sleep of the just.

At four in the morning he was awakened by the well-known signal. Descending to the door, he was filled with astonishment to find Macfarlane with his gig, and in the gig one of those long and ghastly packages with which he was so well acquainted.

"What?" he cried. "Have you been out alone? How did you manage?"

But Macfarlane silenced him roughly, bidding him turn to business. When they had got the body upstairs and laid it on the table, Macfarlane made at first as if he were going away. Then he paused and seemed to hesitate; and then, "You had better look at the face," said he, in tones of some constraint. "You had better," he repeated, as Fettes only stared at him in wonder.

"But where, and how, and when did you come by it?" cried the other.

"Look at the face," was the only answer.

Fettes was staggered; strange doubts assailed him. He looked from the young doctor to the body, and then back again. At last, with a start, he did as he was bidden. He had almost expected the sight that met his eyes, and yet the shock was cruel. To see, fixed in the rigidity of death and naked on that coarse layer of sackcloth, the man whom he had left well clad and full of meat and sin upon the threshold of a tavern, awoke, even in the thoughtless Fettes, some of the terrors of the conscience. It was a *cras tibi* which reechoed in his soul, that two whom he had known should have come to lie upon these icy tables. Yet these were only secondary thoughts. His first concern regarded Wolfe. Unprepared for a challenge so momentous, he knew not how to look his comrade in the face. He durst not meet his eye, and he had neither words nor voice at his command.

It was Macfarlane himself who made the first advance. He came up quietly behind and laid his hand gently but firmly on the other's shoulder.

"Richardson," said he, "may have the head."

Now Richardson was a student who had long been anxious for that portion of the human subject to dissect. There was no answer, and the murderer resumed: "Talking of business, you must pay me; your accounts, you see, must tally."

Fettes found a voice, the ghost of his own: "Pay you!" he cried. "Pay you for that?"

"Why, yes, of course you must. By all means and on every possible account, you must," returned the other. "I dare not give it for nothing, you dare not take it for nothing; it would compromise us both. This is another case like Jane Galbraith's. The more things are wrong the more we must act as if all were right. Where does old K—— keep his money?"

"There," answered Fettes hoarsely, pointing to a cupboard in the corner.

"Give me the key, then," said the other calmly, holding out his hand.

There was an instant's hesitation, and the die was cast. Macfarlane could not suppress a nervous twitch, the infinitesimal mark of an immense relief, as he felt the key between his fingers. He opened the cupboard, brought out pen and ink and a paper book that stood in one compartment, and separated from the funds in a drawer a sum suitable to the occasion.

"Now, look here," he said, "there is the payment made—first proof of your good faith: first step to your security. You have now to clinch it by a second. Enter the payment in your book, and then you for your part may defy the devil."

The next few seconds were for Fettes an agony of thought; but in balancing his terrors it was the most immediate that triumphed. Any future difficulty seemed almost welcome if he could avoid a present quarrel with Macfarlane. He set down the candle which he had been carrying all this time, and with a steady hand entered the date, the nature, and the amount of the transaction.

"And now," said Macfarlane, "it's only fair that you

should pocket the lucre. I've had my share already. By the bye, when a man of the world falls into a bit of luck, has a few shillings extra in his pocket—I'm ashamed to speak of it, but there's a rule of conduct in the case. No treating, no purchase of expensive class books, no squaring of old debts; borrow, don't lend."

"Macfarlane," began Fettes, still somewhat hoarsely, "I have put my neck in a halter to oblige you."

"To oblige me?" cried Wolfe. "Oh, come! You did, as near as I can see the matter, what you downright had to do in self-defense. Suppose I got into trouble, where would you be? This second little matter flows clearly from the first. Mr. Gray is the continuation of Miss Galbraith. You can't begin and then stop. If you begin, you must keep on beginning; that's the truth. No rest for the wicked."

A horrible sense of blackness and the treachery of fate seized hold upon the soul of the unhappy student.

"My God!" he cried, "but what have I done? and when did I begin? To be made a class assistant—in the name of reason, where's the harm in that? Service wanted the position; Service might have got it. Would *he* have been where *I* am now?"

"My dear fellow," said Macfarlane, "what a boy you are! What harm *has* come to you? What harm *can* come to you if you hold your tongue? Why, man, do you know what this life is? There are two squads of us—the lions and the lambs. If you're a lamb, you'll come to lie upon these tables like Gray or Jane Galbraith; if you're a lion, you'll live and drive a horse like me, like K——, like all the world with any wit or courage. You're staggered at the first. But look at K——! My dear fellow, you're clever, you have pluck. I like you, and K—— likes you. You were born to lead the hunt; and I tell you, on my honor and my experience of life, three days from now you'll laugh at all these scarecrows like a high-school boy at a farce."

And with that Macfarlane took his departure and drove off

up the wynd in his gig to get under cover before daylight. Fettes was thus left alone with his regrets. He saw the miserable peril in which he stood involved. He saw, with inexpressible dismay, that there was no limit to his weakness, and that, from concession to concession, he had fallen from the arbiter of Macfarlane's destiny to his paid and helpless accomplice. He would have given the world to have been a little braver at the time, but it did not occur to him that he might still be brave. The secret of Jane Galbraith and the cursed entry in the daybook closed his mouth.

Hours passed; the class began to arrive; the members of the unhappy Gray were dealt out to one and to another, and received without remark. Richardson was made happy with the head; and before the hour of freedom rang Fettes trembled with exultation to perceive how far they had already gone toward safety.

For two days he continued to watch, with increasing joy, the dreadful process of disguise.

On the third day Macfarlane made his appearance. He had been ill, he said; but he made up for lost time by the energy with which he directed the students. To Richardson in particular he extended the most valuable assistance and advice, and that student, encouraged by the praise of the demonstrator, burned high with ambitious hopes, and saw the medal already in his grasp.

Before the week was out Macfarlane's prophecy had been fulfilled. Fettes had outlived his terrors and had forgotten his baseness. He began to plume himself upon his courage, and had so arranged the story in his mind that he could look back on these events with an unhealthy pride. Of his accomplice he saw but little. They met, of course, in the business of the class; they received their orders together from Mr. K——. At times they had a word or two in private, and Macfarlane was from first to last particularly kind and jovial. But it was plain that he avoided any reference to their common secret; and even when Fettes whispered to him that he had cast in his lot with the lions and foresworn the lambs, he only signed to him smilingly to hold his peace.

At length an occasion arose which threw the pair once more into a closer union. Mr. K—— was again short of subjects; pupils were eager, and it was a part of this teacher's pretensions to be always well supplied. At the same time there came the news of a burial in the rustic graveyard of Glencorse. Time has little changed the place in question. It stood then, as now, upon a crossroad, out of call of human habitations, and buried fathom deep in the foliage of six cedar trees. The cries of the sheep upon the neighboring hills, the streamlets upon either hand, one loudly singing among pebbles, the other dripping furtively from pond to pond, the stir of the wind in mountainous old flowering chestnuts, and once in seven days the voice of the bell and the old tunes of the precentor, were the only sounds that disturbed the silence around the rural church. The Resurrection Man—to use a byname of the period—was not to be deterred by any of the sanctities of customary piety. It was part of his trade to despise and desecrate the scrolls and trumpets of old tombs, the paths worn by the feet of worshippers and mourners, and the offerings and the inscriptions of bereaved affection. To rustic neighborhoods, where love is more than commonly tenacious, and where some bonds of blood or fellowship unite the entire society of a parish, the body-snatcher, far from being repelled by natural respect, was attracted by the ease and safety of the task. To bodies that had been laid in earth, in joyful expectation of a far different awakening, there came that hasty, lamp-lit, terror-haunted resurrection of the spade and mattock. The coffin was forced, the cerements torn, and the melancholy relics, clad in sackcloth, after being rattled for hours on moonless byways, were at length exposed to uttermost indignities before a class of gaping boys.

Somewhat as two vultures may swoop upon a dying lamb,

Fettes and Macfarlane were to be let loose upon a grave in that green and quiet resting place. The wife of a farmer, a woman who had lived for sixty years, and been known for nothing but good butter and a godly conversation, was to be rooted from her grave at midnight and carried, dead and naked, to that far-away city that she had always honored with her Sunday's best; the place beside her family was to be empty till the crack of doom; her innocent and almost venerable members to be exposed to that last curiosity of the anatomist.

Late one afternoon the pair set forth, well wrapped in cloaks and furnished with a formidable bottle. It rained without remission—a cold, dense, lashing rain. Now and again there blew a puff of wind, but these sheets of falling water kept it down. Bottle and all, it was a sad and silent drive as far as Penicuik, where they were to spend the evening. They stopped once, to hide their implements in a thick bush not far from the churchyard, and once again at the Fisher's Tryst, to have a toast before the kitchen fire and vary their nips of whisky with a glass of ale. When they reached their journey's end the gig was housed, the horse was fed and comforted, and the two young doctors in a private room sat down to the best dinner and the best wine the house afforded. The lights, the fire, the beating rain upon the window, the cold, incongruous work that lay before them, added zest to their enjoyment of the meal. With every glass their cordiality increased. Soon Macfarlane handed a little pile of gold to his companion.

"A compliment," he said. "Between friends these little d——d accommodations ought to fly like pipe lights."

Fettes pocketed the money, and applauded the sentiment to the echo. "You are a philosopher," he cried. "I was an ass till I knew you. You and K—— between you, by the Lord Harry! But you'll make a man of me."

"Of course we shall," applauded Macfarlane. "A man? I tell you, it required a man to back me up the other morning. There are some big, brawling, forty-year-old cowards who would have turned sick at the look of the d——d thing; but not you—kept your head. I watched you."

"Well, and why not?" Fettes thus vaunted himself. "It was no affair of mine. There was nothing to gain on the one side but disturbance, and on the other I could count on your gratitude, don't you see?" And he slapped his pocket till the gold pieces rang.

Macfarlane somehow felt a certain touch of alarm at these unpleasant words. He may have regretted that he had taught his young companion so successfully, but he had no time to interfere, for the other noisily continued in this boastful strain:

"The great thing is not to be afraid. Now, between you and me, I don't want to hang—that's practical; but for all cant, Macfarlane, I was born with a contempt. Hell, God, Devil, right, wrong, sin, crime, and all the old gallery of curiosities —they may frighten boys, but men of the world, like you and me, despise them. Here's to the memory of Gray!"

It was by this time growing somewhat late. The gig, according to order, was brought round to the door with both lamps brightly shining, and the young men had to pay their bill and take the road. They announced that they were bound for Peebles, and drove in that direction till they were clear of the last houses of the town; then, extinguishing the lamps, returned upon their course, and followed a byroad toward Glencorse. There was no sound but that of their own passage, and the incessant, strident pouring of the rain. It was pitch dark; here and there a white gate or a white stone in the wall guided them for a short space across the night; but for the most part it was at a foot pace, and almost groping, that they picked their way through that resonant blackness to their solemn and isolated destination. In the sunken woods that traverse the neighborhood of the burying ground the last glimmer failed them, and it became necessary to kindle a match and reillumine one of the lanterns of the gig. Thus, under the dripping trees, and environed by huge and moving shadows, they reached the scene of their unhallowed labors.

They were both experienced in such affairs, and powerful with the spade; and they had scarce been twenty minutes at their task before they were rewarded by a dull rattle on the coffin lid. At the same moment Macfarlane, having hurt his hand upon a stone, flung it carelessly above his head. The grave, in which they now stood almost to the shoulders, was close to the edge of the plateau of the graveyard; and the gig lamp had been propped, the better to illuminate their labors, against a tree, and on the immediate verge of the steep bank descending to the stream. Chance had taken a sure aim with the stone. Then came a clang of broken glass; night fell upon them; sounds alternately dull and ringing announced the bounding of the lantern down the bank, and its occasional collision with the trees. A stone or two, which it had dislodged in its descent, rattled behind it into the profundities of the glen; and then silence, like night, resumed its sway; and they might bend their hearing to its utmost pitch, but naught was to be heard except the rain, now marching to the wind, now steadily falling over miles of open country.

They were so nearly at an end of their abhorred task that they judged it wisest to complete it in the dark. The coffin was exhumed and broken open; the body inserted in the dripping sack and carried between them to the gig; one mounted to keep it in its place, and the other, taking the horse by the mouth, groped along by wall and bush until they reached the wider road by the Fisher's Tryst. Here was a faint, diffused radiancy, which they hailed like daylight; by that they pushed the horse to a good pace and began to rattle along merrily in the direction of the town.

They had both been wetted to the skin during their operations, and now, as the gig jumped among the deep ruts, the thing that stood propped between them fell now upon one and now upon the other. At every repetition of the horrid contact each instinctively repelled it with the greater haste; and the process, natural although it was, began to tell upon the nerves of the companions. Macfarlane made some ill-favored jest about the farmer's wife, but it came hollowly from his lips, and was allowed to drop in silence. Still their unnatural burden bumped from side to side; and now the head would be laid, as if in confidence, upon their shoulders, and now the drenching sackcloth would flap icily about their faces. A creeping chill began to possess the soul of Fettes. He peered at the bundle, and it seemed somehow larger than at first. All over the countryside, and from every degree of distance, the farm dogs accompanied their passage with tragic ululations; and it grew and grew upon his mind that some unnatural miracle had been accomplished, that some nameless change had befallen the dead body, and that it was in fear of their unholy burden that the dogs were howling.

"For God's sake," said he, making a great effort to arrive at speech, "for God's sake, let's have a light!"

Seemingly Macfarlane was affected in the same direction; for, though he made no reply, he stopped the horse, passed the reins to his companion, got down, and proceeded to kindle the remaining lamp. They had by that time got no farther than the crossroad down to Auchenclinny. The rain still poured as though the deluge were returning, and it was no easy matter to make a light in such a world of wet and darkness. When at last the flickering blue flame had been transferred to the wick and began to expand and clarify, and shed a wide circle of misty brightness round the gig, it became possible for the two young men to see each other and the thing they had along with them. The rain had molded the rough sacking to the outlines of the body underneath; the head was distinct from the trunk, the shoulders plainly modeled; something at once spectral and human riveted their eyes upon the ghastly comrade of their drive.

For some time Macfarlane stood motionless, holding up

the lamp. A nameless dread was swathed, like a wet sheet, about the body, and tightened the white skin upon the face of Fettes; a fear that was meaningless, a horror of what could not be, kept mounting to his brain. Another beat of the watch, and he had spoken. But his comrade forestalled him.

"That is not a woman," said Macfarlane, in a hushed voice.

"It was a woman when we put her in," whispered Fettes.

"Hold that lamp," said the other. "I must see her face."

And as Fettes took the lamp his companion untied the fastenings of the sack and drew down the cover from the head. The light fell very clear upon the dark, well-molded features and smooth-shaven cheeks of a too familiar countenance, often beheld in dreams of both of these young men. A wild yell rang up into the night; each leaped from his own side into the roadway; the lamp fell, broke, and was extinguished; and the horse, terrified by this unusual commotion, bounded and went off toward Edinburgh at a gallop, bearing along with it, sole occupant of the gig, the body of the dead and long-dissected Gray.

Man-Size in Marble By E. NESBIT

ALTHOUGH EVERY WORD of this story is as true as despair, I do not expect people to believe it. Nowadays a "rational explanation" is required before belief is possible. Let me then, at once, offer the "rational explanation" which finds most favor among those who have heard the tale of my life's tragedy. It is held that we were "under a delusion," Laura and I, on that thirty-first of October; and that this supposition places the whole matter on a satisfactory and believable basis. The reader can judge, when he, too, has heard my story, how far this is an "explanation," and in what sense it is "rational." There were three who took part in this: Laura and I and another man. The other man still lives, and can speak to the truth of the least credible part of my story.

I never in my life knew what it was to have as much money as I required to supply the most ordinary needs—good colors, books, and cab fares—and when we were married we knew quite well that we should only be able to live at all by "strict punctuality and attention to business." I used to paint in those days, and Laura used to write, and we felt sure we could keep the pot at least simmering. Living in town was out of the question, so we went to look for a cottage in the country, which should be at once sanitary and picturesque. So rarely do these two qualities meet in one cottage that our search was for some time quite fruitless. We tried advertisements, but most of the desirable rural residences which we did look at proved to be lacking in both essentials, and when a cottage chanced to have drains it always had stucco as well and was shaped like a tea caddy. And if we found a vine or rose-covered porch, corruption invariably lurked within. Our minds got so befogged by the eloquence of house agents, and the rival disadvantages of the fever traps and outrages to beauty which we had seen and scorned, that I very much doubt whether either of us, on our wedding morning, knew the difference between a house and a haystack. But when we got away from friends and house agents, on our honeymoon, our wits grew clear again, and we knew a pretty cottage when at last we saw one. It was at Brenzett—a little village set on a hill over against the southern marshes. We had gone there, from the seaside village where we were staying, to see the church, and two fields from the church we found this cottage. It stood quite by itself, about two miles from the village. It was a long, low building, with rooms sticking out in unexpected places. There was a bit of stonework—ivy-covered and moss-grown, just two old rooms, all that was left of a big house that had once stood there—and round this stonework the house had grown up. Stripped of its roses and jasmine it would have been hideous. As it stood it was charming, and after a brief examination we took it. It was absurdly cheap. The rest of our honeymoon we spent in grubbing about in secondhand shops in the country town, picking up bits of old oak and Chippendale chairs for our furnishing. We wound up with a run up to town and a visit to Liberty's, and soon the low oak-beamed lattice-windowed rooms began to be home. There was a jolly old-fashioned garden, with grass paths, and no end of hollyhocks and sunflowers, and big lilies. From the window you could see the marsh pastures, and beyond them the blue, thin line of the sea. We were as happy as the summer was glorious, and settled down into work sooner than we ourselves expected. I was never tired of sketching the view and the wonderful cloud effects from the open lattice, and Laura would sit at the table and write verses about them, in which I mostly played the part of foreground.

We got a tall old peasant woman to do for us. Her face and figure were good, though her cooking was of the homeliest; but she understood all about gardening, and told us all the old names of the coppices and cornfields, and the stories of the smugglers and highwaymen, and, better still, of the "things that walked," and of the "sights" which met one in lonely glens of a starlight night. She was a great comfort to us, because Laura hated housekeeping as much as I loved folklore, and we soon came to leave all the domestic business to Mrs. Dorman, and to use her legends in little magazine stories which brought in the jingling guinea.

We had three months of married happiness, and did not have a single quarrel. One October evening I had been down to smoke a pipe with the doctor—our only neighbor—a pleasant young Irishman. Laura had stayed at home to finish a comic sketch of a village episode for the *Monthly Marplot*. I left her laughing over her own jokes, and came in to find her a crumpled heap of pale muslin weeping on the window seat.

"Good heavens, my darling, what's the matter?" I cried, taking her in my arms. She leaned her little dark head against my shoulder and went on crying. I had never seen her cry before—we had always been so happy, you see—and I felt sure some frightful misfortune had happened.

"What *is* the matter? Do speak."

"It's Mrs. Dorman," she sobbed.

121

"What has she done?" I inquired, immensely relieved.

"She says she must go before the end of the month, and she says her niece is ill; she's gone down to see her now, but I don't believe that's the reason, because her niece is always ill. I believe someone has been setting her against us. Her manner was so queer——"

"Never mind, Pussy," I said; "whatever you do, don't cry, or I shall have to cry too, to keep you in countenance, and then you'll never respect your man again!"

She dried her eyes obediently on my handkerchief, and even smiled faintly.

"But you see," she went on, "it is really serious, because these village people are so sheepy, and if one won't do a thing you may be quite sure none of the others will. And I shall have to cook the dinners, and wash up the hateful greasy plates; and you'll have to carry cans of water about, and clean the boots and knives—and we shall never have any time for work, or earn any money, or anything. We shall have to work all day, and only be able to rest when we are waiting for the kettle to boil!"

I represented to her that even if we had to perform these duties, the day would still present some margin for other toils and recreations. But she refused to see the matter in any but the grayest light. She was very unreasonable, my Laura, but I could not have loved her any more if she had been as reasonable as Whately.

"I'll speak to Mrs. Dorman when she comes back, and see if I can't come to terms with her," I said. "Perhaps she wants a rise in her pay. It will be all right. Let's walk up to the church."

The church was a large and lonely one, and we loved to go there, especially upon bright nights. The path skirted a wood, cut through it once, and ran along the crest of the hill through two meadows, and round the churchyard wall, over which the old yews loomed in black masses of shadow. This path, which was partly paved, was called "the bier-balk," for it had long been the way by which the corpses had been carried to burial. The churchyard was richly treed, and was shaded by great elms which stood just outside and stretched their majestic arms in benediction over the happy dead. A large, low porch let one into the building by a Norman doorway and a heavy oak door studded with iron. Inside, the arches rose into darkness, and between them the reticulated windows, which stood out white in the moonlight. In the chancel, the windows were of rich glass, which showed in faint light their noble coloring, and made the black oak of the choir pews hardly more solid than the shadows. But on each side of the altar lay a gray marble figure of a knight in full plate armor lying upon a low slab, with hands held up in everlasting prayer, and these figures, oddly enough, were always to be seen if there was any glimmer of light in the church. Their names were lost, but the peasants told of them that they had been fierce and wicked men, marauders by land and sea, who had been the scourge of their time, and had been guilty of deeds so foul that the house they had lived in—the big house, by the way, that had stood on the site of our cottage—had been stricken by lightning and the vengeance of Heaven. But for all that, the gold of their heirs had bought them a place in the church. Looking at the bad hard faces reproduced in the marble, this story was easily believed.

The church looked at its best and weirdest on that night, for the shadows of the yew trees fell through the windows upon the floor of the nave and touched the pillars with tattered shade. We sat down together without speaking, and watched the solemn beauty of the old church, with some of that awe which inspired its early builders. We walked to the chancel and looked at the sleeping warriors. Then we rested some time on the stone seat in the porch, looking out over the stretch of quiet moonlit meadows, feeling in every fiber of our beings the peace of the night and of our happy love; and came away at last with a sense that even scrubbing and black-leading were but small troubles at their worst.

Mrs. Dorman had come back from the village, and I at once invited her to a *tête-à-tête*.

"Now, Mrs. Dorman," I said, when I had got her into my painting room, "what's all this about your not staying with us?"

"I should be glad to get away, sir, before the end of the month," she answered, with her usual placid dignity.

"Have you any fault to find, Mrs. Dorman?"

"None at all, sir; you and your lady have always been most kind, I'm sure——"

"Well, what is it? Are your wages not high enough?"

"No, sir, I gets quite enough."

"Then why not stay?"

"I'd rather not"—with some hesitation—"my niece is ill."

"But your niece has been ill ever since we came."

No answer. There was a long and awkward silence. I broke it.

"Can't you stay for another month?" I asked.

"No, sir. I'm bound to go by Thursday."

And this was Monday!

"Well, I must say, I think you might have let us know before. There's no time now to get any one else, and your mistress is not fit to do heavy housework. Can't you stay till next week?"

"I might be able to come back next week."

I was now convinced that all she wanted was a brief holiday, which we should have been willing enough to let her have, as soon as we could get a substitute.

"But why must you go this week?" I persisted. "Come, out with it."

Mrs. Dorman drew the little shawl, which she always wore, tightly across her bosom, as though she were cold. Then she said, with a sort of effort:

"They say, sir, as this was a big house in Catholic times, and there was a many deeds done here."

The nature of the "deeds" might be vaguely inferred from the inflection of Mrs. Dorman's voice—which was enough to make one's blood run cold. I was glad that Laura was not in the room. She was always nervous, as highly strung natures are, and I felt that these tales about our house, told by this old peasant woman, with her impressive manner and contagious credulity, might have made our home less dear to my wife.

"Tell me all about it, Mrs. Dorman," I said; "you needn't mind about telling me. I'm not like the young people who make fun of such things."

Which was partly true.

"Well, sir"—she sank her voice—"you may have seen in the church, beside the altar, two shapes."

"You mean the effigies of the knights in armor," I said cheerfully.

"I mean them two bodies, drawed out man-size in marble," she returned, and I had to admit that her description was a thousand times more graphic than mine, to say nothing of a certain weird force and uncanniness about the phrase "drawed out man-size in marble."

"They do say, as on All Saints' Eve them two bodies sits up on their slabs, and gets off of them, and then walks down the aisle, *in their marble*"—(another good phrase, Mrs. Dorman)—"and as the church clock strikes eleven they walks out of the church door, and over the graves, and along the bier-balk, and if it's a wet night there's the marks of their feet in the morning."

"And where do they go?" I asked, rather fascinated.

"They comes back here to their home, sir, and if anyone meets them——"

"Well, what then?" I asked.

But no—not another word could I get from her, save that her niece was ill and she must go. After what I had heard I scorned to discuss the niece, and tried to get from Mrs. Dorman more details of the legend. I could get nothing but warnings.

"Whatever you do, sir, lock the door early on All Saints' Eve, and make the cross sign over the doorstep and on the windows."

"But has anyone ever seen these things?" I persisted.

"That's not for me to say. I know what I know, sir."

"Well, who was here last year?"

"No one, sir; the lady as owned the house only stayed here in summer, and she always went to London a full month afore *the* night. And I'm sorry to inconvenience you and your lady, but my niece is ill and I must go on Thursday."

I could have shaken her for her absurd reiteration of that obvious fiction, after she had told me her real reasons.

She was determined to go, nor could our united entreaties move her in the least.

I did not tell Laura the legend of the shapes that "walked in their marble," partly because a legend concerning our house might perhaps trouble my wife, and partly, I think, from some more occult reason. This was not quite the same to me as any other story, and I did not want to talk about it till the day was over. I had very soon ceased to think of the legend, however. I was painting a portrait of Laura, against the lattice window, and I could not think of much else. I had got a splendid background of yellow and gray sunset, and was working away with enthusiasm at her face. On Thursday Mrs. Dorman went. She relented, at parting, so far as to say:

"Don't you put yourself about too much, ma'am, and if there's any little thing I can do next week, I'm sure I shan't mind."

From which I inferred that she wished to come back to us after Hallowe'en. Up to the last she adhered to the fiction of the niece with touching fidelity.

Thursday passed off pretty well. Laura showed marked

ability in the matter of steak and potatoes, and I confess that my knives, and the plates, which I insisted upon washing, were better done than I had dared to expect.

Friday came. It is about what happened on that Friday that this is written. I wonder if I should have believed it, if anyone had told it to me. I will write the story of it as quickly and plainly as I can. Everything that happened on that day is burnt into my brain. I shall not forget anything, nor leave anything out.

I got up early, I remember, and lighted the kitchen fire, and had just achieved a smoky success when my little wife came running down, as sunny and sweet as the clear October morning itself. We prepared breakfast together, and found it very good fun. The housework was soon done, and when brushes and brooms and pails were quiet again, the house was still indeed. It is wonderful what a difference one makes in a house. We really missed Mrs. Dorman, quite apart from considerations concerning pots and pans. We spent the day in dusting our books and putting them straight, and dined gaily on cold steak and coffee. Laura was, if possible, brighter and gayer and sweeter than usual, and I began to think that a little domestic toil was really good for her. We had never been so merry since we were married, and the walk we had that afternoon was, I think, the happiest time of all my life. When we had watched the deep scarlet clouds slowly pale into leaden gray against a pale-green sky, and saw the white mists curl up along the hedgerows in the distant marsh, we came back to the house, silently, hand in hand.

"You are sad, my darling," I said, half jestingly, as we sat down together in our little parlor. I expected a disclaimer, for my own silence had been the silence of complete happiness. To my surprise she said:

"Yes. I think I am sad, or rather I am uneasy. I don't think I'm very well. I have shivered three or four times since we came in, and it is not cold, is it?"

"No," I said, and hoped it was not a chill caught from the treacherous mists that roll up from the marshes in the dying light. No—she said, she did not think so. Then, after a silence, she spoke suddenly:

"Do you ever have presentiments of evil?"

"No," I said, smiling, "and I shouldn't believe in them if I had."

"I do," she went on; "the night my father died I knew it, though he was right away in the North of Scotland." I did not answer in words.

She sat looking at the fire for some time in silence, gently stroking my hand. At last she sprang up, came behind me, and, drawing my head back, kissed me.

"There, it's over now," she said. "What a baby I am! Come, light the candles, and we'll have some of these new Rubinstein duets."

And we spent a happy hour or two at the piano.

At about half past ten I began to long for the good-night pipe, but Laura looked so white that I felt it would be brutal of me to fill our sitting room with the fumes of strong cavendish.

"I'll take my pipe outside," I said.

"Let me come, too."

"No, sweetheart, not tonight; you're much too tired. I shan't be long. Get to bed, or I shall have an invalid to nurse tomorrow as well as the boots to clean."

I kissed her and was turning to go, when she flung her arms round my neck and held me as if she would never let me go again. I stroked her hair.

"Come, Pussy, you're over-tired. The housework has been too much for you."

She loosened her clasp a little and drew a deep breath.

"No. We've been very happy today, Jack, haven't we? Don't stay out too long."

"I won't, my dearie."

I strolled out of the front door, leaving it unlatched. What a night it was! The jagged masses of heavy dark cloud were rolling at intervals from horizon to horizon, and thin white wreaths covered the stars. Through all the rush of the cloud river, the moon swam, breasting the waves and disappearing again in the darkness. When now and again her light reached the woodlands they seemed to be slowly and noiselessly waving in time to the swing of the clouds above them. There was a strange gray light over all the earth; the fields had that shadowy bloom over them which only comes from the marriage of dew and moonshine, or frost and starlight.

I walked up and down, drinking in the beauty of the quiet earth and the changing sky. The night was absolutely silent. Nothing seemed to be abroad. There was no scurrying of rabbits, or twitter of the half-asleep birds. And though the clouds went sailing across the sky, the wind that drove them never came low enough to rustle the dead leaves in the woodland paths. Across the meadows I could see the church tower standing out black and gray against the sky. I walked there thinking over our three months of happiness—and of my wife, her dear eyes, her loving ways. Oh, my little girl! My own little girl; what a vision came then of a long, glad life for you and me together!

I heard a bell-beat from the church. Eleven already! I turned to go in, but the night held me. I could not go back into our little warm rooms yet. I would go up to the church. I felt vaguely that it would be good to carry my love and thankfulness to the sanctuary whither so many loads of sorrow and gladness had been borne by the men and women of the dead years.

I looked in at the low window as I went by. Laura was half lying on her chair in front of the fire. I could not see her face, only her little head showed dark against the pale blue wall. She was quite still. Asleep, no doubt. My heart reached out to her as I went on. There must be a God, I thought, and a God who was good. How otherwise could anything so sweet and dear as she have ever been imagined?

I walked slowly along the edge of the wood. A sound broke the stillness of the night, it was a rustling in the wood. I stopped and listened. The sound stopped too. I went on, and now distinctly heard another step than mine answer mine like an echo. It was a poacher or a wood stealer, most likely, for these were not unknown in our Arcadian neighborhood. But whoever it was, he was a fool not to step more lightly. I turned into the wood, and now the footstep seemed to come from the path I had just left. It must be an echo, I thought. The wood looked perfect in the moonlight. The large dying ferns and the brushwood showed where through thinning foliage the pale light came down. The tree trunks stood up like Gothic columns all around me. They reminded me of the church, and I turned into the bier-balk, and passed through the corpse gate between the graves to the low porch. I paused for a moment on the stone seat where Laura and I had watched the fading landscape. Then I noticed that the door of the church was open, and I blamed myself for having left it unlatched the other night. We were the only people who ever cared to come to the church except on Sundays, and I was vexed to think that through our carelessness the damp autumn airs had had a chance of getting in and injuring the old fabric. I went in. It will seem strange, perhaps, that I should have gone halfway up the aisle before I remembered—with a sudden chill, followed by as sudden a rush of self-contempt—that this was the very day and hour when, according to tradition, the "shapes drawed out man-size in marble" began to walk.

Having thus remembered the legend, and remembered it with a shiver, of which I was ashamed, I could not do otherwise than walk up towards the altar, just to look at the figures—as I said to myself; really what I wanted was to assure myself, first, that I did not believe the legend, and, secondly, that it was not true. I was rather glad that I had come. I thought now I could tell Mrs. Dorman how vain her fancies were, and how peacefully the marble figures slept on through the ghastly hour. With my hands in my pockets I passed up the aisle. In the gray dim light the eastern end of the church looked larger than usual, and the arches above the two tombs looked larger too. The moon came out and showed me the reason. I stopped short, my heart gave a leap that nearly choked me, and then sank sickeningly.

The "bodies drawed out man-size" *were gone*, and their marble slabs lay wide and bare in the vague moonlight that slanted through the east window.

Were they really gone or was I mad? Clenching my nerves, I stooped and passed my hand over the smooth slabs, and felt their flat unbroken surface. Had someone taken the things away? Was it some vile practical joke? I would make sure, anyway. In an instant I had made a torch of a newspaper, which happened to be in my pocket, and lighting it held it high above my head. Its yellow glare illumined the dark arches and those slabs. The figures *were* gone. And I was alone in the church; or was I alone?

And then a horror seized me, a horror indefinable and indescribable—an overwhelming certainty of supreme and accomplished calamity. I flung down the torch and tore along the aisle and out through the porch, biting my lips as I ran to keep myself from shrieking aloud. Oh, was I mad—or what was this that possessed me? I leaped the churchyard wall and took the straight cut across the fields, led by the light from our windows. Just as I got over the first stile, a dark figure seemed to spring out of the ground. Mad still with that certainty of misfortune, I made for the thing that stood in my path, shouting, "Get out of the way, can't you!"

But my push met with a more vigorous resistance than I had expected. My arms were caught just above the elbow and held as in a vice, and the raw-boned Irish doctor actually shook me.

"Would ye?" he cried, in his own unmistakable accents— "would ye, then?"

"Let me go, you fool," I gasped. "The marble figures have gone from the church; I tell you they've gone."

He broke into a ringing laugh. "I'll have to give ye a draught tomorrow, I see. Ye've bin smoking too much and listening to old wives' tales."

"I tell you, I've seen the bare slabs."

"Well, come back with me. I'm going up to old Palmer's—his daughter's ill; we'll look in at the church and let me see the bare slabs."

"You go, if you like," I said, a little less frantic for his laughter; "I'm going home to my wife."

"Rubbish, man," said he; "d'ye think I'll permit that? Are ye to go saying all yer life that ye've seen solid marble endowed with vitality, and me to go all me life saying ye were a coward? No, sir—ye shan't do ut."

The night air—a human voice—and I think also the physical contact with this six feet of solid common sense, brought me back a little to my ordinary self, and the word "coward" was a mental shower bath.

"Come on, then," I said sullenly; "perhaps you're right."

He still held my arm tightly. We got over the stile and back to the church. All was still as death. The place smelt very damp and earthy. We walked up the aisle. I am not ashamed to confess that I shut my eyes: I knew the figures would not be there. I heard Kelly strike a match.

"Here they are, ye see, right enough; ye've been dreaming or drinking, asking yer pardon for the imputation."

I opened my eyes. By Kelly's expiring vesta I saw two shapes lying "in their marble" on their slabs. I drew a deep breath, and caught his hand.

"I'm awfully indebted to you," I said. "It must have been some trick of light, or I have been working rather hard, perhaps that's it. Do you know, I was quite convinced they were gone."

"I'm aware of that," he answered rather grimly; "ye'll have to be careful of that brain of yours, my friend, I assure ye."

He was leaning over and looking at the right-hand figure, whose stony face was the more villainous and deadly in expression.

"By Jove," he said, "something has been afoot here—this hand is broken."

And so it was. I was certain that it had been perfect the last time Laura and I had been there.

"Perhaps some one has *tried* to remove them," said the young doctor.

"That won't account for my impression," I objected.

"Too much painting and tobacco will account for that, well enough."

"Come along," I said, "or my wife will be getting anxious. You'll come in and have a drop of whisky and drink confusion to ghosts and better sense to me."

"I ought to go up to Palmer's, but it's so late now I'd best leave it till the morning," he replied. "I was kept late at the Union, and I've had to see a lot of people since. All right, I'll come back with ye."

I think he fancied I needed him more than did Palmer's girl, so, discussing how such an illusion could have been possible, and deducing from this experience large generalities concerning ghostly apparitions, we walked up to our cottage. We saw, as we walked up the garden path, that bright light streamed out of the front door, and presently saw that the parlor door was open too. Had she gone out?

"Come in," I said, and Dr. Kelly followed me into the parlor. It was all ablaze with candles, not only the wax ones, but at least a dozen guttering, glaring tallow dips, stuck in vases and ornaments in unlikely places. Light, I knew, was Laura's remedy for nervousness. Poor child! Why had I left her? Brute that I was.

We glanced round the room, and at first we did not see her. The window was open, and the draft set all the candles flaring one way. Her chair was empty and her handkerchief and book lay on the floor. I turned to the window. There, in the recess of the window, I saw her. Oh, my child, my love, had she gone to that window to watch for me? And what had come into the room behind her? To what had she turned with that look of frantic fear and horror? Oh, my little one, had she thought that it was I whose step she heard, and turned to meet—what?

She had fallen back across a table in the window, and her body lay half on it and half on the window seat, and her head hung down over the table, the brown hair loosened and fallen to the carpet. Her lips were drawn back, and her eyes wide, wide open. They saw nothing now. What had they seen last?

The doctor moved towards her, but I pushed him aside and sprang to her; caught her in my arms and cried:

"It's all right, Laura! I've got you safe, wifie."

She fell into my arms in a heap. I clasped her and kissed her, and called her by all her pet names, but I think I knew all the time that she was dead. Her hands were tightly clenched. In one of them she held something fast. When I was quite sure that she was dead, and that nothing mattered at all any more, I let him open her hand to see what she held.

It was a gray marble finger.

Bram Stoker

THE JUDGE'S HOUSE

WHEN THE TIME for his examination drew near, Malcolm Malcolmson made up his mind to go somewhere to read by himself. He feared the attractions of the seaside, and also he feared completely rural isolation, for of old he knew its charms, and so he determined to find some unpretentious little town where there would be nothing to distract him. He refrained from asking suggestions from any of his friends, for he argued that each would recommend some place of which he had knowledge, and where he had already acquaintances. As Malcolmson wished to avoid friends he had no wish to encumber himself with the attention of friends' friends, and so he determined to look out for a place for himself. He packed a portmanteau with some clothes and all the books he required, and then took ticket for the first name on the local timetable which he did not know.

When at the end of three hours' journey he alighted at Benchurch, he felt satisfied that he had so far obliterated his tracks as to be sure of having a peaceful opportunity of pursuing his studies. He went straight to the one inn which the sleepy little place contained, and put up for the night. Benchurch was a market town, and once in three weeks was crowded to excess, but for the remainder of the twenty-one days it was as attractive as a desert. Malcolmson looked around the day after his arrival to try to find quarters more isolated than even so quiet an inn as "The Good Traveler" afforded. There was only one place which took his fancy, and it certainly satisfied his wildest ideas regarding quiet: in fact, quiet was not the proper word to apply to it—desolation was the only term conveying any suitable idea of its isolation. It was an old rambling, heavy-built house of the Jacobean style, with heavy gables and windows, unusually small, and set higher than was customary in such houses, and was surrounded with a high brick wall, massively built. Indeed, on examination, it looked more like a fortified house than an ordinary dwelling. But all these things pleased Malcolmson. "Here," he thought, "is the very spot I have been looking for, and if I can only get opportunity of using it I shall be happy." His joy was increased when he realized beyond doubt that it was not at present inhabited.

From the post office he got the name of the agent, who was rarely surprised at the application to rent a part of the old house. Mr. Cranford, the local lawyer and agent, was a genial old gentleman, and frankly confessed his delight at anyone being willing to live in the house.

"To tell you the truth," said he, "I should be only too happy, on behalf of the owners, to let anyone have the house rent free for a term of years if only to accustom the people here to see it inhabited. It has been so long empty that some kind of absurd prejudice has grown up about it, and this can be best put down by its occupation—if only," he added with a sly glance at Malcolmson, "by a scholar like yourself, who wants its quiet for a time."

Malcolmson thought it needless to ask the agent about the "absurd prejudice"; he knew he would get more information, if he should require it, on that subject from other quarters. He paid his three months' rent, got a receipt, and the name of an old woman who would probably undertake to "do" for him, and came away with the keys in his pocket. He then went to the landlady of the inn, who was a cheerful and most kindly person, and asked her advice as to such stores and provisions as he would be likely to require. She threw up her hands in amazement when he told her where he was going to settle himself.

"Not in the Judge's House!" she said, and grew pale as she spoke. He explained the locality of the house, saying that he did not know its name. When he had finished she answered:

"Aye, sure enough—sure enough the very place! It is the Judge's House sure enough." He asked her to tell him about the place, why so called, and what there was against it. She told him that it was so called locally because it had been many years before—how long she could not say, as she was herself from another part of the country, but she thought it must have been a hundred years or more—the abode of a judge who was held in great terror on account of his harsh sentences and his hostility to prisoners at Assizes. As to what there was against the house itself she could not tell. She had often asked, but no one could inform her; but there was a general feeling that there was *something*, and for her own part she would not take all the money in Drinkwater's Bank and stay in the house an hour by herself. Then she apologized to Malcolmson for her disturbing talk.

"It is too bad of me, sir, and you—and a young gentleman, too—if you will pardon me saying it, going to live there all alone. If you were my boy—and you'll excuse me for saying it—you wouldn't sleep there a night, not if I had to go there myself and pull the big alarm bell that's on the roof!" The good creature was so manifestly in earnest, and was so kindly in her intentions, that Malcolmson, although amused, was touched. He told her kindly how much he appreciated her interest in him, and added:

"But, my dear Mrs. Witham, indeed you need not be concerned about me! A man who is reading for the Mathematical Tripos has too much to think of to be disturbed by any of these mysterious 'somethings,' and his work is of too exact and prosaic a kind to allow of his having any corner in his mind for mysteries of any kind. Harmonical Progression, Permutations and Combinations, and Elliptic Functions have sufficient mysteries for me!" Mrs. Witham kindly undertook to see after his commissions, and he went himself to look for the old woman who had been recommended to him. When he returned to the Judge's House with her, after an interval of a couple of hours, he found Mrs. Witham herself waiting with several men and boys carrying parcels, and an upholsterer's man with a bed in a cart, for she said, though tables and chairs might be all very well, a bed that hadn't been aired for mayhap fifty years was not proper for young bones to lie on. She was evidently curious to see the inside of the house; and though manifestly so afraid of the 'somethings' that at the slightest sound she clutched on to Malcolmson, whom she never left for a moment, went over the whole place.

After his examination of the house, Malcolmson decided to take up his abode in the great dining room, which was big enough to serve for all his requirements; and Mrs. Witham, with the aid of the charwoman, Mrs. Dempster, proceeded to arrange matters. When the hampers were brought in and unpacked, Malcolmson saw that with much kind forethought she had sent from her own kitchen sufficient provisions to last for a few days. Before going she expressed all sorts of kind wishes; and at the door turned and said:

"And perhaps, sir, as the room is big and drafty it might be well to have one of those big screens put round your bed at night—though, truth to tell, I would die myself if I were to be so shut in with all kinds of—of 'things,' that put their heads round the sides, or over the top, and look on me!" The image which she had called up was too much for her nerves, and she fled incontinently.

Mrs. Dempster sniffed in a superior manner as the landlady disappeared, and remarked that for her own part she wasn't afraid of all the bogies in the kingdom.

"I'll tell you what it is, sir," she said; "bogies is all kinds and sorts of things—except bogies! Rats and mice, and beetles; and creaky doors, and loose slates, and broken panes, and stiff drawer handles, that stay out when you pull them and then fall down in the middle of the night. Look at the wainscot of the room! It is old—hundreds of years old! Do you think there's no rats and beetles there? And do you imagine, sir, that you won't see none of them? Rats is bogies, I tell you, and bogies is rats; and don't you get to think anything else!"

"Mrs. Dempster," said Malcolmson gravely, making her a polite bow, "you know more than a Senior Wrangler! And let me say, that, as a mark of esteem for your indubitable soundness of head and heart, I shall, when I go, give you possession of this house, and let you stay here by yourself for the last two months of my tenancy, for four weeks will serve my purpose."

"Thank you kindly, sir!" she answered, "but I couldn't sleep away from home a night. I am in Greenhow's Charity, and if I slept a night away from my rooms I should lose all I have got to live on. The rules is very strict; and there's too many watching for a vacancy for me to run any risks in the matter. Only for that, sir, I'd gladly come here and attend on you altogether during your stay."

"My good woman," said Malcolmson hastily, "I have come here on purpose to obtain solitude; and believe me that I am grateful to the late Greenhow for having so organized his admirable charity—whatever it is—that I am perforce denied the opportunity of suffering from such a form of temptation! Saint Anthony himself could not be more rigid on the point!"

The old woman laughed harshly. "Ah, you young gentlemen," she said, "you don't fear for naught; and belike you'll get all the solitude you want here." She set to work with her cleaning; and by nightfall, when Malcolmson returned from his walk—he always had one of his books to study as he walked—he found the room swept and tidied, a fire burning in the old hearth, the lamp lit, and the table spread for supper with Mrs. Witham's excellent fare. "This is comfort, indeed," he said, as he rubbed his hands.

When he had finished his supper, and lifted the tray to the other end of the great oak dining table, he got out his books again, put fresh wood on the fire, trimmed his lamp, and set himself down to a spell of real hard work. He went on without pause till about eleven o'clock, when he knocked off for a bit to fix his fire and lamp, and to make himself a cup of tea. He had always been a tea drinker, and during his college life had sat late at work and had taken tea late. The rest was a great luxury to him, and he enjoyed it with a sense of delicious, voluptuous ease. The renewed fire leaped and sparkled, and threw quaint shadows through the great old room; and as he sipped his hot tea he reveled in the sense of isolation from his kind. Then it was that he began to notice for the first time what a noise the rats were making.

"Surely," he thought, "they cannot have been at it all the time I was reading. Had they been, I must have noticed it!" Presently, when the noise increased, he satisfied himself that it was really new. It was evident that at first the rats had been frightened at the presence of a stranger, and the light of fire and lamp; but that as the time went on they had grown bolder and were now disporting themselves as was their wont.

How busy they were! And hark to the strange noises! Up and down behind the old wainscot over the ceiling and under the floor they raced, and gnawed, and scratched! Malcolmson smiled to himself as he recalled to mind the saying of Mrs. Dempster, "Bogies is rats, and rats is bogies!" The tea began to have its effect of intellectual and nervous stimulus, he saw with joy another long spell of work to be done before the night was past, and in the sense of security which it gave him, he allowed himself the luxury of a good look round the room. He took his lamp in one hand, and went all around, wondering that so quaint and beautiful an old house had been so long neglected. The carving of the oak on the panels of the wainscot was fine, and on and round the doors and windows it was beautiful and of rare merit. There were some old pictures on the walls, but they were coated so thick with dust and dirt that he could not distinguish any detail of them, though he held his lamp as high as he could over his head. Here and there as he went round he saw some crack or hole blocked for a moment by the face of a rat with its bright eyes glittering in the light, but in an instant it was gone, and a squeak and a scamper followed.

The thing that most struck him, however, was the rope of the great alarm bell on the roof, which hung down in a corner of the room on the right-hand side of the fireplace. He pulled up close to the hearth a great high-backed carved oak chair, and sat down to his last cup of tea. When this was done he made up the fire, and went back to his work, sitting at the corner of the table, having the fire to his left. For a while the rats disturbed him somewhat with their perpetual scampering, but he got accustomed to the noise as one does to the ticking of a clock or to the roar of moving water; and he became so immersed in his work that everything in the world, except the problem which he was trying to solve, passed away from him.

He suddenly looked up, his problem was still unsolved, and there was in the air that sense of the hour before the dawn, which is so dread to doubtful life. The noise of the rats had ceased. Indeed it seemed to him that it must have ceased but lately and that it was the sudden cessation which had disturbed him. The fire had fallen low, but still it threw out a deep red glow. As he looked he started in spite of his *sang-froid*.

There on the great high-backed carved oak chair by the right side of the fireplace sat an enormous rat, steadily glaring at him with baleful eyes. He made a motion to it as though to hunt it away, but it did not stir. Then he made the motion of throwing something. Still it did not stir, but showed its great white teeth angrily, and its cruel eyes shone in the lamplight with an added vindictiveness.

Malcolmson felt amazed, and seizing the poker from the hearth ran at it to kill it. Before, however, he could strike it, the rat, with a squeak that sounded like the concentration of hate, jumped upon the floor, and, running up the rope of the alarm bell, disappeared in the darkness beyond the range of the green-shaded lamp. Instantly, strange to say, the noisy scampering of the rats in the wainscot began again.

By this time Malcolmson's mind was quite off the problem; and as a shrill cock crow outside told him of the approach of morning, he went to bed and to sleep.

He slept so sound that he was not even waked by Mrs. Dempster coming in to make up his room. It was only when she had tidied up the place and got his breakfast ready and tapped on the screen which closed in his bed that he woke. He was a little tired still after his night's hard work, but a strong cup of tea soon freshened him up, and, taking his book, he went out for his morning walk, bringing with him a few sandwiches lest he should not care to return till dinner time. He found a quiet walk between high elms some way outside the town, and here he spent the greater part of the day studying his Laplace. On his return he looked in to see Mrs. Witham and to thank her for her kindness. When she saw him coming through the diamond-paned bay window of her sanctum she came out to meet him and asked him in. She looked at him searchingly and shook her head as she said:

"You must not overdo it, sir. You are paler this morning

than you should be. Too late hours and too hard work on the brain isn't good for any man! But tell me, sir, how did you pass the night? Well, I hope? But, my heart! sir, I was glad when Mrs. Dempster told me this morning that you were all right and sleeping sound when she went in."

"Oh, I was all right," he answered, smiling, "the 'something' didn't worry me, as yet. Only the rats; and they had a circus, I tell you, all over the place. There was one wicked-looking old devil that sat up on my own chair by the fire, and wouldn't go till I took the poker to him, and then he ran up the rope of the alarm bell and got to somewhere up the wall or the ceiling—I couldn't see where, it was so dark."

"Mercy on us," said Mrs. Witham, "an old devil, and sitting on a chair by the fireside! Take care, sir! Take care! There's many a true word spoken in jest."

"How do you mean? 'Pon my word I don't understand."

"An old devil! The old devil, perhaps. There! sir, you needn't laugh," for Malcolmson had broken into a hearty peal. "You young folks thinks it easy to laugh at things that makes older ones shudder. Never mind, sir! never mind! Please God, you'll laugh all the time. It's what I wish you myself!" and the good lady beamed all over in sympathy with his enjoyment, her fears gone for a moment.

"Oh, forgive me!" said Malcolmson presently. "Don't think me rude; but the idea was too much for me—that the old devil himself was on the chair last night!" And at the thought he laughed again. Then he went home to dinner.

This evening the scampering of the rats began earlier; indeed it had been going on before his arrival, and only ceased whilst his presence by its freshness disturbed them. After dinner he sat by the fire for a while and had a smoke; and then, having cleared his table, began to work as before. Tonight the rats disturbed him more than they had done on the previous night. How they scampered up and down and under and over! How they squeaked, and scratched, and gnawed!

How they, getting bolder by degrees, came to the mouths of their holes and to the chinks and cracks and crannies in the wainscoting till their eyes shone like tiny lamps as the firelight rose and fell. But to him, now doubtless accustomed to them, their eyes were not wicked; only their playfulness touched him. Sometimes the boldest of them made sallies out on the floor or along the moldings of the wainscot. Now and again as they disturbed him Malcolmson made a sound to frighten them, smiting the table with his hand or giving a fierce "Hsh, hsh," so that they fled straightway to their holes.

And so the early part of the night wore on; and despite the noise Malcolmson got more and more immersed in his work.

All at once he stopped, as on the previous night, being over-come by a sudden sense of silence. There was not the faintest sound of gnaw, or scratch, or squeak. The silence was as of the grave. He remembered the odd occurrence of the previous night, and instinctively he looked at the chair standing close by the fireside. And then a very odd sensation thrilled through him.

There, on the great high-backed carved oak chair beside the fireplace, sat the same enormous rat, steadily glaring at him with baleful eyes.

Instinctively he took the nearest thing to his hand, a book of logarithms, and flung it at it. The book was badly aimed and the rat did not stir, so again the poker performance of the previous night was repeated; and again the rat, being closely pursued, fled up the rope of the alarm bell. Strangely too, the departure of this rat was instantly followed by the renewal of the noise made by the general rat community. On this occasion, as on the previous one, Malcolmson could not see at what part of the room the rat disappeared, for the green shade of his lamp left the upper part of the room in darkness, and the fire had burned low.

On looking at his watch he found it was close on midnight; and, not sorry for the *divertissement*, he made up his fire and made himself his nightly pot of tea. He had got through a good spell of work, and thought himself entitled to a cigarette; and so he sat on the great carved oak chair before the fire and enjoyed it. Whilst smoking he began to think that he would like to know where the rat disappeared to, for he had certain ideas for the morrow not entirely disconnected with a rattrap. Accordingly he lit another lamp and placed it so that it would shine well into the right-hand corner of the wall by the fireplace. Then he got all the books he had with him, and placed them handy to throw at the vermin. Finally he lifted the rope of the alarm bell and placed the end of it on the table, fixing the extreme end under the lamp. As he handled it he could not help noticing how pliable it was, especially for so strong a rope, and one not in use. "You could hang a man with it," he thought to himself. When his preparations were made he looked around, and said complacently:

"There now, my friend, I think we shall learn something of you this time!" He began his work again, and though as before somewhat disturbed at first by the noise of the rats, soon lost himself in his propositions and problems.

Again he was called to his immediate surroundings suddenly. This time it might not have been the sudden silence only which took his attention; there was a slight movement of the rope, and the lamp moved. Without stirring, he looked to see if his pile of books was within range, and then cast his eye along the rope. As he looked he saw the great rat drop from the rope on the oak armchair and sit there glaring at him. He raised a book in his right hand, and taking careful aim, flung it at the rat. The latter, with a quick movement, sprang aside and dodged the missile. He then took another book, and a third, and flung them one after another at the rat, but each time unsuccessfully. At last, as he stood with a book poised in his hand to throw, the rat squeaked and seemed afraid. This made Malcolmson more than ever eager to strike, and the book flew and struck the rat a resounding blow. It gave a terrified squeak, and turning on its pursuer a look of terrible malevolence, ran up the chair back and made a great jump to the rope of the alarm bell and ran up it like lightning. The lamp rocked under the sudden strain, but it was a heavy one and did not topple over. Malcolmson kept his eyes on the rat, and saw it by the light of the second lamp leap to a molding of the wainscot and disappear through a hole in one of the great pictures which hung on the wall, obscured and invisible through its coating of dirt and dust.

"I shall look up my friend's habitation in the morning," said the student, as he went over to collect his books. "The third picture from the fireplace; I shall not forget." He picked up the books one by one, commenting on them as he lifted them. "*Conic Sections* he does not mind, nor *Cycloidal Oscillations*, nor the *Principia*, nor *Quarternions*, nor *Thermodynamics*. Now for the book that fetched him!" Malcolmson took it up and looked at it. As he did so he started, and a sudden pallor overspread his face. He looked round uneasily and shivered slightly, as he murmured to himself:

"The Bible my mother gave me! What an odd coincidence." He sat down to work again, and the rats in the wainscot renewed their gambols. They did not disturb him, however; somehow their presence gave him a sense of companionship. But he could not attend to his work, and after striving to master the subject on which he was engaged gave it up in despair, and went to bed as the first streak of dawn stole in through the eastern window.

He slept heavily but uneasily, and dreamed much; and when Mrs. Dempster woke him late in the morning he seemed ill at ease, and for a few minutes did not seem to realize exactly where he was. His first request rather surprised the servant.

"Mrs. Dempster, when I am out today I wish you would get the steps and dust or wash those pictures—specially that one the third from the fireplace—I want to see what they are."

Late in the afternoon Malcolmson worked at his books in the shaded walk, and the cheerfulness of the previous day came back to him as the day wore on, and he found that his reading was progressing well. He had worked out to a satisfactory conclusion all the problems which had as yet baffled him, and it was in a state of jubilation that he paid a visit to Mrs. Witham at "The Good Traveler." He found a stranger in the cozy sitting room with the landlady, who was introduced to him as Dr. Thornhill. She was not quite at ease, and this, combined with the doctor's plunging at once into a series of questions, made Malcolmson come to the conclusion that his presence was not an accident, so without preliminary he said:

"Dr. Thornhill, I shall with pleasure answer you any question you may choose to ask me if you will answer me one question first."

The Doctor seemed surprised, but he smiled and answered at once. "Done! What is it?"

"Did Mrs. Witham ask you to come here and see me and advise me?"

Dr. Thornhill for a moment was taken aback, and Mrs. Witham got fiery red and turned away; but the doctor was a frank and ready man, and he answered at once and openly:

"She did; but she didn't intend you to know it. I suppose it was my clumsy haste that made you suspect. She told me that she did not like the idea of your being in that house all by yourself, and that she thought you took too much strong tea. In fact, she wants me to advise you if possible to give up the tea and the very late hours. I was a keen student in my time, so I suppose I may take the liberty of a college man, and without offense, advise you not quite as a stranger."

Malcolmson with a bright smile held out his hand. "Shake! as they say in America," he said. "I must thank you for your kindness and Mrs. Witham too, and your kindness deserves a return on my part. I promise to take no more strong tea—no tea at all till you let me—and I shall go to bed tonight at one o'clock at latest. Will that do?"

"Capital," said the doctor. "Now tell us all that you noticed in the old house." And so Malcolmson then and there told in minute detail all that had happened in the last two nights. He was interrupted every now and then by some exclamation from Mrs. Witham, till finally when he told of the episode of the Bible the landlady's pent-up emotions found vent in a shriek; and it was not till a stiff glass of brandy and water had been administered that she grew composed again. Dr. Thornhill listened with a face of growing gravity, and when the narrative was complete and Mrs. Witham had been restored he asked:

"The rat always went up the rope of the alarm bell?"

"Always."

"I suppose you know," said the doctor after a pause, "what the rope is?"

"No!"

"It is," said the doctor slowly, "the very rope which the hangman used for all the victims of the Judge's judicial rancor!" Here he was interrupted by another scream from Mrs. Witham, and steps had to be taken for her recovery. Malcolmson, having looked at his watch, and found that it was close to his dinner hour, had gone home before her complete recovery.

When Mrs. Witham was herself again she almost assailed the doctor with angry questions as to what he meant by putting such horrible ideas into the poor young man's mind. "He has quite enough there already to upset him," she added. Dr. Thornhill replied:

"My dear madam, I had a distinct purpose in it! I wanted to draw his attention to the bell rope, and to fix it there. It may be that he is in a highly overwrought state, and has been studying too much, although I am bound to say that he seems as sound and healthy a young man, mentally and bodily, as ever I saw—but then the rats—and that suggestion of the devil." The doctor shook his head and went on: "I would have offered to go and stay the first night with him but that I felt sure it would have been a cause of offense. He may get in the night some strange fright or hallucination and if he does I want him to pull that rope. All alone as he is, it will give us warning, and we may reach him in time to be of service. I shall be sitting up pretty late tonight and shall keep my ears open. Do not be alarmed if Benchurch gets a surprise before morning."

"Oh, Doctor, what do you mean? What do you mean?"

"I mean this; that possibly—nay, more probably—we shall hear the great alarm bell from the Judge's House tonight," and the doctor made about as effective an exit as could be thought of.

When Malcolmson arrived home he found that it was a little after his usual time, and Mrs. Dempster had gone away—the rules of Greenhow's Charity were not to be neglected. He was glad to see that the place was bright and tidy with a cheerful fire and a well-trimmed lamp. The evening was colder than might have been expected in April, and a heavy wind was blowing with such rapidly increasing strength that there was every promise of a storm during the night. For a few minutes after his entrance the noise of the rats ceased; but so soon as they became accustomed to his presence they began again. He was glad to hear them, for he felt once more the feeling of companionship in their noise, and his mind ran back to the strange fact that they only ceased to manifest themselves when that other—the great rat with the baleful eyes—came upon the scene. The reading lamp only was lit and its green shade kept the ceiling and the upper part of the room in darkness, so that the cheerful light from the hearth spreading over the floor and shining on the white cloth laid over the end of the table was warm and cheery. Malcolmson sat down to his dinner with a good appetite and a buoyant

151

spirit. After his dinner and a cigarette he sat steadily down to work, determined not to let anything disturb him, for he remembered his promise to the doctor, and made up his mind to make the best of the time at his disposal.

For an hour or so he worked all right, and then his thoughts began to wander from his books. The actual circumstances around him, the calls on his physical attention, and his nervous susceptibility were not to be denied. By this time the wind had become a gale, and the gale a storm. The old house, solid though it was, seemed to shake to its foundations, and the storm roared and raged through its many chimneys and its queer old gables, producing strange, unearthly sounds in the empty rooms and corridors. Even the great alarm bell on the roof must have felt the force of the wind, for the rope rose and fell slightly, as though the bell were moved a little from time to time, and the limber rope fell on the oak floor with a hard and hollow sound.

As Malcolmson listened to it he bethought himself of the doctor's words, "It is the rope which the hangman used for the victims of the Judge's judicial rancor," and he went over to the corner of the fireplace and took it in his hand to look at it. There seemed a sort of deadly interest in it, and as he stood there he lost himself for a moment in speculation as to who these victims were, and the grim wish of the Judge to have such a ghastly relic ever under his eyes. As he stood there the swaying of the bell on the roof still lifted the rope now and again; but presently there came a new sensation—a sort of tremor in the rope, as though something were moving along it.

Looking up instinctively Malcolmson saw the great rat coming slowly down towards him, glaring at him steadily. He dropped the rope and started back with a muttered curse, and the rat turning ran up the rope again and disappeared, and at the same instant Malcolmson became conscious that the noise of the rats, which had ceased for a while, began again.

All this set him thinking, and it occurred to him that he had not investigated the lair of the rat or looked at the pictures, as he had intended. He lit the other lamp without the shade, and, holding it up, went and stood opposite the third picture from the fireplace on the right-hand side where he had seen the rat disappear on the previous night.

At the first glance he started back so suddenly that he almost dropped the lamp, and a deadly pallor overspread his face. His knees shook, and heavy drops of sweat came on his forehead, and he trembled like an aspen. But he was young and plucky, and pulled himself together, and after the pause of a few seconds stepped forward again, raised the lamp, and examined the picture, which had been dusted and washed, and now stood out clearly.

It was of a judge dressed in his robes of scarlet and ermine. His face was strong and merciless, evil, crafty, and vindictive, with a sensual mouth, hooked nose of ruddy color, and shaped like the beak of a bird of prey. The rest of the face was of a cadaverous color. The eyes were of peculiar brilliance and with a terribly malignant expression. As he looked at them, Malcolmson grew cold, for he saw there the very counterpart of the eyes of the great rat. The lamp almost fell from his hand, he saw the rat with its baleful eyes peering out through the hole in the corner of the picture and noted the sudden cessation of the noise of the other rats. However, he pulled himself together, and went on with his examination of the picture.

The Judge was seated in a great high-backed carved oak chair, on the right-hand side of a great stone fireplace where, in the corner, a rope hung down from the ceiling, its end lying coiled on the floor. With a feeling of something like horror, Malcolmson recognized the scene of the room as it stood, and gazed around him in an awe-struck manner as though he expected to find some strange presence behind him. Then he looked over to the corner of the fireplace—and with a loud cry he let the lamp fall from his hand.

There, in the Judge's armchair, with the rope hanging behind, sat the rat with the Judge's baleful eyes, now intensified and with a fiendish leer. Save for the howling of the storm without, there was silence.

The fallen lamp recalled Malcolmson to himself. Fortunately it was of metal, and so the oil was not spilt. However, the practical need of attending to it settled at once his nervous apprehensions. When he had turned it out, he wiped his brow and thought for a moment.

"This will not do," he said to himself. "If I go on like this I shall become a crazy fool. This must stop! I promised the doctor I would not take tea. Faith, he was pretty right! My nerves must have been getting into a queer state. Funny I did not notice it. I never felt better in my life. However, it is all right now, and I shall not be such a fool again."

Then he mixed himself a good stiff glass of brandy and water and resolutely sat down to his work.

It was nearly an hour when he looked up from his book, disturbed by the sudden stillness. Without, the wind howled and roared louder than ever, and the rain drove in sheets against the windows, beating like hail on the glass; but, within, there was no sound whatever save the echo of the wind as it roared in the great chimney, and now and then a hiss as a few raindrops found their way down the chimney in a lull of the storm. The fire had fallen low and had ceased to flame, though it threw out a red glow. Malcolmson listened attentively, and presently heard a thin, squeaking noise, very faint. It came from the corner of the room where the rope hung down, and he thought it was the creaking of the rope on the floor as the swaying of the bell raised and lowered it. Looking up, however, he saw in the dim light the great rat clinging to the rope and gnawing it. The rope was already nearly gnawed through—he could see the lighter color where the strands were laid bare. As he looked the job was completed, and the severed end of the rope fell clattering on the oaken floor, whilst for an instant the great rat remained like a knob or tassel at the end of the rope, which now began to sway to and fro. Malcolmson felt for a moment another pang of terror as he thought that now the possibility of calling the outer world to his assistance was cut off, but an intense anger took its place, and seizing the book he was reading he hurled it at the rat. The blow was well aimed, but before the missile could reach it the rat dropped off and struck the floor with a soft thud. Malcolmson instantly rushed over towards it, but it darted away and disappeared in the darkness of the shadows of the room. Malcolmson felt that his work was over for the night, and determined then and there to vary the monotony of the proceedings by a hunt for the rat, and took off the green shade of the lamp so as to insure a wider-spreading light. As he did so the gloom of the upper part of the room was relieved, and in the new flood of light, great by comparison with the previous darkness, the pictures on the wall stood out boldly. From where he stood, Malcolmson saw right opposite to him the third picture on the wall from the right of the fireplace. He rubbed his eyes in surprise, and then a great fear began to come upon him.

In the center of the picture was a great irregular patch of brown canvas, as fresh as when it was stretched on the frame. The background was as before, with chair and chimney corner and rope, but the figure of the Judge had disappeared.

Malcolmson, almost in a chill of horror, turned slowly round, and then he began to shake and tremble like a man in a palsy. His strength seemed to have left him, and he was incapable of action or movement, hardly even of thought. He could only see and hear.

There, on the great high-backed carved oak chair, sat the Judge in his robes of scarlet and ermine, with his baleful eyes glaring vindictively, and a smile of triumph on the resolute, cruel mouth, as he lifted with his hands a *black cap.* Malcolmson felt as if the blood were running from his heart, as one does in moments of prolonged suspense. There was a singing in his ears. Without, he could hear the roar and howl of the tempest, and through it, swept on the storm, came the striking of midnight by the great chimes in the market place. He stood for a space of time that seemed to him endless, still as a statue and with wide-open, horror-struck eyes, breathless. As the clock struck, so the smile of triumph on the Judge's face intensified, and at the last stroke of midnight he placed the black cap on his head.

Slowly and deliberately the Judge rose from his chair and picked up the piece of rope of the alarm bell which lay on the floor, drew it through his hands as if he enjoyed its touch, and then deliberately began to knot one end of it, fashioning it into a noose. This he tightened and tested with his foot, pulling hard at it till he was satisfied and then making a running noose of it, which he held in his hand. Then he began to move along the table on the opposite side to Malcolmson, keeping his eyes on him until he had passed him, when with a quick movement he stood in front of the door. Malcolmson then began to feel that he was trapped, and tried to think of what he should do. There was some fascination in the Judge's eyes, which he never took off him, and he had, perforce, to look. He saw the Judge approach—still keeping between him and the door—and raise the noose and throw it towards him as if to entangle him. With a great effort he made a quick movement to one side, and saw the rope fall beside him, and heard it strike the oaken floor. Again the Judge raised the noose and tried to ensnare him, ever keeping his baleful eyes fixed on him, and each time by a mighty effort the student just managed to evade it. So this went on for many times, the Judge seeming never discouraged nor discomposed at failure, but playing as a cat does with a mouse. At last in despair, which had reached its climax, Malcolmson cast a quick glance round him. The lamp seemed to have blazed up, and there was a fairly good light in the room. At the many rat holes and in the chinks and crannies of the wainscot he saw the rats' eyes; and this aspect, which was purely physical, gave him a gleam of comfort. He looked around and saw that the rope of the great alarm bell was laden with rats. Every inch of it was covered with them, and more and more were pouring through the small circular hole in the ceiling whence it emerged, so that with their weight the bell was beginning to sway.

Hark! It had swayed till the clapper had touched the bell. The sound was but a tiny one, but the bell was only beginning to sway, and it would increase.

At the sound the Judge, who had been keeping his eyes fixed on Malcolmson, looked up, and a scowl of diabolical anger overspread his face. His eyes fairly glowed like hot coals, and he stamped his foot with a sound that seemed to make the house shake. A dreadful peal of thunder broke overhead as he raised the rope again, whilst the rats kept running up and down the rope as though working against time. This time, instead of throwing it, he drew close to his victim, and held open the noose as he approached. As he came closer there seemed something paralyzing in his very presence, and Malcolmson stood rigid as a corpse. He felt the Judge's icy fingers touch his throat as he adjusted the rope. The noose tightened—tightened. Then the Judge, taking the rigid form of the student in his arms, carried him over and placed him standing in the oak chair, and stepping up beside him, put his hand up and caught the end of the swaying rope of the alarm bell. As he raised his hand the rats fled squeaking, and disappeared through the hole in the ceiling. Taking the end of the noose which was round Malcolmson's neck he tied it to the hanging bell rope, and then descending pulled away the chair.

When the alarm bell of the Judge's House began to sound, a crowd soon assembled. Lights and torches of various kinds appeared, and soon a silent crowd was hurrying to the spot. They knocked loudly at the door, but there was no reply. Then they burst in the door, and poured into the great dining room, the doctor at the head.

There at the end of the rope of the great alarm bell hung the body of the student, and on the face of the Judge in the picture was a malignant smile.

The Shadow of a Shade

TOM HOOD

MY SISTER LETTIE has lived with me ever since I had a home of my own. She was my little housekeeper before I married. Now she is my wife's constant companion, and the "darling Auntie" of my children, who go to her for comfort, advice, and aid in all their little troubles and perplexities.

But, though she has a comfortable home, and loving hearts around her, she wears a grave, melancholy look on her face, which puzzles acquaintances and grieves friends.

A disappointment! Yes, the old story of a lost lover is the reason for Lettie's looks. She has had good offers often; but since she lost the first love of her heart she has never indulged in the happy dream of loving and being beloved.

George Mason was a cousin of my wife's—a sailor by profession. He and Lettie met one another at our wedding, and fell in love at first sight. George's father had seen service before him on the great mysterious sea, and had been especially known as a good Arctic sailor, having shared in more than one expedition in search of the North Pole and the Northwest Passage.

It was not a matter of surprise to me, therefore, when George volunteered to go out in the *Pioneer*, which was being fitted out for a cruise in search of Franklin and his missing expedition. There was a fascination about such an undertaking that I felt I could not have resisted had I been in his place. Of course, Lettie did not like the idea at all, but he silenced her by telling her that men who volunteered for Arctic search were never lost sight of, and that he should not make as much advance in his profession in a dozen years as he would in the year or so of this expedition. I cannot say that Lettie, even after this, was quite satisfied with the notion of his going, but, at all events, she did not argue against it any longer. But the grave look, which is now habitual with her, but was a rare thing in her young and happy days, passed over her face sometimes when she thought no one was looking.

My younger brother, Harry, was at this time an academy student. He was only a beginner then. Now he is pretty well known in the art world, and his pictures command fair prices. Like all beginners in art, he was full of fancies and theories. He would have been a pre-Raphaelite, only pre-Raphaelism had not been invented then. His peculiar craze was for what he styled the Venetian School. Now, it chanced that George had a fine Italian-looking head, and Harry persuaded him to sit to him for his portrait. It was a fair likeness, but a very moderate work of art. The background was so very dark, and George's naval costume so very deep in color, that the face came out too white and staring. It was a three-quarter picture; but only one hand showed in it, leaning on the hilt of a sword. As George said, he looked much more like the commander of a Venetian galley than a modern mate.

However, the picture pleased Lettie, who did not care much about art provided the resemblance was good. So the picture was duly framed—in a tremendously heavy frame, of Harry's ordering—and hung up in the dining room.

And now the time for George's departure was growing

nearer. The *Pioneer* was nearly ready to sail, and her crew only waited orders. The officers grew acquainted with each other before sailing, which was an advantage. George took up very warmly with the surgeon, Vincent Grieve, and, with my permission, brought him to dinner once or twice.

"Poor chap, he has no friends nearer than the Highlands, and it's precious lonely work."

"Bring him by all means, George! You know that any friends of yours will be welcome here."

So Vincent Grieve came. I am bound to say I was not favorably impressed by him, and almost wished I had not consented to his coming. He was a tall, pale, fair young man, with a hard Scotch face and a cold, gray eye. There was something in his expression, too, that was unpleasant—something cruel or crafty, or both.

I considered that it was very bad taste for him to pay such marked attention to Lettie, coming, as he did, as the friend of her fiancé. He kept by her constantly and anticipated George in all the little attentions which a lover delights to pay. I think George was a little put out about it, though he said nothing, attributing his friend's offense to lack of breeding.

Lettie did not like it at all. She knew that she was not to have George with her much longer, and she was anxious to have him to herself as much as possible. But as Grieve was her lover's friend she bore the infliction with the best possible patience.

The surgeon did not seem to perceive in the least that he was interfering where he had no business. He was quite self-possessed and happy, with one exception. The portrait of George seemed to annoy him. He had uttered a little impatient exclamation when he first saw it which drew my attention to him; and I noticed that he tried to avoid looking at it. At last, when dinner came, he was told to sit exactly facing the picture. He hesitated for an instant and then sat down, but almost immediately rose again.

"It's very childish and that sort of thing," he stammered, "but I cannot sit opposite that picture."

"It is not high art," I said, "and may irritate a critical eye."

"I know nothing about art," he answered, "but it's one of those unpleasant pictures whose eyes follow you about the room. I have an inherited horror of such pictures. My mother married against her father's will, and when I was born she was so ill she was hardly expected to live. When she was sufficiently recovered to speak without delirious rambling she implored them to remove a picture of my grandfather that hung in the room, and which she vowed made threatening faces at her. It's superstitious, but constitutional—I have a horror of such paintings!"

I believe George thought this was a ruse of his friend's to get a seat next to Lettie; but I felt sure it was not, for I had seen the alarmed expression of his face.

At night, when George and his friend were leaving, I took an opportunity to ask the former, half in a joke, if he should bring the surgeon to see us again. George made a very hearty assertion to the contrary, adding that he was pleasant enough company among men at an inn, or on board ship, but not where ladies were concerned.

But the mischief was done. Vincent Grieve took advantage of the introduction and did not wait to be invited again. He called the next day, and nearly every day after. He was a more frequent visitor than George now, for George was obliged to attend to his duties, and they kept him on board the *Pioneer* pretty constantly, whereas the surgeon, having seen to the supply of drugs, etc., was pretty well at liberty. Lettie avoided him as much as possible, but he generally brought, or professed to bring, some little message from George to her, so that he had an excuse for asking to see her.

On the occasion of his last visit—the day before the *Pioneer* sailed—Lettie came to me in great distress. The young cub had actually the audacity to tell her he loved her. He knew, he said, about her engagement to George, but that did not prevent another man from loving her too. A man could no more help falling in love than he could help taking a fever. Lettie stood upon her dignity and rebuked him severely; but he told her he could see no harm in telling her of his passion, though he knew it was a hopeless one.

"A thousand things may happen," he said at last, "to bring your engagement with George Mason to an end. Then perhaps you will not forget that another loves you!"

I was very angry, and was forthwith going to give him my opinion on his conduct, when Lettie told me has was gone, that she had bade him go and had forbidden him the house. She only told me in order to protect herself, for she did not intend to say anything to George, for fear it should lead to a duel or some other violence.

That was the last we saw of Vincent Grieve before the *Pioneer* sailed.

George came the same evening, and was with us till daybreak, when he had to tear himself away and join his ship.

After shaking hands with him at the door, in the cold, gray, drizzly dawn, I turned back into the dining room, where poor Lettie was sobbing on the sofa.

I could not help starting when I looked at George's portrait, which hung above her. The strange light of daybreak could hardly account for the extraordinary pallor of the face. I went close to it and looked hard at it. I saw that it was covered with moisture, and imagined that that possibly made it look so pale. As for the moisture, I supposed poor Lettie had been kissing the beloved's portrait, and that the moisture was caused by her tears.

It was not till a long time after, when I was jestingly telling Harry how his picture had been caressed, that I learnt the error of my conjecture. Lettie assured me most solemnly that I was mistaken in supposing she had kissed it.

"It was the varnish blooming, I expect," said Harry. And

thus the subject was dismissed, for I said no more, though I knew well enough, in spite of my not being an artist, that the bloom of varnish was quite another sort of thing.

The *Pioneer* sailed. We received—or, rather, Lettie received —two letters from George, which he had taken the opportunity of sending by homeward-bound whalers. In the second he said it was hardly likely he should have an opportunity of sending another, as they were sailing into high latitudes—into the solitary sea to which none but expedition ships ever penetrated. They were all in high spirits, he said, for they had encountered very little ice and hoped to find clear water farther north than usual. Moreover, he added, Grieve had held a sinecure so far, for there had not been a single case of illness on board.

Then came a long silence, and a year crept away very slowly for poor Lettie. Once we heard of the expedition from the papers. They were reported as pushing on and progressing favorably by a wandering tribe of Esquimaux with whom the captain of a Russian vessel fell in. They had laid the ship up for the winter, and were taking the boats on sledges, and believed they had met with traces of the lost crews that seemed to show they were on the right track.

The winter passed again, and spring came. It was a balmy, bright spring such as we get occasionally, even in this changeable and uncertain climate of ours.

One evening we were sitting in the dining room with the window open, for, although we had long given up fires, the room was so oppressively warm that we were glad of the breath of the cool evening breeze.

Lettie was working. Poor child, though she never murmured, she was evidently pining at George's long absence. Harry was leaning out of the window, studying the evening effect on the fruit blossom, which was wonderfully early and plentiful, the season was so mild. I was sitting at the table, near the lamp, reading the paper.

Suddenly there swept into the room a chill. It was not a gust of cold wind, for the curtain by the open window did not swerve in the least. But the deathly cold pervaded the room—came, and was gone in an instant. Lettie shuddered, as I did, with the intense icy feeling.

She looked up. "How curiously cold it has got all in a minute," she said.

"We are having a taste of poor George's polar weather," I said with a smile.

At the same moment I instinctively glanced towards his portrait. What I saw struck me dumb. A rush of blood, at fever heat, dispelled the numbing influence of the chill breath that had seemed to freeze me.

I have said the lamp was lighted; but it was only that I might read with comfort, for the violet twilight was still so full of sunset that the room was not dark. But as I looked at the picture I saw it had undergone a strange change. I saw it as plainly as possible. It was no delusion, coined for the eye by the brain.

I saw, in the place of George's head, a grinning skull! I stared at it hard; but it was no trick of fancy. I could see the hollow orbits, the gleaming teeth, the fleshless cheekbones—it was the head of death!

Without saying a word, I rose from my chair and walked straight up to the painting. As I drew nearer a sort of mist seemed to pass before it; and as I stood close to it, I saw only the face of George. The spectral skull had vanished.

"Poor George!" I said unconsciously.

Lettie looked up. The tone of my voice had alarmed her, the expression of my face did not reassure her.

"What do you mean? Have you heard anything? Oh, Robert, in mercy tell me!"

She got up and came over to me, laying her hands on my arm, looked up into my face imploringly.

"No, my dear; how should I hear? Only I could not help thinking of the privation and discomfort he must have gone through. I was reminded of it by the cold——"

"Cold!" said Harry, who had left the window by this time. "Cold! What on earth are you talking about? Cold, such an evening as this! You must have had a touch of ague, I should think."

"Both Lettie and I felt it bitterly cold a minute or two ago. Did not you feel it?"

"Not a bit; and as I was three parts out of the window I ought to have felt it if anyone did."

It was curious, but that strange chill had been felt only in the room. It was not the night wind, but some supernatural breath connected with the dread apparition I had seen. It was, indeed, the chill of polar winter—the icy shadow of the frozen North.

"What is the day of the month, Harry?" I asked.

"Today—the twenty-third, I think," he answered; then added, taking up the newspaper I had been reading: "Yes, here you are. Tuesday, February the twenty-third, if the *Daily News* tells truth, which I suppose it does. Newspapers can afford to tell the truth about dates, whatever they may do about art." Harry had been rather roughly handled by the critic of a morning paper for one of his pictures a few days before, and he was a little angry with journalism generally.

Presently Lettie left the room, and I told Harry what I had felt and seen, and told him to take note of the date, for I feared that some mischance had befallen George.

"I'll put it down in my pocket book, Bob. But you and Lettie must have had a touch of the cold shivers, and your stomach or fancy misled you—they're the same thing, you know. Besides, as regards the picture, there's nothing in that! There is a skull there, of course. As Tennyson says:

Any face, however full,
Padded round with flesh and fat,
Is but modeled on a skull.

The skull's there—just as in every good figure-subject the
nude is there under the costumes. You fancy that is a mere
coat of paint. Nothing of the kind! Art lives, sir! That is just
as much a real head as yours is with all the muscles and
bones, just the same. That's what makes the difference between art and rubbish."

This was a favorite theory of Harry's, who had not yet developed from the dreamer into the worker. As I did not care
to argue with him, I allowed the subject to drop after we had
written down the date in our pocket books. Lettie sent down
word presently that she did not feel well and had gone to bed.
My wife came down presently and asked what had happened.
She had been up with the children and had gone in to see
what was the matter with Lettie.

"I think it was very imprudent to sit with the window
open, dear. I know the evenings are warm, but the night air
strikes cold at times—at any rate, Lettie seems to have caught
a violent cold, for she is shivering very much. I am afraid she
has got a chill from the open windows."

I did not say anything to her then, except that both Lettie
and I had felt a sudden coldness; for I did not care to enter
into an explanation again, for I could see Harry was inclined
to laugh at me for being so superstitious.

At night, however, in our own room, I told my wife
what had occurred, and what my apprehensions were. She
was so upset and alarmed that I almost repented having
done so.

The next morning Lettie was better again, and as we did
not either of us refer to the events of the preceding night the
circumstance appeared to be forgotten by us all.

But from that day I was ever inwardly dreading the arrival of bad news. And at last it came, as I expected.

One morning, just as I was coming downstairs to breakfast, there came a knock at the door, and Harry made his appearance. It was a very early visit for him, for he generally used to spend his mornings at the studio, and drop in on his way home at night.

He was looking pale and agitated.

"Lettie's not down, is she, yet?" he asked; and then, before I could answer, added another question: "What newspaper do you take?"

"The *Daily News*," I answered. "Why?"

"She's not down?"

"No."

"Thank God! Look here!"

He took a paper from his pocket and gave it to me, pointing out a short paragraph at the bottom of one of the columns.

I knew what was coming the moment he spoke about Lettie.

The paragraph was headed, "Fatal Accident to one of the Officers of the *Pioneer* Expedition Ship." It stated that news had been received at the Admiralty stating that the expedition had failed to find the missing crews, but had come upon some traces of them. Want of stores and necessaries had compelled them to turn back without following those traces up; but the commander was anxious, as soon as the ship could be refitted, to go out and take up the trail where he had left it. An unfortunate accident had deprived him of one of his most promising officers, Lieutenant Mason, who was precipitated from an iceberg while out shooting with the surgeon. He was beloved by all, and his death had flung a gloom over the gallant little troop of explorers.

"It's not in the *News* today, thank goodness, Bob," said Harry, who had been searching that paper while I was reading the one he brought, "but you must keep a sharp lookout for some days and not let Lettie see it when it appears, as it is certain to do sooner or later."

Then we both of us looked at each other with tears in our eyes. "Poor George!—poor Lettie!" we sighed softly.

"But she must be told at some time or other?" I said despairingly.

"I suppose so," said Harry, "but it would kill her to come on it suddenly like this. Where's your wife?"

She was with the children, but I sent up for her and told her the ill-tidings.

She had a hard struggle to conceal her emotion, for Lettie's sake. But the tears would flow in spite of her efforts.

"How shall I ever find courage to tell her?" she asked.

"Hush!" said Harry, suddenly grasping her arm and looking towards the door.

I turned. There stood Lettie, with her face pale as death, with her lips apart, and with a blind look about her eyes. She had come in without our hearing her. We never learnt how much of the story she had overheard; but it was enough to tell her the worst. We all sprang towards her; but she only waved us away, turned round, and went upstairs again without saying a word. My wife hastened up after her and found her on her knees by the bed, insensible.

The doctor was sent for, and restoratives were promptly administered. She came to herself again, but lay dangerously ill for some weeks from the shock.

It was about a month after she was well enough to come downstairs again that I saw in the paper an announcement of the arrival of the *Pioneer*. The news had no interest for any of us now, so I said nothing about it. The mere mention of the vessel's name would have caused the poor girl pain.

One afternoon shortly after this, as I was writing a letter, there came a loud knock at the front door. I looked up from my writing and listened; for the voice which inquired if I was in sounded strange, but yet not altogether unfamiliar. As I looked up, puzzling whose it could be, my eye rested accidentally upon poor George's portrait. Was I dreaming or awake?

I have told you that the one hand was resting on a sword. I could see now distinctly that the forefinger was raised, as if in warning. I looked at it hard, to assure myself it was no fancy, and then I perceived, standing out bright and distinct on the pale face, two large drops, as if of blood.

I walked up to it, expecting the appearance to vanish, as the skull had done. It did not vanish; but the uplifted finger resolved itself into a little white moth which had settled on the canvas. The red drops were fluid, and certainly not blood, though I was at a loss for the time to account for them.

The moth seemed to be in a torpid state, so I took it off the picture and placed it under an inverted wineglass on the mantelpiece. All this took less time to do than to describe. As I turned from the mantelpiece the servant brought in a card, saying the gentleman was waiting in the hall to know if I would see him.

On the card was the name of "Vincent Grieve, of the exploring vessel *Pioneer.*"

"Thank heaven, Lettie is out," thought I; and then added aloud to the servant, "Show him in here; and Jane, if your mistress and Miss Lettie come in before the gentleman goes, tell them I have someone with me on business and do not wish to be disturbed."

I went to the door to meet Grieve. As he crossed the threshold, and before he could have seen the portrait, he stopped, shuddered, and turned white, even to his thin lips.

"Cover that picture before I come in," he said hurriedly, in a low voice. "You remember the effect it had upon me. Now, with the memory of poor Mason, it would be worse than ever."

I could understand his feelings better now than at first; for I had come to look on the picture with some awe myself. So I took the cloth off a little round table that stood under the window and hung it over the portrait.

When I had done so Grieve came in. He was greatly altered. He was thinner and paler than ever; hollow-eyed and hollow-cheeked. He had acquired a strange stoop, too, and his eyes had lost the crafty look for a look of terror, like that of a hunted beast. I noticed that he kept glancing sideways every instant, as if unconsciously. It looked as if he heard someone behind him.

I had never liked the man; but now I felt an insurmountable repugnance to him—so great a repugnance that, when I came to think of it, I felt pleased that the incident of covering the picture at his request had led to my not shaking hands with him.

I felt that I could not speak otherwise than coldly to him; indeed, I had to speak with painful plainness.

I told him that, of course, I was glad to see him back, but that I could not ask him to continue to visit us. I should be glad to hear the particulars of poor George's death, but that I could not let him see my sister, and hinted, as delicately as I could, at the impropriety of which he had been guilty when he last visited.

He took it all very quietly, only giving a long, weary sigh when I told him I must beg him not to repeat his visit. He looked so weak and ill that I was obliged to ask him to take a glass of wine—an offer which he seemed to accept with great pleasure.

I got out the sherry and biscuits and placed them on the table between us, and he took a glass and drank it off greedily.

It was not without some difficulty that I could get him to tell me of George's death. He related, with evident reluctance, how they had gone out to shoot a white bear which they had seen on an iceberg stranded along the shore. The top of the berg was ridged like the roof of a house, sloping down on one side to the edge of a tremendous overhanging precipice. They had scrambled along the ridge in order to get nearer the game, when George incautiously ventured on the sloping side.

"I called out to him," said Grieve, "and begged him to come back, but too late. The surface was as smooth and slippery as glass. He tried to turn back, but slipped and fell. And then began a horrible scene. Slowly, slowly, but with ever-increasing motion, he began to slide down towards the edge. There was nothing to grasp at—no irregularity or projection on the smooth face of the ice. I tore off my coat, and, hastily attaching it to the stock of my gun, pushed the latter towards him; but it did not reach far enough. Before I could lengthen it, by tying my cravat to it, he had slid yet further away, and more quickly. I shouted in agony; but there was no one within hearing. He, too, saw his fate was sealed; and he could only tell me to bring his last farewell to you, and—and to her!"—here Grieve's voice broke—"and it was all over! He clung to the edge of the precipice instinctively for one second, and was gone!"

Just as Grieve uttered the last word, his jaw fell; his eyeballs seemed ready to start from his head; he sprang to his feet, pointed at something behind me, and then flinging up his arms, fell, with a scream, as if he had been shot. He was seized with an epileptic fit.

I instinctively looked behind me as I hurried to raise him from the floor. The cloth had fallen from the picture, where the face of George, made paler than ever by the gouts of red, looked sternly down.

I rang the bell. Luckily, Harry had come in; and, when the servant told him what was the matter, he came in and assisted me in restoring Grieve to consciousness. Of course, I covered the painting up again.

When he was quite himself again, Grieve told me he was subject to fits occasionally.

He seemed very anxious to learn if he had said or done anything extraordinary while he was in the fit, and appeared reassured when I said he had not. He apologized for the trouble he had given, and said as soon as he was strong enough he would take his leave. He was leaning on the mantelpiece as he said this. The little white moth caught his eye.

"So you have had someone else from the *Pioneer* here before me?" he said, nervously.

I answered in the negative, asking what made him think so.

"Why, this little white moth is never found in such southern latitudes. It is one of the last signs of life northward. Where did you get it?"

"I caught it here, in this room," I answered.

"That is very strange. I never heard of such a thing before. We shall hear of showers of blood soon, I should not wonder."

"What do you mean?" I asked.

"Oh, these little fellows emit little drops of a red-looking fluid at certain seasons, and sometimes so plentifully that the superstitious think it is a shower of blood. I have seen the snow quite stained in places. Take care of it, it is a rarity in the south."

I noticed, after he left, which he did almost immediately, that there was a drop of red fluid on the marble under the wineglass. The bloodstain on the picture was accounted for; but how came the moth here?

And there was another strange thing about the man, which I had scarcely been able to assure myself of in the room, where there were cross-lights, but about which there was no possible mistake when I saw him walking away up the street.

"Harry, here—quick!" I called to my brother, who at once came to the window. "You're an artist, tell me, is there anything strange about that man?"

"No; nothing that I can see," said Harry, but then suddenly, in an altered tone, added, "Yes, there is. By Jove, *he has a double shadow!*"

That was the explanation of his sidelong glances, of the habitual stoop. There was something always at his side, which none could see, but which cast a shadow.

He turned, presently, and saw us at the window. Instantly, he crossed the road to the shady side of the street. I told Harry all that had passed, and we agreed that it would be as well not to say a word to Lettie.

Two days later, when I returned from a visit to Harry's studio, I found the whole house in confusion.

I learnt from Lettie that while my wife was upstairs, Grieve had called, had not waited for the servant to announce him, but had walked straight into the dining room, where Lettie was sitting. She noticed that he avoided looking at the picture, and to make sure of not seeing it, had seated himself on the sofa just beneath it. He had then, in spite of Lettie's angry remonstrances, renewed his offer of love, strengthening it finally by assuring her that poor George with his dying breath had implored him to seek her, and watch over her, and marry her.

"I was so indignant I hardly knew how to answer him," said Lettie. "When, suddenly, just as he uttered the last words, there came a twang like the breaking of the guitar—and—I hardly know how to describe it—but the portrait had fallen, and the corner of the heavy frame had struck him on the head, cutting it open, and rendering him insensible."

They had carried him upstairs, by the direction of the doctor, for whom my wife at once sent on hearing what had occurred. He was laid on the couch in my dressing room, where I went to see him. I intended to reproach him for coming to the house, despite my prohibition, but I found him delirious. The doctor said it was a queer case; for, though the blow was a severe one, it was hardly enough to account for the symptoms of brain fever. When he learnt that Grieve had but just returned in the *Pioneer* from the North, he said it was possible that the privation and hardship had told on his constitution and sown the seeds of the malady.

We sent for a nurse, who was to sit up with him, by the doctor's directions.

The rest of my story is soon told. In the middle of the night I was roused by a loud scream. I slipped on my clothes, and rushed out to find the nurse, with Lettie in her arms, in a faint. We carried her into her room, and then the nurse explained the mystery to us.

It appears that about midnight Grieve sat up in bed, and began to talk. And he said such terrible things that the nurse became alarmed. Nor was she much reassured when she became aware that the light of her single candle flung what seemed to be two shadows of the sick man on the wall.

Terrified beyond measure, she had crept into Lettie's room, and confided her fears to her; and Lettie, who was a courageous and kindly girl, dressed herself, and said she would sit with her. She, too, saw the double shadow—but what she heard was far more terrible.

Grieve was sitting up in bed, gazing at the unseen figure to which the shadow belonged. In a voice that trembled with emotion, he begged the haunting spirit to leave him, and prayed its forgiveness.

"You know the crime was not premeditated. It was a sudden temptation of the devil that made me strike the blow, and fling you over the precipice. It was the devil tempting me with the recollection of her exquisite face—of the tender love that might have been mine, but for you. But she will not listen to me. See, she turns away from me, as if she knew I was your murderer, George Mason!"

It was Lettie who repeated in a horrified whisper this awful confession.

I could see it all now! As I was about to tell Lettie of the many strange things I had concealed from her, the nurse, who had gone to see her patient, came running back in alarm.

Vincent Grieve had disappeared. He had risen in his delirious terror, had opened the window, and leaped out. Two days later his body was found in the river.

A curtain hangs now before poor George's portrait, though

it is no longer connected with any supernatural marvels; and never, since the night of Vincent Grieve's death, have we seen aught of that most mysterious haunting presence—the Shadow of a Shade.

THE MONKEY'S PAW
W. W. JACOBS

I

WITHOUT, THE NIGHT was cold and wet, but in the small parlor of Lakesnam Villa the blinds were drawn and the fire burned brightly. Father and son were at chess, the former, who possessed ideas about the game involving radical changes, putting his king into such sharp and unnecessary perils that it even provoked comment from the white-haired old lady knitting placidly by the fire.

"Hark at the wind," said Mr. White, who, having seen a fatal mistake after it was too late, was amiably desirous of preventing his son from seeing it.

"I'm listening," said the latter, grimly surveying the board as he stretched out his hand. "Check."

"I should hardly think that he'd come tonight," said his father, with his hand poised over the board.

"Mate," replied the son.

"That's the worst of living so far out," bawled Mr. White, with sudden and unlooked-for violence; "of all the beastly, slushy, out-of-the-way places to live in, this is the worst. Pathway's a bog, and the road's a torrent. I don't know what

W. W. Jacobs

people are thinking about. I suppose because only two houses on the road are let, they think it doesn't matter."

"Never mind, dear," said his wife soothingly; "perhaps you'll win the next one."

Mr. White looked up sharply, just in time to intercept a knowing glance between mother and son. The words died away on his lips, and he hid a guilty grin in his thin gray beard.

"There he is," said Herbert White, as the gate banged to loudly and heavy footsteps came toward the door.

The old man rose with hospitable haste, and opening the door, was heard condoling with the new arrival. The new arrival also condoled with himself, so that Mrs. White said, "Tut, tut!" and coughed gently as her husband entered the room, followed by a tall burly man, beady of eye and rubicund of visage.

"Sergeant Major Morris," he said, introducing him.

The sergeant major shook hands, and taking the proffered seat by the fire, watched contentedly while his host got out whisky and tumblers and stood a small copper kettle on the fire.

At the third glass his eyes got brighter, and he began to talk, the little family circle regarding with eager interest this visitor from distant parts, as he squared his broad shoulders in the chair and spoke of strange scenes and doughty deeds, of wars and plagues and strange peoples.

"Twenty-one years of it," said Mr. White, nodding at his wife and son. "When he went away he was a slip of a youth in the warehouse. Now look at him."

"He don't look to have taken much harm," said Mrs. White politely.

"I'd like to go to India myself," said the old man, "just to look round a bit, you know."

"Better where you are," said the sergeant major, shaking his head. He put down the empty glass and, sighing softly, shook it again.

"I should like to see those old temples and fakirs and jugglers," said the old man. "What was that you started telling me the other day about a monkey's paw or something, Morris?"

"Nothing," said the soldier hastily. "Leastways, nothing worth hearing."

"Monkey's paw?" said Mrs. White curiously.

"Well, it's just a bit of what you might call magic, perhaps," said the sergeant major offhandedly.

His three listeners leaned forward eagerly. The visitor absent-mindedly put his empty glass to his lips and then set it down again. His host filled it for him.

"To look at," said the sergeant major, fumbling in his pocket, "it's just an ordinary little paw, dried to a mummy."

He took something out of his pocket and proffered it. Mrs. White drew back with a grimace, but her son, taking it, examined it curiously.

"And what is there special about it?" inquired Mr. White, as he took it from his son and, having examined it, placed it upon the table.

"It had a spell put on it by an old fakir," said the sergeant major, "a very holy man. He wanted to show that fate ruled people's lives, and that those who interfered with it did so to their sorrow. He put a spell on it so that three separate men could have three wishes from it."

His manner was so impressive that his hearers were conscious that their light laughter jarred somewhat.

"Well, why don't you have three, sir?" said Herbert White cleverly.

The soldier regarded him in the way that middle age is wont to regard presumptuous youth. "I have," he said quietly, and his blotchy face whitened.

"And did you really have the three wishes granted?" asked Mrs. White.

"I did," said the sergeant major, and his glass tapped against his strong teeth.

"And has anybody else wished?" inquired the old lady.

"The first man had his three wishes, yes," was the reply. "I don't know what the first two were, but the third was for death. That's how I got the paw."

His tones were so grave that a hush fell upon the group.

"If you've had your three wishes, it's no good to you now, then, Morris," said the old man at last. "What do you keep it for?"

The soldier shook his head. "Fancy, I suppose," he said slowly. "I did have some idea of selling it, but I don't think I will. It has caused enough mischief already. Besides, people won't buy. They think it's a fairy tale, some of them, and those who do think anything of it want to try it first and pay me afterward."

"If you could have another three wishes," said the old man, eyeing him keenly, "would you have them?"

"I don't know," said the other. "I don't know."

He took the paw, and dangling it between his front finger and thumb, suddenly threw it upon the fire. White, with a slight cry, stooped down and snatched it off.

"Better let it burn," said the soldier solemnly.

"If you don't want it, Morris," said the old man, "give it to me."

"I won't," said his friend doggedly. "I threw it on the fire. If you keep it, don't blame me for what happens. Pitch it on the fire again, like a sensible man."

The other shook his head and examined his new possession closely. "How do you do it?" he inquired.

"Hold it up in your right hand and wish aloud," said the sergeant major, "but I warn you of the consequences."

"Sounds like the *Arabian Nights*," said Mrs. White, as she rose and began to set the supper. "Don't you think you might wish for four pairs of hands for me?"

Her husband drew the talisman from his pocket and then all three burst into laughter as the sergeant major, with a look of alarm on his face, caught him by the arm.

"If you must wish," he said gruffly, "wish for something sensible."

Mr. White dropped it back into his pocket, and, placing chairs, motioned his friend to the table. In the business of supper the talisman was partly forgotten, and afterward the three sat listening in an enthralled fashion to a second installment of the soldier's adventures in India.

"If the tale about the monkey's paw is not more truthful than those he has been telling us," said Herbert, as the door closed behind their guest, just in time for him to catch the last train, "we shan't make much out of it."

"Did you give him anything for it, Father?" inquired Mrs. White, regarding her husband closely.

"A trifle," said he, coloring slightly. "He didn't want it, but I made him take it. And he pressed me again to throw it away."

"Likely," said Herbert, with pretended horror. "Why, we're going to be rich, and famous, and happy. Wish to be an emperor, Father, to begin with; then you can't be henpecked."

He darted round the table, pursued by the maligned Mrs. White armed with an antimacassar.

Mr. White took the paw from his pocket and eyed it dubiously. "I don't know what to wish for, and that's a fact," he said slowly. "It seems to me I've got all I want."

"If you only cleared the house, you'd be quite happy, wouldn't you?" said Herbert, with his hand on his shoulder. "Well, wish for two hundred pounds, then; that'll just do it."

His father, smiling shamefacedly at his own credulity, held up the talisman, as his son, with a solemn face somewhat marred by a wink at his mother, sat down at the piano and struck a few impressive chords.

"I wish for two hundred pounds," said the old man distinctly.

A fine crash from the piano greeted the words, interrupted

by a shuddering cry from the old man. His wife and son ran toward him.

"It moved," he cried, with a glance of disgust at the object as it lay on the floor. "As I wished it twisted in my hands like a snake."

"Well, I don't see the money," said his son, as he picked it up and placed it on the table, "and I bet I never shall."

"It must have been your fancy, Father," said his wife, regarding him anxiously.

He shook his head. "Never mind, though; there's no harm done, but it gave me a shock all the same."

They sat down by the fire again while the two men finished their pipes. Outside, the wind was higher than ever, and the old man started nervously at the sound of a door banging upstairs. A silence unusual and depressing settled upon all three, which lasted until the old couple rose to retire for the night.

"I expect you'll find the cash tied up in a big bag in the middle of your bed," said Herbert, as he bade them good night, "and something horrible squatting up on top of the wardrobe watching you as you pocket your ill-gotten gains."

II

In the brightness of the wintry sun next morning as it streamed over the breakfast table, Herbert laughed at his fears. There was an air of prosaic wholesomeness about the room which it had lacked on the previous night, and the dirty, shriveled little paw was pitched on the sideboard with a carelessness which betokened no great belief in its virtues.

"I suppose all old soldiers are the same," said Mrs. White. "The idea of our listening to such nonsense! How could wishes be granted in these days? And if they could, how could two hundred pounds hurt you, Father?"

"Might drop on his head from the sky," said the frivolous Herbert.

"Morris said the things happened so naturally," said his father, "that you might if you so wished attribute it to coincidence."

"Well, don't break into the money before I come back," said Herbert, as he rose from the table. "I'm afraid it'll turn you into a mean, avaricious man, and we shall have to disown you."

His mother laughed, and following him to the door, watched him down the road, and, returning to the breakfast table, was very happy at the expense of her husband's credulity. All of which did not prevent her from scurrying to the door at the postman's knock, nor prevent her from referring somewhat shortly to retired sergeant majors of bibulous habits when she found that the post brought a tailor's bill.

"Herbert will have some more of his funny remarks, I expect, when he comes home," she said, as they sat at dinner.

"I dare say," said Mr. White, pouring himself out some beer; "but for all that, the thing moved in my hand; that I'll swear to."

"You thought it did," said the old lady soothingly.

"I say it did," replied the other. "There was no thought about it; I had just—— What's the matter?"

His wife made no reply. She was watching the mysterious movements of a man outside, who, peering in an undecided fashion at the house, appeared to be trying to make up his mind to enter. In mental connection with the two hundred pounds, she noticed that the stranger was well dressed and wore a silk hat of glossy newness. Three times he paused at the gate, and then walked on again. The fourth time he stood with his hand upon it, and then with sudden resolution flung it open and walked up the path. Mrs. White at the same moment placed her hands behind her, and hurriedly unfastening the strings of her apron, put that useful article of apparel beneath the cushion of her chair.

She brought the stranger, who seemed ill at ease, into the room. He gazed furtively at Mrs. White, and listened in a preoccupied fashion as the old lady apologized for the appearance of the room, and her husband's coat, a garment which he usually reserved for the garden. She then waited as patiently as her sex would permit for him to broach his business, but he was at first strangely silent.

"I—was asked to call," he said at last, and stooped and picked a piece of cotton from his trousers. "I come from Maw and Meggins."

The old lady started. "Is anything the matter?" she asked breathlessly. "Has anything happened to Herbert? What is it? What is it?"

Her husband interposed. "There, there, Mother," he said hastily. "Sit down, and don't jump to conclusions. You've not brought bad news, I'm sure, sir," and he eyed the other wistfully.

"I'm sorry——" began the visitor.

"Is he hurt?" demanded the mother.

The visitor bowed in assent. "Badly hurt," he said quietly, "but he is not in any pain."

"Oh, thank God!" said the old woman, clasping her hands. "Thank God for that! Thank——"

She broke off suddenly as the sinister meaning of the assurance dawned upon her and she saw the awful confirmation of her fears in the other's averted face. She caught her breath, and turning to her slower-witted husband, laid her trembling old hand upon his. There was a long silence.

"He was caught in the machinery," said the visitor at length, in a low voice.

"Caught in the machinery," repeated Mr. White, in a dazed fashion, "yes."

He sat staring blankly out at the window, and, taking his wife's hand between his own, pressed it as he had been wont to do in their old courting days nearly forty years before.

"He was the only one left us," he said, turning gently to the visitor. "It is hard."

The other coughed, and rising, walked slowly to the window. "The firm wished me to convey their sincere sympathy with you in your great loss," he said, without looking round. "I beg that you will understand I am only their servant and merely obeying orders."

There was no reply; the old woman's face was white, her eyes staring, and her breath inaudible; on the husband's face was a look such as his friend the sergeant might have carried into his first action.

"I was to say that Maw and Meggins disclaim all responsibility," continued the other. "They admit no liability at all, but in consideration of your son's services they wish to present you with a certain sum as compensation."

Mr. White dropped his wife's hand, and rising to his feet, gazed with a look of horror at his visitor. His dry lips shaped the words, "How much?"

"Two hundred pounds," was the answer.

Unconscious of his wife's shriek, the old man smiled faintly, put out his hands like a sightless man, and dropped, a senseless heap, to the floor.

III

In the huge new cemetery, some two miles distant, the old people buried their dead, and came back to a house steeped in shadow and silence. It was all over so quickly that at first they could hardly realize it, and remained in a state of expectation as though of something else to happen—something else which was to lighten this load, too heavy for old hearts to bear. But the days passed, and expectation gave place to resignation—the hopeless resignation of the old, sometimes miscalled apathy. Sometimes they hardly exchanged a word, for now they had nothing to talk about, and their days were long to weariness.

It was about a week after that that the old man, waking suddenly in the night, stretched out his hand and found himself alone. The room was in darkness, and the sound of subdued weeping came from the window. He raised himself in bed and listened.

"Come back," he said tenderly. "You will be cold."

"It is colder for my son," said the old woman, and wept afresh.

The sound of her sobs died away on his ears. The bed was warm, and his eyes heavy with sleep. He dozed fitfully, and then slept until a sudden wild cry from his wife awoke him with a start.

"The monkey's paw!" she cried wildly. "The monkey's paw!"

He started up in alarm. "Where? Where is it? What's the matter?"

She came stumbling across the room toward him. "I want it," she said quietly. "You've not destroyed it?"

"It's in the parlor, on the bracket," he replied, marveling. "Why?"

She cried and laughed together, and bending over, kissed his cheek.

"I only just thought of it," she said hysterically. "Why didn't I think of it before? Why didn't you think of it?"

"Think of what?" he questioned.

"The other two wishes," she replied rapidly. "We've only had one."

"Was not that enough?" he demanded fiercely.

"No," she cried triumphantly; "we'll have one more. Go down and get it quickly, and wish our boy alive again."

The man sat up in bed and flung the bedclothes from his quaking limbs. "Good God, you are mad!" he cried, aghast.

"Get it," she panted; "get it quickly, and wish—— Oh, my boy, my boy!"

Her husband struck a match and lit the candle. "Get back to bed," he said unsteadily. "You don't know what you are saying."

"We had the first wish granted," said the old woman feverishly; "why not the second?"

"A coincidence," stammered the old man.

"Go and get it and wish," cried the old woman, and dragged him toward the door.

He went down in the darkness, and felt his way to the parlor, and then to the mantelpiece. The talisman was in its place, and a horrible fear that the unspoken wish might bring his mutilated son before him ere he could escape from the room seized upon him, and he caught his breath as he found that he had lost the direction of the door. His brow cold with sweat, he felt his way round the table, and groped along the wall until he found himself in the small passage with the unwholesome thing in his hand.

Even his wife's face seemed changed as he entered the room. It was white and expectant, and to his fears seemed to have an unusual look upon it. He was afraid of her.

"Wish!" she cried, in a strong voice.

"It is foolish and wicked," he faltered.

"Wish!" repeated his wife.

He raised his hand. "I wish my son alive again."

The talisman fell to the floor, and he regarded it shudderingly. Then he sank trembling into a chair as the old woman, with burning eyes, walked to the window and raised the blind.

He sat until he was chilled with the cold, glancing occasionally at the figure of the old woman peering through the window. The candle end, which had burnt below the rim of the china candlestick, was throwing pulsating shadows on the ceiling and walls, until, with a flicker larger than the rest, it expired. The old man, with an unspeakable sense of relief at the failure of the talisman, crept back to his bed, and a minute or two afterward the old woman came silently and apathetically beside him.

Neither spoke, but both lay silently listening to the ticking of the clock. A stair creaked, and a squeaky mouse scurried noisily through the wall. The darkness was oppressive, and after lying for some time screwing up his courage, the husband took the box of matches, and striking one, went downstairs for a candle.

At the foot of the stairs the match went out, and he paused to strike another, and at the same moment a knock, so quiet and stealthy as to be scarcely audible, sounded on the front door.

The matches fell from his hand. He stood motionless, his breath suspended until the knock was repeated. Then he turned and fled swiftly back to his room, and closed the door behind him. A third knock sounded through the house.

"*What's that?*" cried the old woman, starting up.

"A rat," said the old man, in shaking tones, "a rat. It passed me on the stairs."

His wife sat up in bed, listening. A loud knock resounded through the house.

"It's Herbert!" she screamed. "It's Herbert!"

She ran to the door, but her husband was before her, and catching her by the arm, held her tightly.

"What are you going to do?" he whispered hoarsely.

"It's my boy; it's Herbert!" she cried, struggling mechanically. "I forgot it was two miles away. What are you holding me for? Let go. I must open the door."

"For God's sake don't let it in," cried the old man, trembling.

"You're afraid of your own son," she cried, struggling. "Let me go. I'm coming, Herbert; I'm coming."

There was another knock, and another. The old woman

with a sudden wrench broke free and ran from the room. Her husband followed to the landing, and called after her appealingly as she hurried downstairs. He heard the chain rattle back and the bottom bolt drawn slowly and stiffly from the socket. Then the old woman's voice, strained and panting.

"The bolt," she cried loudly. "Come down. I can't reach it."

But her husband was on his hands and knees groping wildly on the floor in search of the paw. If he could only find it before the thing outside got in. A perfect fusillade of knocks reverberated through the house, and he heard the scraping of a chair as his wife put it down in the passage against the door. He heard the creaking of the bolt as it came slowly back, and at the same moment, he found the monkey's paw, and frantically breathed his third and last wish.

The knocking ceased suddenly, although the echoes of it were still in the house. He heard the chair drawn back and the door opened. A cold wind rushed up the staircase, and a long loud wail of disappointment and misery from his wife gave him courage to run down to her side, and then to the gate beyond. The street lamp flickering opposite shone on a quiet and deserted road.

I

I HAD NOT been settled much more than six weeks in my country practice, when I was sent for to a neighboring town, to consult with the resident medical man there, on a case of very dangerous illness.

My horse had come down with me, at the end of a long ride the night before, and had hurt himself, luckily much more than he had hurt his master. Being deprived of the animal's services, I started for my destination by the coach (there were no railways at that time); and I hoped to get back again, towards the afternoon, in the same way.

After the consultation was over I went to the principal inn of the town to wait for the coach. When it came up, it was full inside and out. There was no resource left me but to get home as cheaply as I could, by hiring a gig. The price asked for this accommodation struck me as being so extortionate, that I determined to look out for an inn of inferior pretensions, and to try if I could not make a better bargain with a less prosperous establishment.

I soon found a likely-looking house, dingy and quiet, with

an old-fashioned sign that had evidently not been repainted for many years past. The landlord, in this case, was not above making a small profit; and as soon as we came to terms, he rang the yard bell to order the gig.

"Has Robert not come back from that errand?" asked the landlord, appealing to the waiter, who answered the bell.

"No, sir, he hasn't."

"Well, then, you must wake up Isaac."

"Wake up Isaac?" I repeated; "that sounds rather odd. Do your ostlers go to bed in the daytime?"

"This one does," said the landlord, smiling to himself in rather a strange way.

"And dreams, too," added the waiter.

"Never you mind about that," retorted his master; "you go and rouse Isaac up. The gentleman's waiting for his gig."

The landlord's manner and the waiter's manner expressed a great deal more than they either of them said. I began to suspect that I might be on the trace of something professionally interesting to me, as a medical man; and I thought I should like to look at the ostler before the waiter awakened him.

"Stop a minute," I interposed; "I have rather a fancy for seeing this man before you wake him up. I am a doctor; and if this queer sleeping and dreaming of his comes from anything wrong in his brain, I may be able to tell you what to do with him."

"I rather think you will find his complaint past all doctoring, sir," said the landlord. "But if you would like to see him, you're welcome, I'm sure."

He led the way across a yard and down a passage to the stables; opened one of the doors; and waiting outside himself, told me to look in.

I found myself in a two-stall stable. In one of the stalls a horse was munching his corn. In the other, an old man was lying asleep on the litter.

I stooped and looked at him attentively. It was a withered,

woebegone face. The eyebrows were painfully contracted; the mouth was set fast, and drawn down at the corners. The hollow, wrinkled cheeks, and the scanty, grizzled hair, told their own tale of past sorrow or suffering. He was drawing his breath convulsively when I first looked at him; and in a moment more he began to talk in his sleep.

"Wake up!" I heard him say in a quick whisper, through his clenched teeth. "Wake up, there! Murder!"

He moved one lean arm slowly till it rested over his throat, shuddered a little, and turned on the straw. Then the arm left his throat, the hand stretched itself out, and clutched at the side towards which he had turned, as if he fancied himself to be grasping at the edge of something. I saw his lips move, and bent lower over him. He was still talking in his sleep.

"Light gray eyes," he murmured, "and a droop in the left eyelid—flaxen hair, with a gold-yellow streak in it—all right, Mother—fair white arms, with a down on them—little lady's hand, with a reddish look under the fingernails. The knife—always the cursed knife—first on one side, then on the other. Aha! you she-devil, where's the knife?"

At the last word his voice rose, and he grew restless on a sudden. I saw him shudder on the straw; his withered face became distorted, and he threw up both his hands with a quick, hysterical gasp. They struck against the bottom of the manger under which he lay, and the blow awakened him. I had just time to slip through the door, and close it, before his eyes were fairly open and his senses his own again.

"Do you know anything about that man's past life?" I said to the landlord.

"Yes, sir. I know pretty well all about it," was the answer, "and an uncommon queer story it is. Most people don't believe it. It's true, though, for all that. Why, just look at him," continued the landlord, opening the stable door again. "Poor devil! He's so worn out with his restless nights that he's dropped back into his sleep already."

"Don't wake him," I said; "I'm in no hurry for the gig. Wait till the other man comes back from his errand. And, in the meantime, suppose I have some lunch, and a bottle of sherry; and suppose you come and help me to get through it."

The heart of mine host, as I had anticipated, warmed to me over his own wine. He soon became communicative on the subject of the man asleep in the stable; and by little and little, I drew the whole story out of him. Extravagant and incredible as the events must appear to everybody, they are related here just as I heard them, and just as they happened.

II

Some years ago there lived in the suburbs of a large seaport town, on the west coast of England, a man in humble circumstances, by name Isaac Scatchard. His means of subsistence were derived from any employment he could get as an ostler, and occasionally, when times went well with him, from temporary engagements in service as stable helper in private houses. Though a faithful, steady, and honest man, he got on badly in his calling. His ill-luck was proverbial among his neighbors. He was always missing good opportunities by no fault of his own; and always living longest in service with amiable people who were not punctual payers of wages. "Unlucky Isaac" was his nickname in his own neighborhood —and no one could say that he did not richly deserve it.

With far more than one man's fair share of adversity to endure, Isaac had but one consolation to support him—and that was of the dreariest and most negative kind. He had no wife and children to increase his anxieties and add to the bitterness of his various failures in life. It might have been from mere insensibility, or it might have been from generous unwillingness to involve another in his own unlucky destiny— but the fact undoubtedly was, that he had arrived at the middle term of life without marrying; and, what is much more remarkable, without once exposing himself from eighteen to eight-and-thirty, to the genial imputation of ever having had a sweetheart.

When he was out of service he lived alone with his widowed mother. Mrs. Scatchard was a woman above the average in her lowly station, as to capacity and manners. She had seen better days, as the phrase is; but she never referred to them in the presence of curious visitors; and, though perfectly polite to everyone who approached her, never cultivated any intimacies among her neighbors. She contrived to provide hardly enough for her simple wants, by doing rough work for the tailors; and always managed to keep a decent home for her son to return to whenever his ill-luck drove him out helpless into the world.

One bleak autumn, when Isaac was getting fast towards forty, and when he was, as usual, out of place through no fault of his own, he set forth from his mother's cottage on a long walk inland to a gentleman's seat, where he had heard that a stable helper was required.

It wanted then but two days of his birthday; and Mrs. Scatchard, with her usual fondness, made him promise before he started that he would be back in time to keep that anniversary with her in as festive a way as their poor means would allow. It was easy for him to comply with her request, even supposing he slept a night each way on the road.

He was to start from home on Monday morning, and whether he got the new place or not he was to be back for his birthday dinner on Wednesday at two o'clock.

Arriving at his destination too late on the Monday night to make application for the stable helper's place, he slept at the village inn, and, in good time on the Tuesday morning presented himself at the gentleman's house to fill the vacant situation. Here, again, his ill-luck pursued him as inexorably as ever. The excellent written testimonials to his character which he was able to produce availed him nothing; his long walk had been taken in vain—only the day before, the stable helper's place had been given to another man.

Isaac accepted this new disappointment resignedly, and as a matter of course. Naturally slow in capacity, he had the bluntness of sensibility and phlegmatic patience of disposition which frequently distinguish men with sluggishly working mental powers. He thanked the gentleman's steward, with his usual quiet civility, for granting him an interview, and took his departure with no appearance of unusual depression in his face or manner.

Before starting on his homeward walk, he made some inquiries at the inn and ascertained that he might save a few miles, on his return, by following a new road. Furnished with full instructions, several times repeated, as to the various turnings he was to take, he set forth on his homeward journey and walked on all day with only one stoppage for bread and cheese. Just as it was getting towards dark the rain came on and the wind began to rise; and he found himself, to make matters worse, in a part of the country with which he was entirely unacquainted, though he knew himself to be some fifteen miles from home. The first house he found to inquire at was a lonely roadside inn, standing on the outskirts of a thick wood. Solitary as the place looked, it was welcome to a lost man who was also hungry, thirsty, footsore, and wet. The landlord was civil and respectable-looking; and the price he asked for a bed was reasonable enough. Isaac, therefore, decided on stopping comfortably at the inn for that night.

He was constitutionally a temperate man. His supper simply consisted of two rashers of bacon, a slice of homemade bread, and a pint of ale. He did not go to bed immediately after this moderate meal, but sat up with the landlord, talking about his bad prospects and his long run of ill-luck, and diverging from these topics to the subjects of horseflesh and racing. Nothing was said, either by himself, his host, or the few laborers who strayed into the taproom, which could, in the slightest degree, excite the very small and very dull imaginative faculty which Isaac Scatchard possessed.

At a little after eleven the house was closed. Isaac went round with the landlord and held the candle while the doors and lower windows were being secured. He noticed, with surprise, the strength of the bolts, bars, and iron-sheathed shutters.

"You see, we are rather lonely here," said the landlord. "We never have had any attempts made to break in yet, but it's always as well to be on the safe side. When nobody is sleeping here I am the only man in the house. My wife and daughter are timid, and the servant girl takes after her missuses. Another glass of ale before you turn in?—No!—Well, how such a sober man as you comes to be out of a place is more than I can make out, for one. . . . Here's where you're to sleep. You're the only lodger tonight, and I think you'll say my missus has done her best to make you comfortable. You're quite sure you won't have another glass of ale?—Very well. Good night."

It was half past eleven by the clock in the passage as they went upstairs to the bedroom, the window of which looked on to the wood at the back of the house.

Isaac locked the door, set his candle on the chest of drawers, and wearily got ready for bed. The bleak autumn wind was still blowing, and the solemn, surging moan of it in the wood was dreary and awful to hear through the night silence. Isaac felt strangely wakeful. He resolved, as he lay down in bed, to keep the candle alight until he began to grow sleepy; for there was something unendurably depressing in the bare idea of lying awake in the darkness, listening to the dismal, ceaseless moan of the wind in the wood.

Sleep stole on him before he was aware of it. His eyes closed, and he fell off insensibly to rest, without having so much as thought of extinguishing the candle.

The first sensation of which he was conscious, after sinking into slumber, was a strange shivering that ran through him suddenly from head to foot, and a dreadful sinking pain at the heart, such as he had never felt before. The shivering only disturbed his slumbers—the pain woke him instantly. In one moment he passed from a state of sleep to a state of wakefulness—his eyes wide open—his mental perceptions cleared on a sudden as if by a miracle.

The candle had burnt down nearly to the last morsel of tallow, but the top of the unsnuffed wick had just fallen off, and the light in the little room was, for the moment, fair and full.

Between the foot of his bed and the closed door, there stood a woman with a knife in her hand, looking at him.

He was stricken speechless with terror, but he did not lose the preternatural clearness of his faculties; and he never took his eyes off the woman. She said not a word as they stared each other in the face; but she began to move slowly towards the left-hand side of the bed.

His eyes followed her. She was a fair, fine woman, with yellowish flaxen hair, and light gray eyes, with a droop in the left eyelid. He noticed these things, and fixed them on his mind, before she was round at the side of the bed. Speechless, with no expression in her face, with no noise following her footfall, she came closer and closer—stopped—and slowly raised the knife. He laid his right arm over his throat to save it; but, as he saw the knife coming down, threw his hand across the bed to the right side, and jerked his body over that way, just as the knife descended on the mattress within an inch of his shoulder.

His eyes fixed on her arm and hand, as she slowly drew her knife out of the bed. A white, well-shaped arm, with a pretty down lying lightly over the fair skin. A delicate, lady's hand, with the crowning beauty of a pink flush under and round the fingernails.

She drew the knife out, and passed back again slowly to the foot of the bed; stopped there for a moment looking at him; then came on—still speechless, still with no expression on the beautiful face, still with no sound following the stealthy footfalls—came on to the right side of the bed where he now lay.

As she approached, she raised the knife again, and he drew himself away to the left side. She struck, as before, right into the mattress, with a deliberate, perpendicularly downward action of the arm. This time his eyes wandered from her to the knife. It was like the large clasp knives which he had often seen laboring men use to cut their bread and bacon with. Her delicate little fingers did not conceal more than two-thirds of the handle; he noticed that it was made of buckhorn, clean and shining as the blade was, and looking like new.

For the second time she drew the knife out, concealed it in the wide sleeve of her gown, then stopped by the bedside, watching him. For an instant he saw her standing in that position—then the wick of the spent candle fell over into the socket. The flame diminished to a little blue point, and the room grew dark.

A moment, or less if possible, passed so—and then the wick flamed up, smokily, for the last time. His eyes were still looking eagerly over the right-hand side of the bed when the final flash of light came, but they discerned nothing. The fair woman with the knife was gone.

The conviction that he was alone again weakened the hold of the terror that had struck him dumb up to this time. The preternatural sharpness, which the very intensity of his panic had mysteriously imparted to his faculties, left them suddenly. His brain grew confused—his heart beat wildly—his ears opened, for the first time since the appearance of the woman, to a sense of the woeful, ceaseless moaning of the wind among the trees. With the dreadful conviction of the reality of what he had seen still strong within him, he leapt out of bed, and screaming "Murder! Wake up there, wake up!" dashed headlong through the darkness to the door.

It was fast locked, exactly as he had left it on going to bed.

His cries, on starting up, had alarmed the house. He heard the terrified, confused exclamations of women; he saw the master of the house approaching along the passage, with his burning rush candle in one hand and his gun in the other.

"What is it?" asked the landlord breathlessly.

Isaac could only answer in a whisper. "A woman, with a knife in her hand," he gasped out. "In my room—a fair, yellow-haired woman; she jabbed at me with the knife, twice over."

The landlord's pale cheek grew paler. He looked at Isaac eagerly by the flickering light of his candle; and his face began to get red again—his voice altered, too, as well as his complexion.

"She seems to have missed you twice," he said.

"I dodged the knife as it came down," Isaac went on, in the same scared whisper. "It struck the bed each time."

The landlord took his candle into the bedroom immediately. In less than a minute he came out again into the passage in a violent passion.

"The devil fly away with you and your woman with the knife! There isn't a mark in the bedclothes anywhere. What do you mean by coming into a man's place and frightening his family out of their wits by a dream?"

"I'll leave your house," said Isaac faintly. "Better out on the road, in rain and dark, on my way home, than back again in that room, after what I've seen in it. Lend me a light to get my clothes by, and tell me what I'm to pay."

"Pay!" cried the landlord, leading the way with his light sulkily into the bedroom. "You'll find your score on the slate when you go downstairs. I wouldn't have taken you in for all the money you've got about you, if I'd known your dreaming, screeching ways beforehand. Look at the bed. Where's the cut of a knife in it? Look at the window—is the lock bursted?

Look at the door (which I heard you fasten yourself) is it broke in? A murdering woman with a knife in my house! You ought to be ashamed of yourself!"

Isaac answered not a word. He huddled on his clothes: and then they went downstairs together.

"Nigh on twenty minutes past two!" said the landlord, as they passed the clock. "A nice time in the morning to frighten honest people out of their wits!"

Isaac paid his bill, and the landlord let him out at the front door, asking, with a grin of contempt, as he undid the strong fastenings, whether "the murdering woman got in that way?"

They parted without a word on either side. The rain had ceased; but the night was dark, and the wind bleaker than ever. Little did the darkness, or the cold, or the uncertainty about the way home matter to Isaac. If he had been turned out into a wilderness in a thunderstorm, it would have been a relief, after what he had suffered in the bedroom of the inn.

What was the fair woman with the knife? The creature of a dream, or that other creature from the unknown world, called among men by the name of ghost? He could make nothing of the mystery—had made nothing of it, even when it was midday on Wednesday, and when he stood, at last, after many times missing his road, once more on the doorstep of home.

III

His mother came out eagerly to receive him. His face told her in a moment that something was wrong.

"I've lost the place; but that's my luck. I dreamed an ill dream last night, Mother—or, maybe, I saw a ghost. Take it either way, it scared me out of my senses, and I'm not my own man again yet."

"Isaac! Your face frightens me. Come in to the fire. Come in, and tell Mother all about it."

He was as anxious to tell as she was to hear; for it had been his hope, all the way home, that his mother, with her quicker capacity and superior knowledge, might be able to throw some light on the mystery which he could not clear up for himself. His memory of the dream was still mechanically vivid, though his thoughts were entirely confused by it.

His mother's face grew paler and paler as he went on. She never interrupted him by so much as a single word; but when he had done, she moved her chair close to his, put her arm round his neck, and said to him:

"Isaac, you dreamed your ill dream on this Wednesday morning. What time was it when you saw the fair woman with the knife in her hand?"

Isaac reflected on what the landlord had said when they had passed by the clock on his leaving the inn—allowed as nearly as he could for the time that must have elapsed between the unlocking of his bedroom door and the paying of his bill just before going away, and answered:

"Somewhere about two o'clock in the morning."

His mother suddenly quitted her hold of his neck, and struck her hands together with a gesture of despair.

"This Wednesday is your birthday, Isaac; and two o'clock in the morning is the time when you were born!"

Isaac's capacities were not quick enough to catch the infection of his mother's superstitious dread. He was amazed, and a little startled also, when she suddenly rose from her chair, opened her old writing desk, took pen, ink, and paper, and then said to him:

"Your memory is but a poor one, Isaac, and now I'm an old woman, mine's not much better. I want all about this dream of yours to be as well known to both of us, years hence, as it is now. Tell me over again all you told me a minute ago, when you spoke of what the woman with the knife looked like."

Isaac obeyed, and marveled much as he saw his mother carefully set down on paper the very words that he was saying.

"Light gray eyes," she wrote as they came to the descriptive part, "with a droop in the left eyelid. Flaxen hair, with a gold-yellow streak in it. White arms, with a down upon them. Little lady's hand, with a reddish look about the fingernails. Clasp knife with a buckhorn handle, that seemed as good as new." To these particulars, Mrs. Scatchard added the year, month, day of the week, and time in the morning, when the woman of the dream appeared to her son. She then locked up the paper carefully in her writing desk.

Neither on that day, nor on any day after, could her son induce her to return to the matter of the dream. She obstinately kept her thoughts about it to herself, and even refused to refer again to the paper in her writing desk. Ere long, Isaac grew weary of attempting to make her break her resolute silence; and time, which sooner or later wears out all things, gradually wore out the impression produced on him by the dream. He began by thinking of it carelessly, and he ended by not thinking of it at all.

This result was the more easily brought about by the advent of some important changes for the better in his prospects, which commenced not long after his terrible night's experience at the inn. He reaped at last the reward of his long and patient suffering under adversity, by getting an excellent place, keeping it for seven years, and leaving it, on the death of his master, not only with an excellent character, but also with a comfortable annuity bequeathed to him as a reward for saving his mistress's life in a carriage accident. Thus it happened that Isaac Scatchard returned to his old mother, seven years after the time of the dream at the inn, with an annual sum of money at his disposal, sufficient to keep them both in ease and independence for the rest of their lives.

The mother, whose health had been bad of late years, profited so much by the care bestowed on her and by freedom from money anxieties, that when Isaac's birthday came round she was able to sit up comfortably at table and dine with him.

On that day, as the evening drew on, Mrs. Scatchard discovered that a bottle of tonic medicine—which she was accustomed to take, and in which she had fancied that a dose
or more was still left—happened to be empty. Isaac immediately volunteered to go to the chemist's, and get it filled
again. It was as rainy and bleak an autumn night as on the
memorable past occasion when he lost his way and slept at
the roadside inn.

On going into the chemist's shop, he was passed hurriedly
by a poorly dressed woman coming out of it. The glimpse
he had of her face struck him, and he looked back after her as
she descended the door steps.

"You're noticing that woman?" said the chemist's appren-
tice behind the counter. "It's my opinion there's something
wrong with her. She's been asking for laudanum to put to a bad
tooth. Master's out for half an hour; and I told her I wasn't allowed to sell poison to strangers in his absence. She laughed
in a queer way, and said she would come back in half an hour.
If she expects master to serve her, I think she'll be disap-
pointed. It's a case of suicide, sir, if ever there was one yet."

These words added immeasurably to the sudden interest
in the woman which Isaac had felt at the first sight of her
face. After he had got the medicine bottle filled, he looked
about anxiously for her as soon as he was out in the street.
She was walking slowly up and down on the opposite side
of the road. With his heart, very much to his own surprise,
beating fast, Isaac crossed over and spoke to her.

He asked if she was in any distress. She pointed to her
torn shawl, her scanty dress, her crushed, dirty bonnet—then
moved under a lamp so as to let the light fall on her stern,
pale, but still most beautiful face.

"I look like a comfortable, happy woman—don't I?" she
said, with a bitter laugh.

She spoke with a purity of intonation which Isaac had
never heard before from other than ladies' lips. Her slightest

actions seemed to have the easy, negligent grace of a thoroughbred woman. Her skin, for all its poverty-stricken paleness, was as delicate as if her life had been passed in the enjoyment of every social comfort that wealth can purchase. Even her small, finely shaped hands, gloveless as they were, had not lost their whiteness.

Little by little, in answer to his questions, the sad story of the woman came out. There is no need to relate it here; it is told over and over again in police reports and paragraphs descriptive of attempted suicides.

"My name is Rebecca Murdoch," said the woman, as she ended. "I have ninepence left, and I thought of spending it at the chemist's over the way in securing a passage to the other world. Whatever it is, it can't be worse to me than this—so why should I stop here?"

Besides the natural compassion and sadness moved in his heart by what he heard, Isaac felt within him some mysterious influence at work all the time the woman was speaking, which utterly confused his ideas and almost deprived him of his powers of speech. All that he could say in answer to her last reckless words was that he would prevent her from attempting her own life, if he followed her about all night to do it. His rough, trembling earnestness seemed to impress her.

"I won't occasion you that trouble," she answered, when he repeated his threat. "You have given me a fancy for living by speaking kindly to me. No need for the mockery of protestations and promises. You may believe me without them. Come to Fuller's Meadow tomorrow at twelve, and you will find me alive, to answer for myself. No!—no money. My ninepence will do to get me as good a night's lodgings as I want."

She nodded and left him. He made no attempt to follow—he felt no suspicion that she was deceiving him.

"It's strange, but I can't help believing her," he said to himself, and walked away bewildered towards home.

On entering the house, his mind was still so completely

absorbed by its new subject of interest, that he took no notice of what his mother was doing when he came in with the bottle of medicine. She had opened her old writing desk in his absence, and was now reading a paper attentively that lay inside it. On every birthday of Isaac's since she had written down the particulars of his dream from his own lips, she had been accustomed to read that same paper, and ponder over it in private.

The next day he went to Fuller's Meadow.

He had done only right in believing her so implicitly—she was there, punctual to a minute, to answer for herself. The last-left faint defenses in Isaac's heart, against the fascination which a word or look from her began inscrutably to exercise over him, sank down and vanished before her forever on that memorable morning.

When a man, previously insensible to the influence of women, forms an attachment in middle life, the instances are rare indeed, let the warning circumstances be what they may, in which he is found capable of freeing himself from the tyranny of the new ruling passion. The charm of being spoken to familiarly, fondly, and gratefully by a woman whose language and manners still retained enough of their early refinement to hint at the high social station that she had lost, would have been a dangerous luxury to a man of Isaac's rank at the age of twenty. But it was far more than that—it was certain ruin to him—now that his heart was opening unworthily to a new influence at that middle time of life when strong feelings of all kinds, once implanted, strike root most stubbornly in a man's moral nature. A few more stolen interviews after that first morning in Fuller's Meadow completed his infatuation. In less than a month from the time when he first met her, Isaac Scatchard had consented to give Rebecca Murdoch a new interest in existence, and a chance of recovering the character she had lost, by promising to make her his wife.

She had taken possession not of his passions only, but of his faculties as well. All the mind he had he put into her keeping. She directed him on every point, even instructing him how to break the news of his approaching marriage in the safest manner to his mother.

"If you tell her how you met me, and who I am at first," said the cunning woman, "she will move heaven and earth to prevent our marriage. Say I am the sister of one of your fellow servants—ask her to see me before you go into any more particulars—and leave it to me to do the rest. I mean to make her love me next best to you, Isaac, before she knows anything of who I really am."

The motive of the deceit was sufficient to sanctify it to Isaac. The stratagem proposed relieved him of his one great anxiety, and quieted his uneasy conscience on the subject of his mother. Still, there was something wanting to perfect his happiness, something that he could not realize, something mysteriously untraceable, and yet something that perpetually made itself felt—not when he was absent from Rebecca Murdoch, but, strange to say, when he was actually in her presence! She was kindness itself with him; she never made him feel his inferior capacities and inferior manners—she showed the sweetest anxiety to please him in the smallest trifles; but, in spite of all these attractions, he never could feel quite at his ease with her. At their first meeting, there had mingled with his admiration, when he looked in her face, a faint, involuntary feeling of doubt whether that face was entirely strange to him. No after-familiarity had the slightest effect on this inexplicable, wearisome uncertainty.

Concealing the truth, as he had been directed, he announced his marriage engagement precipitately and confusedly to his mother on the day when he contracted it. Poor Mrs. Scatchard showed her perfect confidence in her son by flinging her arms round his neck, and giving him joy of having found at last, in the sister of one of his fellow servants, a woman to comfort and care for him after his mother was gone. She was all eagerness to see the woman of her son's choice, and the next day was fixed for the introduction.

It was a bright, sunny morning, and the little cottage parlor was full of light, as Mrs. Scatchard, happy and expectant, dressed for the occasion in her Sunday gown, sat waiting for her son and her future daughter-in-law.

Punctual to the appointed time, Isaac hurriedly and nervously led his promised wife into the room. His mother rose to receive her—advanced a few steps, smiling—looked Rebecca full in the eyes—and suddenly stopped. Her face, which had been flushed the moment before, turned white in an instant —her eyes lost their expression of softness and kindness, and assumed a blank look of terror—her outstretched hands fell to her sides, and she staggered back a few steps with a low cry to her son.

"Isaac!" she whispered, clutching him fast by the arm, when he asked, alarmedly, if she was taken ill. "Isaac! Does that woman's face remind you of nothing?"

Before he could answer, before he could look round to where Rebecca stood, astonished and angered by her reception, at the lower end of the room, his mother pointed impatiently to her writing desk and gave him the key.

"Open it," she said, in a quick, breathless whisper.

"What does this mean? Why am I treated as if I had no business here? Does your mother want to insult me?" asked Rebecca angrily.

"Open it, and give me the paper in the left-hand drawer. Quick! quick! for heaven's sake!" said Mrs. Scatchard, shrinking further back in terror.

Isaac gave her the paper. She looked it over eagerly for a moment—then followed Rebecca, who was now turning away haughtily to leave the room, and caught her by the shoulder—abruptly raised the long, loose sleeve of her gown—and glanced at her hand and arm. Something like fear began to

214

steal over the angry expression of Rebecca's face, as she shook herself free from the old woman's grasp. "Mad!" she said to herself, "and Isaac never told me." With those few words she left the room.

Isaac was hastening after her, when his mother turned and stopped his further progress. It wrung his heart to see the misery and terror in her face as she looked at him.

"Light gray eyes," she said, in low, mournful, awestruck tones, pointing towards the open door. "A droop in the left eyelid; flaxen hair, with a gold-yellow streak in it; white arms with a down on them; little, lady's hand, with a reddish look under the fingernails. *The Dream Woman!* Isaac, the Dream Woman!"

That faint cleaving doubt, which he had never been able to shake off in Rebecca Murdoch's presence, was fatally set at rest for ever. He *had* seen her face, then, before—seven years before, on his birthday, in the bedroom of the lonely inn.

"Be warned! Oh, my son, be warned! Isaac! Isaac! Let her go, and do you stop with me!"

Something darkened the parlor window as those words were said. A sudden chill ran through him, and he glanced sidelong at the shadow. Rebecca Murdoch had come back. She was peering in curiously at them over the low window blind.

"I have promised to marry, Mother," he said, "and marry I must."

The tears came into his eyes as he spoke, and dimmed his sight; but he could just discern the fatal face outside, moving away again from the window.

His mother's head sank lower.

"Are you faint?" he whispered.

"Brokenhearted, Isaac."

He stooped down and kissed her. The shadow, as he did so, returned to the window; and the fatal face peered in curiously once more.

I V

Three weeks after that day Isaac and Rebecca were man and wife. All that was hopelessly dogged and stubborn in the man's moral nature seemed to have closed round his fatal passion, and to have fixed it unassailably in his heart.

After that first interview in the cottage parlor, no consideration could induce Mrs. Scatchard to see her son's wife again, or even to talk of her when Isaac tried hard to plead her cause after their marriage.

This course of conduct was not in any degree occasioned by a discovery of the degradation in which Rebecca had lived. There was no question of that between mother and son. There was no question of anything but the fearfully exact resemblance between the living, breathing woman, and the specter-woman of Isaac's dream.

Rebecca, on her side, neither felt nor expressed the slightest sorrow at the estrangement between herself and her mother-in-law. Isaac, for the sake of peace, had never contradicted her first idea that age and long illness had affected Mrs. Scatchard's mind. He even allowed his wife to upbraid him for not having confessed this to her at the time of their marriage engagement, rather than risk anything by hinting at the truth. The sacrifice of his integrity before his one all-mastering delusion, seemed but a small thing, and cost his conscience but little, after the sacrifices he had already made.

The time of waking from his delusion—the cruel and the rueful time—was not far off. After some quiet months of married life, as the summer was ending, and the year was getting on towards the month of his birthday, Isaac found his wife altering towards him. She grew sullen and contemptuous; she formed acquaintances of the most dangerous kind, in defiance of his objections, his entreaties, and his commands; and, worst of all, she learnt, ere long, after every fresh difference with her husband, to seek the deadly self-oblivion of drink. Little by little, after the first miserable discovery that his wife was keeping company with drunkards, the shocking certainty forced itself on Isaac that she had grown to be a drunkard herself.

He had been in a sadly desponding state for some time before the occurrence of these domestic calamities. His mother's health, as he could but too plainly discern every time he went to see her at the cottage, was failing fast; and he upbraided himself in secret as the cause of the bodily and mental suffering she endured. When to his remorse on his mother's account was added the shame and misery occasioned by the discovery of his wife's degradation, he sank under the double trial, his face began to alter fast, and he looked what he was, a spirit-broken man.

His mother, still struggling bravely against the illness that was hurrying her to her grave, was the first to notice the sad alteration in him, and the first to hear of his last, worst trouble with his wife. She could only weep bitterly on the day when he made his humiliating confession; but on the next occasion when he went to see her, she had taken a resolution, in reference to his domestic afflictions, which astonished and even alarmed him. He found her dressed to go out, and on asking the reason, received this answer:

"I am not long for this world, Isaac," she said; "and I shall not feel easy on my death-bed, unless I have done my best to the last to make my son happy. I mean to put my own fears and my own feelings out of the question, and to go with you to your wife and try what I can do to reclaim her. Give me your arm, Isaac; and let me do the last thing I can in this world to help my son, before it is too late."

He could not disobey her; and they walked together slowly towards his miserable home.

It was only one o'clock in the afternoon when they reached the cottage where he lived. It was their dinner hour, and Rebecca was in the kitchen. He was thus able to take his mother quietly into the parlor and then prepare his wife for the interview. She had fortunately drunk but little at that early hour, and she was less sullen and capricious than usual.

He returned to his mother, with his mind tolerably at ease. His wife soon followed him into the parlor, and the meeting between her and Mrs. Scatchard passed off better than he had ventured to anticipate; though he observed, with secret apprehension, that his mother, resolutely as she controlled herself in other respects, could not look his wife in the face when she spoke to her. It was a relief to him, therefore, when Rebecca began to lay the cloth.

She laid the cloth, brought in the bread tray, and cut a slice from the loaf for her husband, then returned to the kitchen. At that moment, Isaac, still anxiously watching his mother, was startled by seeing the same ghastly change pass over her face which had altered it so awfully on the morning when Rebecca and she first met. Before he could say a word, she whispered with a look of horror:

"Take me back! Home, home, again, Isaac! Come with me and never go back again!"

He was afraid to ask for an explanation; he could only sign to her to be silent, and help her quickly to the door. As they passed the bread tray on the table, she stopped and pointed to it.

"Did you see what your wife cut your bread with?" she asked in a low whisper.

"No, Mother; I was not noticing. What was it?"

"Look!"

He did look. A new clasp knife, with a buckhorn handle, lay with the loaf in the bread tray. He stretched out his hand, shudderingly, to possess himself of it; but at the same time there was a noise in the kitchen, and his mother caught at his arm.

"The knife of the dream! Isaac, I'm faint with fear—take me away, before she comes back!"

He was hardly able to support her. The visible, tangible reality of the knife struck him with a panic, and utterly destroyed any faint doubts he might have entertained up to this time in relation to the mysterious dream-warning of nearly eight years before. By a last desperate effort, he summoned self-possession enough to help his mother out of the house—so quietly that the "Dream Woman" (he thought of her by that name now) did not hear their departure.

"Don't go back, Isaac, don't go back!" implored Mrs. Scatchard, as he turned to go away, after seeing her safely seated again in her own room.

"I must get the knife," he answered under his breath. His mother tried to stop him again; but he hurried out without another word.

On his return, he found that his wife had discovered their secret departure from the house. She had been drinking, and was in a fury of passion. The dinner in the kitchen was flung under the grate; the cloth was off the parlor table. Where was the knife?

Unwisely, he asked for it. She was only too glad of the opportunity of irritating him, which the request afforded her. He wanted the knife, did he? Could he give her a reason why? —No? Then he should not have it—not if he went down on his knees to ask for it. Further recriminations elicited the fact that she had bought it as a bargain, and that she considered it her own especial property. Isaac saw the uselessness of attempting to get the knife by fair means, and determined to search for it, later in the day, in secret. The search was unsuccessful. Night came on, and he left the house to walk about the streets. He was afraid, now, to sleep in the same room with her.

Three weeks passed. Still sullenly enraged with him, she would not give up the knife; and still that fear of sleeping in the same room with her possessed him. He walked about at night, or dozed in the parlor, or sat watching by his mother's bedside. Before the expiration of the first week in the new month his mother died. It wanted then but ten days of her son's birthday. She had longed to live till that anniversary. Isaac was present at her death; and her last words in this world were addressed to him:

"Don't go back, my son—don't go back!"

He was obliged to go back, if it were only to watch his wife. Exasperated to the last degree by his distrust of her, she had revengefully sought to add a sting to his grief, during the last days of his mother's illness, by declaring that she would assert her right to attend the funeral. In spite of all that he could do or say, she held with wicked pertinacity to her word; and on the day appointed for the burial, forced herself—inflamed and shameless with drink—into her husband's presence, and declared that she would walk in the funeral procession to his mother's grave.

This last, worst outrage, accompanied by all that was most insulting in word and look, maddened him for the moment. He struck her.

The instant the blow was dealt he repented it. She crouched down, silent, in a corner of the room, and eyed him steadily; it was a look that cooled his hot blood and made him tremble. But there was no time now to think of a means of making atonement. Nothing remained but to risk the worst till the funeral was over. There was but one way of making sure of her. He locked her into her bedroom.

When he came back, some hours after, he found her sitting, very much altered in look and bearing, by the bedside, with a bundle on her lap. She rose and faced him quietly, and spoke with a strange stillness in her voice, a strange repose in her eyes, a strange composure in her manner.

"No man has ever struck me twice," she said; "and my husband shall have no second opportunity. Set the door open and let me go. From this day forth we see each other no more."

Before he could answer she passed him and left the room. He saw her walk away up the street.

Would she return?

All that night he watched and waited; but no footstep came near the house. The next night, overcome by fatigue, he lay down in bed in his clothes, with the door locked, the key on the table, and the candle burning. His slumber was not disturbed. The third night, the fourth, the fifth, the sixth passed, and nothing happened. He lay down on the seventh, still in his clothes, still with the door locked, the key on the table, and the candle burning; but easier in his mind.

Easier in his mind, and in perfect health of body, when he fell off to sleep. But his rest was disturbed. He woke twice, without any sensation of uneasiness. But the third time it was that never-to-be-forgotten shivering of the night at the lonely inn, that dreadful sinking pain at the heart, which once more aroused him in an instant.

His eyes opened towards the left-hand side of the bed, and there stood . . .

The Dream Woman again? No! His wife; the living reality, with the dream-specter's face—in the dream-specter's attitude; the fair arm up; the knife clasped in the delicate, white hand.

He sprang upon her almost at the instant of seeing her, and yet not quickly enough to prevent her from hiding the knife. Without a word from him, without a cry from her, he pinioned her in a chair. With one hand he felt up her sleeve; and there, where the Dream Woman had hidden the knife, his wife had hidden it—the knife with the buckhorn handle that looked like new.

In the despair of that fearful moment his brain was steady, his heart was calm. He looked at her fixedly, with the knife in his hand, and said these last words:

"You told me we should see each other no more, and you have come back. It is my turn now to go, and to go for ever. *I* say that we shall see each other no more; and *my* word shall not be broken."

He left her and set forth into the night. There was a bleak wind abroad, and the smell of recent rain was in the air. The distant church clocks chimed the quarter as he walked rapidly beyond the last houses in the suburb. He asked the first policeman he met what hour that was of which the quarter past had just struck.

The man referred sleepily to his watch, and answered, "Two o'clock." Two in the morning. What day of the month was this day that had just begun? He reckoned it up from the date of his mother's funeral. The fatal parallel was complete —it was his birthday!

Had he escaped the mortal peril which his dream foretold? Or had he only received a second warning?

As this ominous doubt forced itself on his mind, he stopped, reflected, and turned back again towards the city. He was still resolute to hold to his word, and never to let her see him more; but there was a thought now in his mind of having her watched and followed. The knife was in his possession; the world was before him; but a new distrust of her—a vague, unspeakable, superstitious dread—had overcome him.

"I must know where she goes, now she thinks I have left her," he said to himself, as he stole back wearily to the precincts of his house.

It was still dark. He had left the candle burning in the bedchamber, but when he looked up to the window of the room now, there was no light in it. He crept cautiously to the house door. On going away, he remembered to have closed it; on trying it now, he found it open.

He waited outside, never losing sight of the house till daylight. Then he ventured indoors—listened, and heard nothing —looked into kitchen, scullery, parlor; and found nothing: went up at last into the bedroom—it was empty. A picklock lay on the floor, betraying how she had gained entrance in the night, and that was the only trace of her.

Whither had she gone? No mortal tongue could tell him.

The darkness had covered her flight; and when the day broke no man could say where the light found her.

Before leaving the house and the town for ever, he gave instructions to a friend and neighbor to sell his furniture for anything that it would fetch, and to apply the proceeds towards employing the police to trace her. The directions were honestly followed, and the money was all spent; but the inquiries led to nothing. The picklock on the bedroom floor remained the last useless trace of the Dream Woman.

At this part of the narrative the landlord paused; and, turning towards the window of the room in which we were sitting, looked in the direction of the stable yard.

"So far," he said, "I tell you what was told to me. The little that remains to be added lies within my own experience. Between two and three months after the events I have just been relating, Isaac Scatchard came to me, withered and old-looking before his time, just as you saw him today. He had his testimonials to character with him, and he asked me for employment here. Knowing that my wife and he were distantly related, I gave him a trial in consideration of that relationship, and liked him in spite of his queer habits. He is as sober, honest, and willing a man as there is in England. As for his restlessness at night, and his sleeping away his leisure time in the day, who can wonder at it after hearing his story? Besides, he never objects to being roused up when he's wanted, so there's not much inconvenience to complain of, after all."

"I suppose he is afraid of a return of that dreadful dream, and of waking out of it in the dark?"

"No," returned the landlord. "The dream comes back to him so often that he has got to bear with it by this time resignedly enough. It's his wife keeps him waking at night, as he has often told me."

"What! Has she never been heard of yet?"

"Never. Isaac himself has the one perpetual thought that she is alive and looking for him. I believe he wouldn't let himself drop off to sleep towards two in the morning for a king's ransom. Two in the morning, he says, is the time she will find him, one of these days. Two in the morning is the time, all the year round, when he likes to be most certain that he has got the clasp knife safe about him. He does not mind being alone, as long as he is awake, except on the night before his birthday, when he firmly believes himself to be in peril of his life. The birthday has only come round once since he has been here, and then he sat up along with the night porter. 'She's looking for me,' is all he says when anybody speaks to him about the one anxiety of his life; 'she's looking for me.' He may be right. She *may* be looking for him. Who can tell?"

"Who can tell?" said I.

Casting the Runes by M. R. JAMES

DEAR SIR,—I am requested by the Council of the ———
Association to return to you the draft of a paper on *The Truth
of Alchemy*, which you have been good enough to offer to
read at our forthcoming meeting, and to inform you that the
Council do not see their way to including it in the program.

> I am,
> Yours faithfully,
> ——— *Secretary*

APRIL 18TH

DEAR SIR,—I am sorry to say that my engagements do not
permit of my affording you an interview on the subject of
your proposed paper. Nor do our laws allow of your discussing
the matter with a committee of our Council, as you suggest.
Please allow me to assure you that the fullest consideration
was given to the draft which you submitted, and that it was
not declined without having been referred to the judgment of

a most competent authority. No personal question (it can hardly be necessary for me to add) can have had the slightest influence on the decision of the Council.

Believe me (*ut supra*),

The Secretary of the —— Association begs respectfully to inform Mr. Karswell that it is impossible for him to communicate the name of any person or persons to whom the draft of Mr. Karswell's paper may have been submitted; and further desires to intimate that he cannot undertake to reply to any further letters on this subject.

"And who *is* Mr. Karswell?" inquired the Secretary's wife. She had called at his office, and (perhaps unwarrantably) had picked up the last of these three letters, which the typist had just brought in.

"Why, my dear, just at present Mr. Karswell is a very angry man. But I don't know much about him otherwise, except that he is a person of wealth, his address is Lufford Abbey, Warwickshire, and he's an alchemist, apparently, and wants to tell us all about it; and that's about all—except that I don't want to meet him for the next week or two. Now, if you're ready to leave this place, I am."

"What have you been doing to make him angry?" asked Mrs. Secretary.

"The usual thing, my dear, the usual thing: he sent in a draft of a paper he wanted to read at the next meeting, and we referred it to Edward Dunning—almost the only man in England who knows about these things—and he said it was perfectly hopeless, so we declined it. So Karswell has been pelting me with letters ever since. The last thing he wanted was the name of the man we referred his nonsense to; you saw my answer to that. But don't you say anything about it, for goodness' sake."

"I should think not, indeed. Did I ever do such a thing? I do hope, though, he won't get to know that it was poor Mr. Dunning."

"Poor Mr. Dunning? I don't know why you call him that; he's a very happy man, is Dunning. Lots of hobbies and a comfortable home, and all his time to himself."

"I only meant I should be sorry for him if this man got hold of his name, and came and bothered him."

"Oh, ah! yes. I dare say he would be poor Mr. Dunning then."

The Secretary and his wife were lunching out, and the friends to whose house they were bound were Warwickshire people. So Mrs. Secretary had already settled it in her own mind that she would question them judiciously about Mr. Karswell. But she was saved the trouble of leading up to the subject, for the hostess said to the host, before many minutes had passed, "I saw the Abbot of Lufford this morning." The host whistled. "*Did* you? What in the world brings him up to town?" "Goodness knows; he was coming out of the British Museum gate as I drove past." It was not unnatural that Mrs. Secretary should inquire whether this was a real abbot who was being spoken of. "Oh no, my dear: only a neighbor of ours in the country who bought Lufford Abbey a few years ago. His real name is Karswell." "Is he a friend of yours?" asked Mr. Secretary, with a private wink to his wife. The question let loose a torrent of declamation. There was really nothing to be said for Mr. Karswell. Nobody knew what he did with himself: his servants were a horrible set of people; he had invented a new religion for himself, and practiced no one could tell what appalling rites; he was very easily offended, and never forgave anybody; he had a dreadful face (so the lady insisted, her husband somewhat demurring); he never did a kind action, and whatever influence he did exert was mischievous. "Do the poor man justice, dear," the husband interrupted. "You forget the treat he gave the school children." "Forget it, indeed! But I'm glad you mentioned it, because it gives an idea of the man. Now, Florence, listen to this. The first winter he was at Lufford this delightful neighbor of ours wrote to the clergyman of his parish (he's not ours, but we know him very well) and offered to show the school children some magic-lantern slides. He said he had some new kinds, which he thought would interest them. Well, the clergyman was rather surprised, because Mr. Karswell had shown himself inclined to be unpleasant to the children—complaining of their trespassing, or something of the sort; but of course he accepted, and the evening was fixed, and our friend went himself to see that everything went right. He said he never had been so thankful for anything as that his own children were all prevented from being there: they were at a children's party at our house, as a matter of fact. Because this Mr. Karswell had evidently set out with the intention of frightening these poor village children out of their wits, and I do believe, if he had been allowed to go on, he would actually have done so. He began with some comparatively mild things. Red Riding Hood was one, and even then, Mr. Farrer said, the wolf was so dreadful that several of the smaller children had to be taken out: and he said Mr. Karswell began the story by producing a noise like a wolf howling in the distance, which was the most gruesome thing he had ever heard. All the slides he showed, Mr. Farrer said, were most clever; they were absolutely realistic, and where he had got them or how he worked them he could not imagine. Well, the show went on, and the stories kept on becoming a little more terrifying each time, and the children were mesmerized into complete silence. At last he produced a series which represented a little boy passing through his own park—Lufford, I mean—in the evening. Every child in the room could recognize the place from the pictures. And this poor boy was followed, and at last pursued and over-taken, and either torn in pieces or somehow made away with, by a horrible hopping creature in white, which you saw first dodging about among the trees, and gradually it appeared more and more plainly. Mr. Farrer said it gave him one of the worst nightmares he ever remembered, and what it must have meant to the children doesn't bear thinking of. Of course this was too much, and he spoke very sharply indeed to Mr. Kars-well, and said it couldn't go on. All *he* said was: 'Oh, you think it's time to bring our little show to an end and send them home to their beds? *Very* well!' And then, if you please, he switched on another slide, which showed a great mass of snakes, centipedes, and disgusting creatures with wings, and somehow or other he made it seem as if they were climbing out of the picture and getting in amongst the audience; and this was accompanied by a sort of dry rustling noise which sent the children nearly mad, and of course they stampeded. A good many of them were rather hurt in getting out of the room, and I don't suppose one of them closed an eye that night. There was the most dreadful trouble in the village afterwards. Of course the mothers threw a good part of the blame on poor Mr. Farrer, and, if they could have got past the gates, I believe the fathers would have broken every window in the Abbey. Well, now, that's Mr. Karswell: that's the Abbot of Lufford, my dear, and you can imagine how we covet *his* society."

"Yes, I think he has all the possibilities of a distinguished criminal, has Karswell," said the host. "I should be sorry for anyone who got into his bad books."

"Is he the man, or am I mixing him up with someone else?" asked the Secretary (who for some minutes had been wearing the frown of the man who is trying to recollect something). "Is he the man who brought out a *History of Witchcraft* some time back—ten years or more?"

"That's the man; do you remember the reviews of it?"

"Certainly I do; and what's equally to the point, I knew the author of the most incisive of the lot. So did you: you must remember John Harrington; he was at John's in our time."

"Oh, very well indeed, though I don't think I saw or heard anything of him between the time I went down and the day I read the account of the inquest on him."

"Inquest?" said one of the ladies. "What has happened to him?"

"Why, what happened was that he fell out of a tree and broke his neck. But the puzzle was, what could have induced him to get up there. It was a mysterious business, I must say. Here was this man—not an athletic fellow, was he? and with no eccentric twist about him that was ever noticed—walking home along a country road late in the evening—no tramps about—well known and liked in the place—and he suddenly begins to run like mad, loses his hat and stick, and finally shins up a tree—quite a difficult tree—growing in the hedgerow: a dead branch gives way, and he comes down with it and breaks his neck, and there he's found next morning with the most dreadful face of fear on him that could be imagined. It was pretty evident, of course, that he had been chased by something, and people talked of savage dogs, and beasts escaped out of menageries; but there was nothing to be made of that. That was in '89, and I believe his brother Henry (whom I remember as well at Cambridge, but *you* probably don't) has been trying to get on the track of an explanation ever since. He, of course, insists there was malice in it, but I don't know. It's difficult to see how it could have come in."

After a time the talk reverted to the *History of Witchcraft*. "Did you ever look into it?" asked the host.

"Yes, I did," said the Secretary. "I went so far as to read it."

"Was it as bad as it was made out to be?"

"Oh, in point of style and form, quite hopeless. It deserved all the pulverizing it got. But, besides that, it was an evil book. The man believed every word of what he was saying, and I'm very much mistaken if he hadn't tried the greater part of his receipts."

"Well, I only remember Harrington's review of it, and I must say if I'd been the author it would have quenched my literary ambition for good. I should never have held up my head again."

"It hasn't had that effect in the present case. But come, it's half past three; I must be off."

On the way home the Secretary's wife said, "I do hope that horrible man won't find out that Mr. Dunning had anything to do with the rejection of his paper." "I don't think there's much chance of that," said the Secretary. "Dunning won't mention it himself, for these matters are confidential, and none of us will for the same reason. Karswell won't know his name, for Dunning hasn't published anything on the same subject yet. The only danger is that Karswell might find out, if he was to ask the British Museum people who was in the habit of consulting alchemical manuscripts: I can't very well tell them not to mention Dunning, can I? It would set them talking at once. Let's hope it won't occur to him."

However, Mr. Karswell was an astute man.

This much is in the way of prologue. On an evening rather later in the same week, Mr. Edward Dunning was returning from the British Museum, where he had been engaged in research, to the comfortable house in a suburb where he lived alone, tended by two excellent women who had been long with him. There is nothing to be added by way of description of him to what we have heard already. Let us follow him as he takes his sober course homewards.

A train took him to within a mile or two of his house, and an electric tram a stage farther. The line ended at a point some three hundred yards from his front door. He had had enough of reading when he got into the car, and indeed the light was not such as to allow him to do more than study the advertisements on the panes of glass that faced him as he sat. As was not unnatural, the advertisements in this particular line of cars were objects of his frequent contemplation, and, with the possible exception of the brilliant and convincing dialogue between Mr. Lamplough and an eminent K. C. on the subject of Pyretic Saline, none of them afforded much scope to his imagination. I am wrong: there was one at the corner of the car farthest from him which did not seem familiar. It was in blue letters on a yellow ground, and all that he could read of it was a name—John Harrington—and something like a date. It could be of no interest to him to know more; but for all that, as the car emptied, he was just curious enough to move along the seat until he could read it well. He felt to a slight extent repaid for his trouble; the advertisement was *not* of the usual type. It ran thus: "In memory of John Harrington, F.S.A., of The Laurels, Ashbrooke. Died Sept. 18th, 1889. Three months were allowed."

The car stopped. Mr. Dunning, still contemplating the blue letters on the yellow ground, had to be stimulated to rise by a word from the conductor. "I beg your pardon," he said, "I was looking at that advertisement; it's a very odd one, isn't it?" The conductor read it slowly. "Well, my word," he said, "I never see that one before. Well, that is a cure, ain't it? Someone bin up to their jokes 'ere, I should think." He got out a duster and applied it, not without saliva, to the pane and then to the outside. "No," he said, returning, "that ain't no transfer; seems to me as if it was reg'lar *in* the glass, what I mean in the substance, as you may say. Don't you think so, sir?" Mr. Dunning examined it and rubbed it with his glove, and agreed. "Who looks after these advertisements, and gives leave for them to be put up? I wish you would inquire. I will just take a note of the words." At this moment there came a call from the driver: "Look alive, George, time's up." "All right, all right; there's something else what's up at this end. You come and look at this 'ere glass." "What's gorn with the glass?" said the driver, approaching. "Well, and oo's 'Arrington? What's it all about?" "I was just asking who was responsible for putting the advertisements up in your cars, and saying it would be as well to make some inquiry about this one." "Well, sir, that's all done at the company's orfice, that work is: it's our Mr. Timms, I believe, looks into that. When we put up tonight I'll leave word, and per'aps I'll be able to tell you tomorrer if you 'appen to be coming this way."

This was all that passed that evening. Mr. Dunning did just go to the trouble of looking up Ashbrooke, and found that it was in Warwickshire.

Next day he went to town again. The car (it was the same car) was too full in the morning to allow of his getting a word with the conductor: he could only be sure that the curious advertisement had been made away with. The close of the day brought a further element of mystery into the transaction. He had missed the tram, or else preferred walking home, but at a rather late hour, while he was at work in his study, one of the maids came to say that two men from the tramways were very anxious to speak to him. This was a reminder of the advertisement, which he had, he says, nearly forgotten. He had the men in—they were the conductor and driver of the car— and when the matter of refreshment had been attended to, asked what Mr. Timms had had to say about the advertisement. "Well, sir, that's what we took the liberty to step round about," said the conductor. "Mr. Timms 'e give William 'ere the rough side of his tongue about that: 'cordin' to 'im there warn't no advertisement of that description sent in, nor ordered, nor paid for, nor put up, nor nothink, let alone not bein' there, and we was playing the fool takin' up his time. 'Well,' I says, 'if that's the case, all I ask of you, Mr. Timms,' I says, 'is to take and look at it for yourself,' I says. 'Of course if it ain't there,' I says, 'you may take and call me what you like.' 'Right,' he says, 'I will': and we went straight off. Now, I leave it to you, sir, if that ad, as we term 'em, with 'Arrington on it warn't as plain as ever you see anything—blue letters on yeller glass, and as I says at the time, and you borne me out, reg'lar *in* the glass, because, if you remember, you recollect of me swabbing it with my duster." "To be sure I do, quite clearly—well?" "You may say well, I don't think. Mr. Timms he gets in that car with a light—no, he told William to 'old the light outside. 'Now,' he says, 'where's your precious ad what we've 'eard so much about?' 'Ere it is,' I says, 'Mr. Timms,' and I laid my 'and on it." The conductor paused.

"Well," said Mr. Dunning, "it was gone, I suppose. Broken?"

"Broke!—not it. There warn't, if you'll believe me, no more trace of them letters—blue letters they was—on that piece o' glass, than—well, it's no good *me* talkin'. *I* never see such a thing. I leave it to William here if—but there, as I says, where's the benefit in me going on about it?"

"And what did Mr. Timms say?"

"Why 'e did what I give 'im leave to—called us pretty much anythink he liked, and I don't know as I blame him so much neither. But what we thought, William and me did, was as we seen you take down a bit of a note about that—well, that letterin'——"

"I certainly did that, and I have it now. Did you wish me to speak to Mr. Timms myself, and show it to him? Was that what you came in about?"

"There, didn't I say as much?" said William. "Deal with a gent if you can get on the track of one, that's my word. Now perhaps, George, you'll allow as I ain't took you very far wrong tonight."

"Very well, William, very well; no need for you to go on as if you'd 'ad to frog's-march me 'ere. I come quiet, didn't I? All the same for that, we 'adn't ought to take up your time this way, sir; but if it so 'appened you could find time to step round to the company's office in the morning and tell Mr. Timms what you seen for yourself, we should lay under a very 'igh obligation to you for the trouble. You see it ain't bein' called—well, one thing and another, as we mind, but if they got it into their 'ead at the orfice as we seen things as warn't there, why, one thing leads to another, and where we should be a twelvemunce 'ence—well, you can understand what I mean."

Amid further elucidations of the proposition, George, conducted by William, left the room.

The incredulity of Mr. Timms (who had a nodding acquaintance with Mr. Dunning) was greatly modified on the following day by what the latter could tell and show him; and any bad mark that might have been attached to the names of William and George was not suffered to remain on the company's books; but explanation there was none.

Mr. Dunning's interest in the matter was kept alive by an incident of the following afternoon. He was walking from his club to the train, and he noticed some way ahead a man with a handful of leaflets such as are distributed to passers-by by agents of enterprising firms. This agent had not chosen a very crowded street for his operations: in fact, Mr. Dunning did not see him get rid of a single leaflet before he himself reached the spot. One was thrust into his hand as he passed: the hand that gave it touched his, and he experienced a sort of little shock as it did so. It seemed unnaturally rough and hot. He looked in passing at the giver, but the impression he got was so unclear that, however much he tried to reckon it up subsequently, nothing would come. He was walking quickly, and as he went on glanced at the paper. It was a blue one. The name of Harrington in large capitals caught his eye. He stopped, startled, and felt for his glasses. The next instant the leaflet was twitched out of his hand by a man who hurried past, and was irrecoverably gone. He ran back a few paces, but where was the passer-by? And where the distributor?

It was in a somewhat pensive frame of mind that Mr. Dunning passed on the following day into the Select Manuscript Room of the British Museum, and filled up tickets for Harley 3586, and some other volumes. After a few minutes they were brought to him, and he was settling the one he wanted first upon the desk, when he thought he heard his own name whispered behind him. He turned round hastily, and in doing so, brushed his little portfolio of loose papers on to the floor. He saw no one he recognized except one of the staff in charge of the room, who nodded to him, and he proceeded to pick up his papers. He thought he had them all, and was turning to begin work, when a stout gentleman at the table behind him, who was just rising to leave, and had collected his own belongings, touched him on the shoulder, saying, "May I give you this? I think it should be yours," and handed him a missing quire. "It is mine, thank you," said Mr. Dunning. In another moment the man had left the room. Upon finishing his work for the afternoon, Mr. Dunning had some conversation with the assistant in charge, and took occasion to ask who the stout gentleman was. "Oh, he's a man named Karswell," said the assistant; "he was asking me a week ago who were the great authorities on alchemy, and of course I told him you were the only one in the country. I'll see if I can't catch him: he'd like to meet you, I'm sure."

"For heaven's sake don't dream of it!" said Mr. Dunning, "I'm particularly anxious to avoid him."

"Oh! very well," said the assistant, "he doesn't come here often: I dare say you won't meet him."

More than once on the way home that day Mr. Dunning confessed to himself that he did not look forward with his usual cheerfulness to a solitary evening. It seemed to him that something ill-defined and impalpable had stepped in between him and his fellow men—had taken him in charge, as it were. He wanted to sit close up to his neighbors in the train and in the tram, but as luck would have it both train and car were markedly empty. The conductor George was thoughtful, and appeared to be absorbed in calculations as to the number of passengers. On arriving at his house he found Dr. Watson, his medical man, on his doorstep. "I've had to upset your household arrangements, I'm sorry to say, Dunning. Both your servants *hors de combat*. In fact, I've had to send them to the nursing home."

"Good heavens! What's the matter?"

"It's something like ptomaine poisoning, I should think: you've not suffered yourself, I can see, or you wouldn't be walking about. I think they'll pull through all right."

"Dear, dear! Have you any idea what brought it on?"

"Well, they tell me they bought some shellfish from a hawker at their dinnertime. It's odd. I've made inquiries, but I can't find that any hawker has been to other houses in the street. I couldn't send word to you; they won't be back for a bit yet. You come and dine with me tonight, anyhow, and we can make arrangements for going on. Eight o'clock. Don't be too anxious."

The solitary evening was thus obviated; at the expense of some distress and inconvenience, it is true. Mr. Dunning spent the time pleasantly enough with the doctor (a rather recent settler), and returned to his lonely home at about eleven thirty. The night he passed is not one on which he looks back with any satisfaction. He was in bed and the light was out. He was wondering if the charwoman would come early enough to get him hot water next morning, when he heard the unmistakable sound of his study door opening. No step followed it on the passage floor, but the sound must mean mischief, for he knew that he had shut the door that evening after putting his papers away in his desk. It was rather shame than courage that induced him to slip out into the passage and lean over the banister in his nightgown, listening. No light was visible; no further sound came: only a gust of warm, or even hot air played for an instant round his shins. He went back and decided to lock himself into his room. There was more unpleasantness, however. Either an economical suburban company had decided that their light would not be required in the small hours, and had stopped working, or else something was wrong with the meter; the effect was in any case that the electric light was off. The obvious course was to find a match, and also to consult his watch: he might as well know how many hours of discomfort awaited him. So he put his hand into the well-known nook under the pillow: only, it did not get so far. What he touched was, according to his account, a mouth, with teeth, and with hair about it, and, he declares, not the mouth of a human being. I do not think it is any use to guess what he said or did; but he was in a spare room with the door locked and his ear to it before he was clearly conscious again. And there he spent the rest of a most miserable night, looking every moment for some fumbling at the door: but nothing came.

The venturing back to his own room in the morning was attended with many listenings and quiverings. The door stood open, fortunately, and the blinds were up (the servants had been out of the house before the hour of drawing them down); there was, to be short, no trace of an inhabitant. The watch, too, was in its usual place; nothing was disturbed, only the wardrobe door had swung open, in accordance with its confirmed habit. A ring at the back door now announced the charwoman, who had been ordered the night before, and nerved Mr. Dunning, after letting her in, to continue his search in other parts of the house. It was equally fruitless.

The day thus begun went on dismally enough. He dared not go to the museum: in spite of what the assistant had said, Karswell might turn up there, and Dunning felt he could not cope with a probably hostile stranger. His own house was odious; he hated sponging on the doctor. He spent some little time in a call at the nursing home, where he was slightly cheered by a good report of his housekeeper and maid. Towards lunch time he betook himself to his club, again experiencing a gleam of satisfaction at seeing the Secretary of the Association. At luncheon Dunning told his friend the more material of his woes, but could not bring himself to speak of those that weighed most heavily on his spirits. "My poor dear man," said the Secretary, "what an upset! Look here: we're alone at home, absolutely. You must put up with us. Yes! no excuse: send your things in this afternoon." Dunning was unable to stand out: he was, in truth, becoming acutely anxious, as the hours went on, as to what that night might have waiting for him. He was almost happy as he hurried home to pack up.

His friends, when they had time to take stock of him, were rather shocked at his lorn appearance, and did their best to keep him up to the mark. Not altogether without success: but, when the two men were smoking alone later, Dunning became dull again. Suddenly he said, "Gayton, I believe that alchemist man knows it was I who got his paper rejected." Gayton whistled. "What makes you think that?" he said. Dunning told of his conversation with the museum assistant, and Gayton could only agree that the guess seemed likely to be correct. "Not that I care much," Dunning went on, "only it might be a nuisance if we were to meet. He's a bad-tempered party, I imagine." Conversation dropped again; Gayton became more and more strongly impressed with the desolateness that came over Dunning's face and bearing, and finally —though with a considerable effort—he asked him point-blank whether something serious was not bothering him. Dunning gave an exclamation of relief. "I was perishing to get it off my mind," he said. "Do you know anything about a man named John Harrington?" Gayton was thoroughly startled, and at the moment could only ask why. Then the complete story of Dunning's experiences came out—what had happened in the tramcar, in his own house, and in the street, the troubling of

spirit that had crept over him, and still held him; and he
ended with the question he had begun with. Gayton was at a
loss how to answer him. To tell the story of Harrington's end
would perhaps be right; only, Dunning was in a nervous state,
the story was a grim one, and he could not help asking himself whether there were not a connecting link between these
two cases, in the person of Karswell. It was a difficult concession for a scientific man, but it could be eased by the phrase
"hypnotic suggestion." In the end he decided that his answer
tonight should be guarded; he would talk the situation over
with his wife. So he said that he had known Harrington at
Cambridge, and believed he had died suddenly in 1889,
adding a few details about the man and his published work.
He did talk over the matter with Mrs. Gayton, and, as he had
anticipated, she leapt at once to the conclusion which had
been hovering before him. It was she who reminded him of
the surviving brother, Henry Harrington, and she also who
suggested that he might be got hold of by means of their hosts
of the day before. "He might be a hopeless crank," objected
Gayton. "That could be ascertained from the Bennetts, who
knew him," Mrs. Gayton retorted; and she undertook to see
the Bennetts the very next day.

It is not necessary to tell in further detail the steps by
which Henry Harrington and Dunning were brought together.

The next scene that does require to be narrated is a conversation that took place between the two. Dunning had told Harrington of the strange ways in which the dead man's name
had been brought before him, and had said something, besides, of his own subsequent experiences. Then he had asked
if Harrington was disposed, in return, to recall any of the circumstances connected with his brother's death. Harrington's
surprise at what he heard can be imagined: but his reply was
readily given.

"John," he said, "was in a very odd state, undeniably, from time to time, during some weeks before, though not immediately before, the catastrophe. There were several things; the principal notion he had was that he thought he was being followed. No doubt he was an impressionable man, but he never had had such fancies as this before. I cannot get it out of my mind that there was ill-will at work, and what you tell me about yourself reminds me very much of my brother. Can you think of any possible connecting link?"

"There is just one that has been taking shape vaguely in my mind. I've been told that your brother reviewed a book very severely not long before he died, and just lately I have happened to cross the path of the man who wrote that book in a way he would resent."

"Don't tell me the man was called Karswell."

"Why not? that is exactly his name."

Henry Harrington leant back. "That is final to my mind. Now I must explain further. From something he said, I feel sure that my brother John was beginning to believe—very much against his will—that Karswell was at the bottom of his trouble. I want to tell you what seems to me to have a bearing on the situation. My brother was a great musician, and used to run up to concerts in town. He came back, three months before he died, from one of these, and gave me his program to look at—an analytical program: he always kept them. 'I nearly missed this one,' he said. 'I suppose I must have dropped it: anyhow, I was looking for it under my seat and in my pockets and so on, and my neighbor offered me his: said "might he give it me, he had no further use for it," and he went away just afterwards. I don't know who he was—a stout, clean-shaven man. I should have been sorry to miss it; of course I could have bought another, but this cost me nothing.' At another time he told me that he had been very uncomfortable both on the way to his hotel and during the night. I piece things together now in thinking it over. Then, not very long after, he was going over these programs, putting them in order to have them bound up, and in this particular one (which by the way I had hardly glanced at), he found quite near the beginning a strip of paper with some very odd writing on it in red and black—most carefully done—it looked to me more like Runic letters than anything else. 'Why,' he said, 'this must belong to my fat neighbor. It looks as if it might be worth returning to him; it may be a copy of something; evidently someone has taken trouble over it. How can I find his address?' We talked it over for a little and agreed that it wasn't worth advertising about, and that my brother had better look out for the man at the next concert, to which he was going very soon. The paper was lying on the book and we were both by the fire; it was a cold, windy summer evening. I suppose the door blew open, though I didn't notice it: at any rate a gust—a warm gust it was—came quite suddenly between us, took the paper, and blew it straight into the fire: it was light, thin paper, and flared and went up the chimney in a single ash. 'Well,' I said, 'you can't give it back now.' He said nothing for a minute: then rather crossly, 'No, I can't; but why you should keep on saying so I don't know.' I remarked that I didn't say it more than once. 'Not more than four times, you mean,' was all he said. I remember all that very clearly, without any good reasons; and now to come to the point. I don't know if you looked at that book of Karswell's which my unfortunate brother reviewed. It's not likely that you should: but I did, both before his death and after it. The first time we made game of it together. It was written in no style at all—split infinitives, and every sort of thing that makes an Oxford gorge rise. Then there was nothing that the man didn't swallow: mixing up classical myths, and stories out of the *Golden Legend* with reports of savage customs of today—all very proper, no doubt, if you know how to use them, but he didn't: he seemed to put the *Golden Legend* and the *Golden Bough* exactly on a par, and to believe both: a pitiable exhibition, in short. Well, after the misfortune, I looked over the book again. It was no better than before, but the impression which it left this time on my mind was different. I suspected—as I told you—that Karswell had borne ill-will to my brother, even that he was in some way responsible for what had happened; and now his book seemed to me to be a very sinister performance indeed. One chapter in particular struck me, in which he spoke of 'casting the Runes' on people, either for the purpose of gaining their affection or of getting them out of the way—perhaps more especially the latter: he spoke of all this in a way that really seemed to me to imply actual knowledge. I've not time to go into details, but the upshot is that I am pretty sure from information received that the civil man at the concert was Karswell: I suspect—I more than suspect—that the paper was of importance: and I do believe that if my brother had been able to give it back, he might have been alive now. Therefore, it occurs to me to ask you whether you have anything to put beside what I have told you."

By way of answer, Dunning had the episode in the Manuscript Room at the British Museum to relate. "Then he did actually hand you some papers; have you examined them? No? Because we must, if you'll allow it, look at them at once, and very carefully."

They went to the still empty house—empty, for the two servants were not yet able to return to work. Dunning's portfolio of papers was gathering dust on the writing table. In it were the quires of small-sized scribbling paper which he used for his transcripts: and from one of these, as he took it up, there slipped and fluttered out into the room with uncanny quickness, a strip of thin light paper. The window was open, but Harrington slammed it to, just in time to intercept the paper, which he caught. "I thought so," he said; "it might be the identical thing that was given to my brother. You'll have to look out, Dunning; this may mean something quite serious for you."

A long consultation took place. The paper was narrowly examined. As Harrington had said, the characters on it were more like Runes than anything else, but not decipherable by either man, and both hesitated to copy them, for fear, as they confessed, of perpetuating whatever evil purpose they might conceal. So it has remained impossible (if I may anticipate a little) to ascertain what was conveyed in this curious message or commission. Both Dunning and Harrington are firmly convinced that it had the effect of bringing its possessors into very undesirable company. That it must be returned to the source whence it came they were agreed, and further, that the only safe and certain way was that of personal service; and here contrivance would be necessary, for Dunning was known by sight to Karswell. He must, for one thing, alter his appearance by shaving his beard. But then might not the blow fall first? Harrington thought they could time it. He knew the date of the concert at which the "black spot" had been put on his brother: it was June eighteenth. The death had followed on September eighteenth. Dunning reminded him that three months had been mentioned on the inscription on the car window. "Perhaps," he added, with a cheerless laugh, "mine may be a bill at three months too. I believe I can fix it by my diary. Yes, April twenty-third was the day at the Museum; that brings us to July twenty-third. Now, you know, it becomes extremely important to me to know anything you will tell me about the progress of your brother's trouble, if it is possible for you to speak of it." "Of course. Well, the sense of being watched whenever he was alone was the most distressing thing to him. After a time I took to sleeping in his room, and he was the better for that: still, he talked a great deal in his sleep. What about? Is it wise to dwell on that, at least before things are straightened out? I think not, but I can tell you this: two things came for him by post during those weeks, both with a London postmark, and addressed in a commercial hand. One was a woodcut of Bewick's, roughly torn out of the page: one which shows a moonlit road and a man walking along it, followed by an awful demon creature. Under it were written the lines out of *The Ancient Mariner* (which I suppose the cut illustrates) about one who, having once looked round—

> *walks on,*
> *And turns no more his head,*
> *Because he knows a frightful fiend*
> *Doth close behind him tread.*

The other was a calendar, such as tradesmen often send. My brother paid no attention to this, but I looked at it after his death, and found that everything after September eighteenth had been torn out. You may be surprised at his having gone out alone the evening he was killed, but the fact is that during the last ten days or so of his life he had been quite free from the sense of being followed or watched."

The end of the consultation was this. Harrington, who knew a neighbor of Karswell's, thought he saw a way of keeping a watch on his movements. It would be Dunning's part to be in readiness to try to cross Karswell's path at any moment, to keep the paper safe and in a place of ready access.

They parted. The next weeks were no doubt a severe strain upon Dunning's nerves: the intangible barrier which had seemed to rise about him on the day when he received the paper gradually developed into a brooding blackness that cut him off from the means of escape to which one might have thought he might resort. No one was at hand who was likely to suggest them to him, and he seemed robbed of all initiative. He waited with inexpressible anxiety as May, June, and early July passed on, for a mandate from Harrington. But all this time Karswell remained immovable at Lufford.

At last, in less than a week before the date he had come to look upon as the end of his earthly activities, came a telegram: "Leaves Victoria by boat train Thursday night. Do not miss. I come to you tonight. Harrington."

He arrived accordingly, and they concocted plans. The train left Victoria at nine and its last stop before Dover was Croydon West. Harrington would mark down Karswell at Victoria, and look out for Dunning at Croydon, calling to him if need were by a name agreed upon. Dunning, disguised as far as might be, was to have no label or initials on any hand luggage, and must at all costs have the paper with him.

Dunning's suspense as he waited on the Croydon platform I need not attempt to describe. His sense of danger during the last days had only been sharpened by the fact that the cloud about him had perceptibly been lighter; but relief was an ominous symptom, and, if Karswell eluded him now, hope was gone: and there were so many chances of that. The rumor of the journey might be itself a device. The twenty minutes in which he paced the platform and persecuted every porter with inquiries as to the boat train were as bitter as any he had spent. Still, the train came, and Harrington was at the window. It was important, of course, that there should be no recognition: so Dunning got in at the farther end of the corridor carriage, and only gradually made his way to the compartment where Harrington and Karswell were. He was pleased, on the whole, to see that the train was far from full.

Karswell was on the alert, but gave no sign of recognition. Dunning took the seat not immediately facing him, and attempted, vainly at first, then with increasing command of his faculties, to reckon the possibilities of making the desired transfer. Opposite to Karswell, and next to Dunning, was a heap of Karswell's coats on the seat. It would be of no use to slip the paper into these—he would not be safe, or would not feel so, unless in some way it could be proffered by him and accepted by the other. There was a handbag, open, and with papers in it. Could he manage to conceal this (so that perhaps Karswell might leave the carriage without it), and then find and give it to him? This was the plan that suggested itself. If he could only have counseled with Harrington! But that could not be. The minutes went on. More than once Karswell rose and went out into the corridor. The second time Dunning was on the point of attempting to make the bag fall off the seat, but he caught Harrington's eye, and read in it a warning. Karswell, from the corridor, was watching: probably to see if the two men recognized each other. He returned, but was evidently restless: and, when he rose the third time, hope dawned, for something did slip off his seat and fall with hardly a sound to the floor. Karswell went out once more, and passed out of range of the corridor window. Dunning picked up what had fallen, and saw that the key was in his hands in the form of one of Cook's ticket cases, with tickets in it. These cases have a pocket in the cover, and within very few seconds the paper of which we have heard was in the pocket of this one. To make the operation more secure, Harrington stood in the doorway of the compartment and fiddled with the blind. It was done, and done at the right time, for the train was now slowing down towards Dover.

In a moment more Karswell re-entered the compartment. As he did so, Dunning, managing, he knew not how, to suppress the tremble in his voice, handed him the ticket case, saying, "May I give you this, sir? I believe it is yours." After a brief glance at the ticket inside, Karswell uttered the hoped-for response, "Yes, it is; much obliged to you, sir," and he placed it in his breast pocket.

Even in the few moments that remained—moments of tense anxiety, for they knew not to what a premature finding of the paper might lead—both men noticed that the carriage seemed to darken about them and to grow warmer; that Karswell was fidgety and oppressed; that he drew the heap of loose coats near to him and cast it back as if it repelled him; and that he then sat upright and glanced anxiously at both. They, with sickening anxiety, busied themselves in collecting their belongings; but they both thought that Karswell was on the point of speaking when the train stopped at Dover Town. It was natural that in the short space between town and pier they should both go into the corridor.

At the pier they got out, but so empty was the train that they were forced to linger on the platform until Karswell should have passed ahead of them with his porter on the way to the boat, and only then was it safe for them to exchange a pressure of the hand and a word of concentrated congratulation. The effect upon Dunning was to make him almost faint. Harrington made him lean up against the wall, while he himself went forward a few yards within sight of the gangway to the boat, at which Karswell had now arrived. The man at the head of it examined his ticket, and, laden with coats, he passed down into the boat. Suddenly the official called after him, "You sir, beg pardon, did the other gentleman show his ticket?" "What the devil do you mean by the other gentleman?" Karswell's snarling voice called back from the deck. The man bent over and looked at him. "The devil? Well, I don't know, I'm sure," Harrington heard him say to himself, and then aloud, "My mistake, sir; must have been your rugs! Ask your pardon." And then, to a subordinate near him, " 'Ad he got a dog with him, or what? Funny thing: I could 'a' swore 'e wasn't alone. Well, whatever it was, they'll 'ave to see to it aboard. She's off now. Another week and we shall be gettin' the 'oliday customers." In five minutes more there was nothing but the lessening lights of the boat, the long line of the Dover lamps, the night breeze, and the moon.

Long and long the two sat in their room at the "Lord Warden." In spite of the removal of their greatest anxiety, they were oppressed with a doubt, not of the lightest. Had they been justified in sending a man to his death, as they believed they had? Ought they not to warn him, at least? "No," said Harrington; "if he is the murderer I think him, we have done no more than is just. Still, if you think it better—but how and where can you warn him?" "He was booked to Abbeville only," said Dunning. "I saw that. If I wired to the hotels there in Joanne's Guide, 'Examine your ticket case, Dunning,' I should feel happier. This is the twenty-first: he will have a day. But I am afraid he has gone into the dark." So telegrams were left at the hotel office.

It is not clear whether these reached their destination, or whether, if they did, they were understood. All that is known is that, on the afternoon of the twenty-third, an English traveler, examining the front of St. Wulfram's Church at Abbeville, then under extensive repair, was struck on the head and instantly killed by a stone falling from the scaffold erected round the northwestern tower, there being, as was clearly proved, no workman on the scaffold at that moment: and the traveler's papers identified him as Mr. Karswell.

Only one detail shall be added. At Karswell's sale a set of Bewick, sold with all faults, was acquired by Harrington. The page with the woodcut of the traveler and the demon was, as he had expected, mutilated. Also, after a judicious interval, Harrington repeated to Dunning something of what he had heard his brother say in his sleep: but it was not long before Dunning stopped him.

ABOUT THE CONTRIBUTORS

EDWARD GOREY (1925–2000) was born in Chicago. He studied briefly at the Art Institute of Chicago, spent three years in the army, and attended Harvard College, where he majored in French literature and roomed with the poet Frank O'Hara. In 1953 Gorey published *The Unstrung Harp*, the first of his many extraordinary illustrated books, which include *The Curious Sofa*, *The Haunted Tea Cosy*, and *The Epiplectic Bicycle*.

ALGERNON BLACKWOOD (1869–1951) wrote many novels and stories dealing with the supernatural and occult (*The Empty House, John Silence, A Prisoner in Fairyland, Shocks*, etc.) and several books for children, including *Dudley and Gilderoy*.

WILLIAM FRYER HARVEY (1885–1937) published, among other books, three collections of ghost stories: *Midnight House*, *The Beast with Five Fingers* (which is also the name of his best-known story), *Moods and Tenses*, and a children's book, *Caprimulgus*.

CHARLES DICKENS (1812–1870) is probably the most famous of all English novelists. Many of his stories were written for *Household Words* and *All the Year Round*, magazines that he founded and edited.

LESLIE POLES HARTLEY (1895–1972) is the author of four volumes of stories (*Night Fears, The Killing Bottle, The Travelling*

Grave, The White Wand), many of which are concerned with the supernatural.

RICHARD HENRY MALDEN (1879–1951) was dean of Wells Cathedral and the author of a collection of ghost stories, in the manner of M. R. James, entitled *Thirteen Ghosts*.

ROBERT LOUIS STEVENSON (1850–1894), the author of *Treasure Island*, *Kidnapped*, and *The Black Arrow*, also wrote many stories of the fantastic and supernatural, and a macabre novel, *Dr. Jekyll and Mr. Hyde*.

EDITH NESBIT (1858–1924) is now best remembered for her children's books, including *Five Children and It*, but she also wrote novels, poems, and a number of ghost stories.

BRAM STOKER (1847–1912) was the creator of the most famous of all vampires, Dracula, and the author of other novels and stories in a similar vein.

TOM HOOD (1779–1845) was the son of the poet Thomas Hood, and himself wrote humorous verse, stories, and a half-dozen novels.

WILLIAM WYMARK JACOBS (1863–1943) was a short-story writer, most of whose work is humorous and deals with coasting vessels and their crews; however, "The Brown Man's Servant" and several other stories are horror tales like "The Monkey's Paw."

WILKIE COLLINS (1824–1889) wrote two of the earliest and most famous mystery novels, *The Woman in White* and *The Moonstone*, and many stories of the supernatural.

MONTAGUE RHODES JAMES (1862–1936) was a medieval scholar, paleographer, Provost of Eton, and possibly the greatest modern ghost-story writer. His stories first appeared in four volumes: *Ghost Stories of an Antiquary*, *More Ghost Stories*, *A Thin Ghost and Others*, and *A Warning to the Curious*. Later, with a few ad-di-tional stories, they appeared in a collected one-volume edition. He also wrote a book for children, *The Five Jars*.

TITLES IN SERIES

For a complete list of titles, visit www.nyrb.com or write to:
Catalog Requests, NYRB, 435 Hudson Street, New York, NY 10014

J.R. ACKERLEY Hindoo Holiday*
J.R. ACKERLEY My Dog Tulip*
J.R. ACKERLEY My Father and Myself*
J.R. ACKERLEY We Think the World of You*
HENRY ADAMS The Jeffersonian Transformation
RENATA ADLER Pitch Dark*
RENATA ADLER Speedboat*
AESCHYLUS Prometheus Bound; translated by Joel Agee*
CÉLESTE ALBARET Monsieur Proust
DANTE ALIGHIERI The Inferno
DANTE ALIGHIERI The New Life
KINGSLEY AMIS The Alteration*
KINGSLEY AMIS Dear Illusion: Collected Stories*
KINGSLEY AMIS Ending Up*
KINGSLEY AMIS Girl, 20*
KINGSLEY AMIS The Green Man*
KINGSLEY AMIS Lucky Jim*
KINGSLEY AMIS The Old Devils*
KINGSLEY AMIS One Fat Englishman*
KINGSLEY AMIS Take a Girl Like You*
ROBERTO ARLT The Seven Madmen*
WILLIAM ATTAWAY Blood on the Forge
W.H. AUDEN (EDITOR) The Living Thoughts of Kierkegaard
W.H. AUDEN W.H. Auden's Book of Light Verse
ERICH AUERBACH Dante: Poet of the Secular World
DOROTHY BAKER Cassandra at the Wedding*
DOROTHY BAKER Young Man with a Horn*
J.A. BAKER The Peregrine
S. JOSEPHINE BAKER Fighting for Life*
HONORÉ DE BALZAC The Human Comedy: Selected Stories*
HONORÉ DE BALZAC The Unknown Masterpiece *and* Gambara*
SYBILLE BEDFORD A Legacy*
MAX BEERBOHM The Prince of Minor Writers: The Selected Essays of Max Beerbohm
MAX BEERBOHM Seven Men
STEPHEN BENATAR Wish Her Safe at Home*
FRANS G. BENGTSSON The Long Ships*
ALEXANDER BERKMAN Prison Memoirs of an Anarchist
GEORGES BERNANOS Mouchette
MIRON BIAŁOSZEWSKI A Memoir of the Warsaw Uprising*
ADOLFO BIOY CASARES Asleep in the Sun
ADOLFO BIOY CASARES The Invention of Morel
EVE BABITZ Eve's Hollywood*
CAROLINE BLACKWOOD Corrigan*
CAROLINE BLACKWOOD Great Granny Webster*
RONALD BLYTHE Akenfield: Portrait of an English Village*
NICOLAS BOUVIER The Way of the World
EMMANUEL BOVE Henri Duchemin and His Shadows*

* *Also available as an electronic book.*

MALCOLM BRALY On the Yard*

MILLEN BRAND The Outward Room*

SIR THOMAS BROWNE Religio Medici and Urne-Buriall*

JOHN HORNE BURNS The Gallery

ROBERT BURTON The Anatomy of Melancholy

CAMARA LAYE The Radiance of the King

GIROLAMO CARDANO The Book of My Life

DON CARPENTER Hard Rain Falling*

J.L. CARR A Month in the Country*

BLAISE CENDRARS Moravagine

EILEEN CHANG Love in a Fallen City

EILEEN CHANG Naked Earth

JOAN CHASE During the Reign of the Queen of Persia*

UPAMANYU CHATTERJEE English, August: An Indian Story

NIRAD C. CHAUDHURI The Autobiography of an Unknown Indian

ANTON CHEKHOV Peasants and Other Stories

ANTON CHEKHOV The Prank: The Best of Young Chekhov

GABRIEL CHEVALLIER Fear: A Novel of World War I*

RICHARD COBB Paris and Elsewhere

COLETTE The Pure and the Impure

JOHN COLLIER Fancies and Goodnights

CARLO COLLODI The Adventures of Pinocchio*

IVY COMPTON-BURNETT A House and Its Head

IVY COMPTON-BURNETT Manservant and Maidservant

BARBARA COMYNS The Vet's Daughter

BARBARA COMYNS Our Spoons Came from Woolworths*

EVAN S. CONNELL The Diary of a Rapist

ALBERT COSSERY The Jokers*

ALBERT COSSERY Proud Beggars*

HAROLD CRUSE The Crisis of the Negro Intellectual

ASTOLPHE DE CUSTINE Letters from Russia*

LORENZO DA PONTE Memoirs

ELIZABETH DAVID A Book of Mediterranean Food

ELIZABETH DAVID Summer Cooking

L.J. DAVIS A Meaningful Life*

AGNES DE MILLE Dance to the Piper

VIVANT DENON No Tomorrow/Point de lendemain

MARIA DERMOÛT The Ten Thousand Things

DER NISTER The Family Mashber

TIBOR DÉRY Niki: The Story of a Dog

ARTHUR CONAN DOYLE The Exploits and Adventures of Brigadier Gerard

CHARLES DUFF A Handbook on Hanging

BRUCE DUFFY The World As I Found It*

DAPHNE DU MAURIER Don't Look Now: Stories

ELAINE DUNDY The Dud Avocado*

ELAINE DUNDY The Old Man and Me*

G.B. EDWARDS The Book of Ebenezer Le Page

JOHN EHLE The Land Breakers*

MARCELLUS EMANTS A Posthumous Confession

EURIPIDES Grief Lessons: Four Plays; translated by Anne Carson

J.G. FARRELL Troubles*

J.G. FARRELL The Siege of Krishnapur*

J.G. FARRELL The Singapore Grip*

ELIZA FAY Original Letters from India

KENNETH FEARING The Big Clock

KENNETH FEARING Clark Gifford's Body

FÉLIX FÉNÉON Novels in Three Lines*

M.I. FINLEY The World of Odysseus

THOMAS FLANAGAN The Year of the French*

SANFORD FRIEDMAN Conversations with Beethoven*

SANFORD FRIEDMAN Totempole*

MASANOBU FUKUOKA The One-Straw Revolution*

MARC FUMAROLI When the World Spoke French

CARLO EMILIO GADDA That Awful Mess on the Via Merulana

BENITO PÉREZ GÁLDOS Tristana*

MAVIS GALLANT The Cost of Living: Early and Uncollected Stories*

MAVIS GALLANT Paris Stories*

MAVIS GALLANT Varieties of Exile*

GABRIEL GARCÍA MÁRQUEZ Clandestine in Chile: The Adventures of Miguel Littín

LEONARD GARDNER Fat City*

ALAN GARNER Red Shift*

WILLIAM H. GASS In the Heart of the Heart of the Country: And Other Stories*

WILLIAM H. GASS On Being Blue: A Philosophical Inquiry*

THÉOPHILE GAUTIER My Fantoms

JEAN GENET Prisoner of Love

ÉLISABETH GILLE The Mirador: Dreamed Memories of Irène Némirovsky by Her Daughter*

JOHN GLASSCO Memoirs of Montparnasse*

P.V. GLOB The Bog People: Iron-Age Man Preserved

NIKOLAI GOGOL Dead Souls*

EDMOND AND JULES DE GONCOURT Pages from the Goncourt Journals

PAUL GOODMAN Growing Up Absurd: Problems of Youth in the Organized Society*

EDWARD GOREY (EDITOR) The Haunted Looking Glass

JEREMIAS GOTTHELF The Black Spider*

A.C. GRAHAM Poems of the Late T'ang

WILLIAM LINDSAY GRESHAM Nightmare Alley*

EMMETT GROGAN Ringolevio: A Life Played for Keeps

VASILY GROSSMAN An Armenian Sketchbook*

VASILY GROSSMAN Everything Flows*

VASILY GROSSMAN Life and Fate*

VASILY GROSSMAN The Road*

OAKLEY HALL Warlock

PATRICK HAMILTON The Slaves of Solitude

PATRICK HAMILTON Twenty Thousand Streets Under the Sky

PETER HANDKE Short Letter, Long Farewell

PETER HANDKE Slow Homecoming

ELIZABETH HARDWICK The New York Stories of Elizabeth Hardwick*

ELIZABETH HARDWICK Seduction and Betrayal*

ELIZABETH HARDWICK Sleepless Nights*

L.P. HARTLEY Eustace and Hilda: A Trilogy*

L.P. HARTLEY The Go-Between*

NATHANIEL HAWTHORNE Twenty Days with Julian & Little Bunny by Papa

ALFRED HAYES In Love*

ALFRED HAYES My Face for the World to See*

PAUL HAZARD The Crisis of the European Mind: 1680–1715*

GILBERT HIGHET Poets in a Landscape
RUSSELL HOBAN Turtle Diary*
JANET HOBHOUSE The Furies
HUGO VON HOFMANNSTHAL The Lord Chandos Letter*
JAMES HOGG The Private Memoirs and Confessions of a Justified Sinner
RICHARD HOLMES Shelley: The Pursuit*
ALISTAIR HORNE A Savage War of Peace: Algeria 1954–1962*
GEOFFREY HOUSEHOLD Rogue Male*
WILLIAM DEAN HOWELLS Indian Summer
BOHUMIL HRABAL Dancing Lessons for the Advanced in Age*
BOHUMIL HRABAL The Little Town Where Time Stood Still*
DOROTHY B. HUGHES The Expendable Man*
RICHARD HUGHES A High Wind in Jamaica*
RICHARD HUGHES In Hazard*
RICHARD HUGHES The Fox in the Attic (The Human Predicament, Vol. 1)*
RICHARD HUGHES The Wooden Shepherdess (The Human Predicament, Vol. 2)*
INTIZAR HUSAIN Basti*
MAUDE HUTCHINS Victorine
YASUSHI INOUE Tun-huang*
HENRY JAMES The Ivory Tower
HENRY JAMES The New York Stories of Henry James*
HENRY JAMES The Other House
HENRY JAMES The Outcry
TOVE JANSSON Fair Play *
TOVE JANSSON The Summer Book*
TOVE JANSSON The True Deceiver*
TOVE JANSSON The Woman Who Borrowed Memories: Selected Stories*
RANDALL JARRELL (EDITOR) Randall Jarrell's Book of Stories
DAVID JONES In Parenthesis
JOSEPH JOUBERT The Notebooks of Joseph Joubert; translated by Paul Auster
KABIR Songs of Kabir; translated by Arvind Krishna Mehrotra*
FRIGYES KARINTHY A Journey Round My Skull
ERICH KÄSTNER Going to the Dogs: The Story of a Moralist*
HELEN KELLER The World I Live In
YASHAR KEMAL Memed, My Hawk
YASHAR KEMAL They Burn the Thistles
MURRAY KEMPTON Part of Our Time: Some Ruins and Monuments of the Thirties*
RAYMOND KENNEDY Ride a Cockhorse*
DAVID KIDD Peking Story*
ROBERT KIRK The Secret Commonwealth of Elves, Fauns, and Fairies
ARUN KOLATKAR Jejuri
DEZSŐ KOSZTOLÁNYI Skylark*
TÉTÉ-MICHEL KPOMASSIE An African in Greenland
GYULA KRÚDY The Adventures of Sindbad*
GYULA KRÚDY Sunflower*
SIGIZMUND KRZHIZHANOVSKY Autobiography of a Corpse*
SIGIZMUND KRZHIZHANOVSKY The Letter Killers Club*
SIGIZMUND KRZHIZHANOVSKY Memories of the Future
K'UNG SHANG-JEN The Peach Blossom Fan*
GIUSEPPE TOMASI DI LAMPEDUSA The Professor and the Siren
GERT LEDIG The Stalin Front*
MARGARET LEECH Reveille in Washington: 1860–1865*

PATRICK LEIGH FERMOR Between the Woods and the Water*
PATRICK LEIGH FERMOR The Broken Road*
PATRICK LEIGH FERMOR Mani: Travels in the Southern Peloponnese*
PATRICK LEIGH FERMOR Roumeli: Travels in Northern Greece*
PATRICK LEIGH FERMOR A Time of Gifts*
PATRICK LEIGH FERMOR A Time to Keep Silence*
PATRICK LEIGH FERMOR The Traveller's Tree*
D.B. WYNDHAM LEWIS AND CHARLES LEE (EDITORS) The Stuffed Owl
SIMON LEYS The Death of Napoleon*
SIMON LEYS The Hall of Uselessness: Collected Essays*
GEORG CHRISTOPH LICHTENBERG The Waste Books
JAKOV LIND Soul of Wood and Other Stories
H.P. LOVECRAFT AND OTHERS Shadows of Carcosa: Tales of Cosmic Horro
DWIGHT MACDONALD Masscult and Midcult: Essays Against the American Grain*
NORMAN MAILER Miami and the Siege of Chicago*
CURZIO MALAPARTE Kaputt
CURZIO MALAPARTE The Skin
JANET MALCOLM In the Freud Archives
JEAN-PATRICK MANCHETTE Fatale*
JEAN-PATRICK MANCHETTE The Mad and the Bad*
OSIP MANDELSTAM The Selected Poems of Osip Mandelstam
OLIVIA MANNING Fortunes of War: The Balkan Trilogy*
OLIVIA MANNING Fortunes of War: The Levant Trilogy*
OLIVIA MANNING School for Love*
JAMES VANCE MARSHALL Walkabout*
GUY DE MAUPASSANT Afloat
GUY DE MAUPASSANT Alien Hearts*
JAMES McCOURT Mawrdew Czgowchwz*
WILLIAM McPHERSON Testing the Current*
DAVID MENDEL Proper Doctoring: A Book for Patients and Their Doctors*
HENRI MICHAUX Miserable Miracle
JESSICA MITFORD Hons and Rebels
JESSICA MITFORD Poison Penmanship*
NANCY MITFORD Frederick the Great*
NANCY MITFORD Madame de Pompadour*
NANCY MITFORD The Sun King*
NANCY MITFORD Voltaire in Love*
MICHEL DE MONTAIGNE Shakespeare's Montaigne; translated by John Florio*
HENRY DE MONTHERLANT Chaos and Night
BRIAN MOORE The Lonely Passion of Judith Hearne*
BRIAN MOORE The Mangan Inheritance*
ALBERTO MORAVIA Agostino*
ALBERTO MORAVIA Boredom*
ALBERTO MORAVIA Contempt*
JAN MORRIS Conundrum*
JAN MORRIS Hav*
PENELOPE MORTIMER The Pumpkin Eater*
ÁLVARO MUTIS The Adventures and Misadventures of Maqroll
L.H. MYERS The Root and the Flower*
NESCIO Amsterdam Stories*
DARCY O'BRIEN A Way of Life, Like Any Other
SILVINA OCAMPO Thus Were Their Faces*

YURI OLESHA Envy*

IONA AND PETER OPIE The Lore and Language of Schoolchildren

IRIS OWENS After Claude*

RUSSELL PAGE The Education of a Gardener

ALEXANDROS PAPADIAMANTIS The Murderess

BORIS PASTERNAK, MARINA TSVETAYEVA, AND RAINER MARIA RILKE Letters, Summer 1926

CESARE PAVESE The Moon and the Bonfires

CESARE PAVESE The Selected Works of Cesare Pavese

LUIGI PIRANDELLO The Late Mattia Pascal

JOSEP PLA The Gray Notebook

ANDREY PLATONOV The Foundation Pit

ANDREY PLATONOV Happy Moscow

ANDREY PLATONOV Soul and Other Stories

J.F. POWERS Morte d'Urban*

J.F. POWERS The Stories of J.F. Powers*

J.F. POWERS Wheat That Springeth Green*

CHRISTOPHER PRIEST Inverted World*

BOLESŁAW PRUS The Doll*

GEORGE PSYCHOUNDAKIS The Cretan Runner: His Story of the German Occupation*

ALEXANDER PUSHKIN The Captain's Daughter*

QIU MIAOJIN Last Words from Montmartre*

RAYMOND QUENEAU We Always Treat Women Too Well

RAYMOND QUENEAU Witch Grass

RAYMOND RADIGUET Count d'Orgel's Ball

FRIEDRICH RECK Diary of a Man in Despair*

JULES RENARD Nature Stories*

JEAN RENOIR Renoir, My Father

GREGOR VON REZZORI An Ermine in Czernopol*

GREGOR VON REZZORI Memoirs of an Anti-Semite*

GREGOR VON REZZORI The Snows of Yesteryear: Portraits for an Autobiography*

TIM ROBINSON Stones of Aran: Labyrinth

TIM ROBINSON Stones of Aran: Pilgrimage

MILTON ROKEACH The Three Christs of Ypsilanti*

FR. ROLFE Hadrian the Seventh

GILLIAN ROSE Love's Work

LINDA ROSENKRANTZ Talk*

WILLIAM ROUGHEAD Classic Crimes

CONSTANCE ROURKE American Humor: A Study of the National Character

SAKI The Unrest-Cure and Other Stories; illustrated by Edward Gorey

TAYEB SALIH Season of Migration to the North

TAYEB SALIH The Wedding of Zein*

JEAN-PAUL SARTRE We Have Only This Life to Live: Selected Essays. 1939–1975

GERSHOM SCHOLEM Walter Benjamin: The Story of a Friendship*

DANIEL PAUL SCHREBER Memoirs of My Nervous Illness

JAMES SCHUYLER Alfred and Guinevere

JAMES SCHUYLER What's for Dinner?*

SIMONE SCHWARZ-BART The Bridge of Beyond*

LEONARDO SCIASCIA The Day of the Owl

LEONARDO SCIASCIA Equal Danger

LEONARDO SCIASCIA The Moro Affair

LEONARDO SCIASCIA To Each His Own

LEONARDO SCIASCIA The Wine-Dark Sea

VICTOR SEGALEN René Leys*

ANNA SEGHERS Transit*

PHILIPE-PAUL DE SÉGUR Defeat: Napoleon's Russian Campaign

GILBERT SELDES The Stammering Century*

VICTOR SERGE The Case of Comrade Tulayev*

VICTOR SERGE Conquered City*

VICTOR SERGE Memoirs of a Revolutionary

VICTOR SERGE Midnight in the Century*

VICTOR SERGE Unforgiving Years

SHCHEDRIN The Golovlyov Family

ROBERT SHECKLEY The Store of the Worlds: The Stories of Robert Sheckley*

GEORGES SIMENON Act of Passion*

GEORGES SIMENON Dirty Snow*

GEORGES SIMENON Monsieur Monde Vanishes*

GEORGES SIMENON Pedigree*

GEORGES SIMENON Three Bedrooms in Manhattan*

GEORGES SIMENON Tropic Moon*

GEORGES SIMENON The Widow*

CHARLES SIMIC Dime-Store Alchemy: The Art of Joseph Cornell

MAY SINCLAIR Mary Olivier: A Life*

WILLIAM SLOANE The Rim of Morning: Two Tales of Cosmic Horror*

SASHA SOKOLOV A School for Fools*

VLADIMIR SOROKIN Ice Trilogy*

VLADIMIR SOROKIN The Queue

NATSUME SŌSEKI The Gate*

DAVID STACTON The Judges of the Secret Court*

JEAN STAFFORD The Mountain Lion

CHRISTINA STEAD Letty Fox: Her Luck

GEORGE R. STEWART Names on the Land

STENDHAL The Life of Henry Brulard

ADALBERT STIFTER Rock Crystal

THEODOR STORM The Rider on the White Horse

JEAN STROUSE Alice James: A Biography*

HOWARD STURGIS Belchamber

ITALO SVEVO As a Man Grows Older

HARVEY SWADOS Nights in the Gardens of Brooklyn

A.J.A. SYMONS The Quest for Corvo

MAGDA SZABÓ The Door*

ANTAL SZERB Journey by Moonlight*

ELIZABETH TAYLOR Angel*

ELIZABETH TAYLOR A Game of Hide and Seek*

ELIZABETH TAYLOR A View of the Harbour*

ELIZABETH TAYLOR You'll Enjoy It When You Get There: The Stories of Elizabeth Taylor*

HENRY DAVID THOREAU The Journal: 1837–1861*

ALEKSANDAR TIŠMA The Use of Man*

TATYANA TOLSTAYA The Slynx

TATYANA TOLSTAYA White Walls: Collected Stories

EDWARD JOHN TRELAWNY Records of Shelley, Byron, and the Author

LIONEL TRILLING The Liberal Imagination*

LIONEL TRILLING The Middle of the Journey*

THOMAS TRYON The Other*

IVAN TURGENEV Virgin Soil

JULES VALLÈS The Child

RAMÓN DEL VALLE-INCLÁN Tyrant Banderas*

MARK VAN DOREN Shakespeare

CARL VAN VECHTEN The Tiger in the House

ELIZABETH VON ARNIM The Enchanted April*

EDWARD LEWIS WALLANT The Tenants of Moonbloom

ROBERT WALSER Berlin Stories*

ROBERT WALSER Jakob von Gunten

ROBERT WALSER A Schoolboy's Diary and Other Stories*

REX WARNER Men and Gods

SYLVIA TOWNSEND WARNER Lolly Willowes*

SYLVIA TOWNSEND WARNER Mr. Fortune*

SYLVIA TOWNSEND WARNER Summer Will Show*

JAKOB WASSERMANN My Marriage*

ALEKSANDER WAT My Century*

C.V. WEDGWOOD The Thirty Years War

SIMONE WEIL On the Abolition of All Political Parties*

SIMONE WEIL AND RACHEL BESPALOFF War and the Iliad

GLENWAY WESCOTT Apartment in Athens*

GLENWAY WESCOTT The Pilgrim Hawk*

REBECCA WEST The Fountain Overflows

EDITH WHARTON The New York Stories of Edith Wharton*

KATHARINE S. WHITE Onward and Upward in the Garden

PATRICK WHITE Riders in the Chariot

T.H. WHITE The Goshawk*

JOHN WILLIAMS Augustus*

JOHN WILLIAMS Butcher's Crossing*

JOHN WILLIAMS Stoner*

ANGUS WILSON Anglo-Saxon Attitudes

EDMUND WILSON Memoirs of Hecate County

RUDOLF AND MARGARET WITTKOWER Born Under Saturn

GEOFFREY WOLFF Black Sun*

FRANCIS WYNDHAM The Complete Fiction

JOHN WYNDHAM Chocky

JOHN WYNDHAM The Chrysalids

BÉLA ZOMBORY-MOLDOVÁN The Burning of the World: A Memoir of 1914*

STEFAN ZWEIG Beware of Pity*

STEFAN ZWEIG Chess Story*

STEFAN ZWEIG Confusion *

STEFAN ZWEIG Journey Into the Past*

STEFAN ZWEIG The Post-Office Girl*